He wore a black leather, studed jeans, and a brown Henley. His black hair was cut short and cropped close to the head without a hint of product. Stubble darkened his jaw, circled his sensuous mouth, and crept down his throat. He had the blackest eyes I'd ever seen fringed with long, thick lashes. He was a demon (or so I'd guessed) and one of New York's finest. He'd helped during Ty's disappearance the previous month and I'd been lusting after him ever since.

Not willingly, of course. See, Ash wasn't any old demon. He oozed sex appeal (rather than green slime) and women couldn't seem to resist him. Nix your ordinary *Exorcist* variety. This guy was a bona fide incubus.

Which meant that said fantasies were totally NOT my fault. An incubus doesn't just reek of S-E-X, he inspires it.

Still, let's say for the sake of argument that I *had* been thinking about him, so what? It wasn't like Ty and I had an actual relationship. I hadn't seen or talked to him in a month. No phone calls. No e-mails. No text messages. Not even a measly comment on MySpace or Facebook. Nothing since our goodbye sex marathon.

Also by Kimberly Raye
published by Ballantine Books

DEAD END DATING
DEAD AND DATELESS
YOUR COFFIN OR MINE?

Just One Bite

A Dead-End Dating Novel

KIMBERLY RAYE

BALLANTINE BOOKS • NEW YORK

Just One Bite is a work of fiction. Names, characters, places, and incidents are the products of the author's imagination or are used fictitiously. Any resemblance to actual events, locales, or persons, living or dead, is entirely coincidental.

A Ballantine Books Mass Market Original

Published in the United States by Ballantine Books, an imprint of The Random House Publishing Group, a division of Random House, Inc., New York.

BALLANTINE and colophon are registered trademarks of Random House, Inc.

This book contains an excerpt from the forthcoming book *Sucker for Love* by Kimberly Raye. This excerpt has been set for this edition only and may not reflect the final content of the forthcoming edition.

ISBN 978-0-345-50365-7

Cover illustration: Peter Lott

Printed in the United States of America

www.ballantinebooks.com

OPM 9 8 7 6 5 4 3 2 1

For my husband, Curt Groff,
for always listening no matter
how much I complain.
I love you, baby!

Acknowledgments

I feel truly blessed to be able to do what I love to do—and that's write. Sometimes it's lonely, sometimes it's stressful, but it's always the coolest job on earth. To those key people who make that job MUCH easier—my wonderful agent, Natasha Kern, my writing BFFs Nina Bangs and Gerry Bartlett, the most supportive producer in Hollywood, Ksana Golod, all of the fabulous people at Ballantine who work so hard to help my books succeed—thank you all SO much!

And many thanks to my fab readers who send notes and e-mails and visit me on MySpace. You guys are the best!!!

One
♥ ♥ ♥

Being a five-hundred-year-old (and holding) born vampire, I've pretty much seen the worst of the worst.

War.

Famine.

Natural disasters.

Stock market crashes.

Powdered wigs (my father is *so* not living that one down).

Bottom line, there isn't much that can shock me, the Countess Lilliana Arrabella Guinevere du Marchette (Lil for short), Manhattan's *numero uno* when it comes to matchmakers.

Except walking into the tastefully decorated office of my hook-up service—Dead End Dating—to find an Anthony Soprano clone holding a very lethal-looking stake.

I came to an abrupt stop in the doorway, my Constanca Basto sandals refusing to carry me the rest of the way inside.

Twisted, right? I had the whole super-vamp package working for me. HD vision, enhanced hearing, mind-reading ability. Throw in the glamour trick—the power to mesmerize and persuade the opposite sex with my deep, entrancing stare—and I really had little to fear despite the nuclear toothpick in his meaty hands.

Then again, he *was* wearing a pair of pitch-black Ray-Bans, which sort of put a crimp on the mind reading and the glam thing. He sat behind my desk, his feet propped on the glass and chrome. He had thinning brown hair and a recessed hairline that said he was in his late thirties, maybe early forties. A black Gucci jacket hugged his potbelly. Black slacks, argyle socks, and gleaming black loafers completed the outfit. He shuffled the stake from one hand to the other. Back and forth. And eyed me.

My heart shifted into overdrive and I drank in a deep, calming breath (NOT a necessity for my kind, but after years of blending with humans, it's become something of a habit). The scent of garlic and sausage spiraled through my nostrils.

I tamped down the urge to bolt (hey, my feet were *frozen*) and decided to go for Plan A—faking my way out of a very difficult (and somewhat smelly) situation.

I gave up the breathing and pasted on my most

mesmerizing smile. "Can I help you with something?"

"Lil Marchette?" he asked, a Bolívar cigar hanging from the corner of his mouth. He had a thick Jersey accent and the cold, emotionless tone of a man who would rather see me with concrete blocks strapped to my ankles than prancing around in my latest La Perla thong.

"Um, no," I blurted. "I'm Evie. Lil's assistant. She's on vacation right now. A really long vacation."

"Evie, huh?" The Ray-Bans swept over me once, twice. "Funny, but I met an Evie about an hour ago." He took a puff and waved the cigar at me. "You don't look anything like her." A stream of smoke spiraled in the air between us. "Granted, you're both blondes, but your hair is longer. And you're taller. And you're a vampire."

So much for Plan A.

Enter Plan B—charming my way out.

"Nice jacket," I told the guy.

"You like? My mother bought it for me."

"She has excellent taste."

He actually smiled. "Damn straight she does. She's a saint, that woman." The Ray-Bans zeroed in on my face. "Goes to Mass every Saturday *and* Sunday. And she don't like liars. She can spot a liar at fifty paces. She's got intuition. Every time she meets a liar, she gets a cramp."

"Maybe it's just gas."

"Have you ever met a saint with gas?"

I'd actually never met a saint, period, which was

saying a lot considering that I've been around *forever*. But saints and vampires don't exactly connect, if you know what I mean, and so I've made it my business to avoid any and all visits to the Vatican, pilgrimages to holy places, and eBay auctions featuring religious artifacts (although I did sneak a peek at the Jesus grilled cheese).

Not that vamps are these anti-spiritual creatures who cringe in the face of a crucifix or double over when someone recites a scripture. It's just somewhat annoying. Really, who wants to get doused with holy water at every turn? Talk about a quick way to ruin a silk blouse.

"I'm not really Evie," I admitted, just in case he'd inherited the whole cramp thing. After all, he was sitting in my favorite chair. "I just thought you were another fan from *MMW* and I wanted to avoid a confrontation."

Manhattan's Most Wanted was a local reality dating show fashioned after *The Bachelor* that paired Manhattan's hottest guys with a bevy of beautiful, buxom women. While I hadn't made the final cut for the actual show, I had made it into the outtakes that had aired a few short weeks ago.

"I saw you riding that carriage through Central Park." He grinned. "You're a real celebrity."

"That's me." Unfortunately.

"I bet they've been climbing out of the woodwork since then. TV always brings out the crazies."

"Not really. I mean, there *was* this one guy who wanted to lick my toes and another who asked me to spit on him. But most are just desperate. And lonely. They just want a date." I eyed the stake and swallowed against the sudden lump in my throat. "There's no chance that you're here for that, is there?"

He shrugged. "Maybe. I mean, I *am* here to kill you, but I might consider a date instead."

"Seriously?" When he nodded, hope blossomed in the pit of my stomach. Along with a bud of *not-in-this-afterlife*. I mean, really. He wasn't exactly my dream guy. But a vamp had to do what a vamp had to do. I squared my shoulders, fought my gag reflex, and smiled. "Just name the time and place, and I'm there."

"Slow down, vamp." He made a face. "You're not exactly my type."

True, so why did the comment make me feel so crappy? Oh, yeah. Because I was a hot, megalicious vampire usually wanted by any and all males, and so this was a stab at my already fragile ego.

We're talking paper-thin, ultradelicate, *this* close to snapping in two—thanks to one hot, hunky bounty hunter/made vampire. About a month ago, we'd had fabulous sex several times and then he'd walked.

Uh, yeah. You both agreed that there was no chance of a future, remember?

I was a born vampire (I'd come into the world via eighteen hours of labor, done the toddler and adolescent thing, and had stopped aging like all my born-vamp brethren when I'd lost my virginity at twenty-two) and he was made (a human who'd been bitten and turned); the two DO NOT go together.

BVs lived to make money and procreate. I was planning on doing both someday, just as soon as I paid down a monumental Visa bill and found my eternity mate (also known as a born vamp with great taste in clothes and a high fertility rating—a little digit that reflected the likelihood that a male vamp could hit a bull's-eye when it came to procreation). Made Vampires, on the other hand, lived to drink blood and have gratuitous sex. No bull's-eye needed.

While Ty Bonner didn't come across as the typical MV (he seemed more interested in hunting dangerous criminals than sucking and humping any and everything with a vagina), he still wasn't the guy for me.

My head knew that, but my undead heart . . .

Let's just say I'd had more than one sob fest since we'd called it quits.

"What's your name?" I asked the man with the stake.

"Vinnie Balducci."   •

The name echoed in my head and stirred a big *aha!* My thoughts started racing and suddenly everything made sense. Thanks to my *MMW* notoriety, I'd obviously attracted the attention of the local representative of the SOBs, short for Snipers of Otherworldly Beings. They were a worldwide organization committed to the extermination of any and all paranormal creatures. I'd heard my father mention Vinnie on occasion, along with the juicy tidbit that the man could be bought off if the price was right.

For my father, that meant a monthly delivery of free file folders and Liquid Paper courtesy of Moe's (think copy machines and office supplies and printing services and *major* boredom).

Moe's was the family business and my biggest fear should my dating service go bust. All three of my brothers managed various locations while my father ran things at the corporate level. I had my own stash of Moe's uniforms (beige Dockers and lime green polo shirts) hanging in my closet just waiting for me to fail.

"I can get you free toner cartridges." I launched into Plan C—bribery.

"Your father already threw in a stash last month."

"Hi-liters?"

He shook his head.

"Copy paper?"

"Got it."

"New business cards?"

He seemed to think before shaking his head. "No, forget it. I need kids. See, Mama wants grandchildren and it's high time I settled down and gave her a couple. Which means I need someone who can squeeze them out on account of the only thing I can squeeze out is a—"

"Gotcha," I cut in. Obviously, the meatball hadn't rolled very far from the pot of spaghetti sauce. "No need to elaborate."

He grinned. "That's where you come in. I want you to help me find the right broad."

O-kay. "So what sort of, um, *broad* are you interested in?"

"Somebody nice. Sweet. Wholesome. Catholic.

That's what Mama always says. 'You need somebody nice and sweet and wholesome and Catholic. Don't go bringing home any atheist bimbos. I don't like atheist bimbos in my house.' "

I snatched a pen and paper off my desk and made a quick note. "No atheist bimbos. Gotcha. How about a Catholic bimbo?"

He shrugged. "That would work, as long as she behaves herself in front of my mama. Oh, and she ought to be demure. My mama likes demure. And she has to be Italian."

"Those sort of cancel each other out, don't you think?"

"You'd better hope not. Otherwise, you'll be getting a one-way ticket to Hell along with the rest of the paranormal creatures in this town." He held up the stake. "Make no mistake, I know how to use this. You'll be my five hundredth kill in the born-vamp category. That's a record, you know. One whack straight into your heart"—he made a motion with his hands to illustrate—"a twist to the left, one to the right. The blood spurts and runs all over the floor, and it's *adios* afterlife."

A major rush of ickiness went through me. FYI— while I might be a blood-drinking vamp, I don't really do the bite-and-suck part very well. I'd rather uncork a bottle of the imported stuff in the comfort of my own living room. No spurting or running required.

"If I take you out"—he pointed the stake at me— "I make SOB history. The bigwigs in administration already promised a nice little bonus package to any-one who meets company goals this year. We're talk-ing a steak dinner. A gold watch. An extra twenty grand for my 401(k). A lifetime supply of Girl Scout cookies." When I arched an eyebrow, he added, "Charlie—he's the main guy—has a couple of little girls and his wife is a troop leader. He's pledged all the Thin Mints I can eat if I break the standing record." He pushed to his feet and rounded the desk. "Thin Mints are mama's second favorite food."

"What's her first?"

"Spaghetti with lots of garlic."

That explained the smell. My feet thawed at the speed of light and I inched backward.

"Go ahead. Run. You might even get away. For now. But when you come back"—he whacked his palm with the stake for emphasis—"I'll be waiting."

"And if I skip the country and head for Costa Rica? Or Switzerland? Or the Bahamas?"

"You move into someone else's territory. Someone who might not have a saintly mother who wants grandchildren."

Which meant I could go somewhere else and even-tually get whacked. Or I could stay in Manhattan and get whacked right here and now. Or I could match up Vinnie with his ideal—no atheist bimbos need apply—and NOT get whacked. *Or* I could ask my family for help and risk dragging them into Vinnie's line of fire.

Number three won hands down.

"Okay, I'll do it," I told him. I motioned to his

weapon. "Just put down the stake and you've got yourself a deal."

He placed the piece of wood on the corner of my desk and we eyeballed each other.

My super-vamp gaze zeroed in on his jacket. "If we're going to do this, you have to be one hundred percent committed. I'll do everything I can, but I need to feel confident that you won't double-cross me and plug me with a couple of .45s when I'm not looking."

He pushed to his feet, shrugged off his coat, and tossed the gun next to the stake.

"Or slip a little garlic into my afternoon cocktail." Not that the big G could actually kill me. At least not in small quantities. But we're talking major digestive upset.

He toed off one loafer and fished out a couple of clear packets filled with the deadly powder. "You want the toothpicks sewn into my underwear, too?" He reached for the waistband of his pants.

"Hold it." I held up a hand to stall him. "Why do you have toothpicks sewn into your underwear?"

"In case I'm captured and my weapons are confiscated." He unfastened his belt. "I can still defend myself."

"With a toothpick?"

"One stab"—the belt slid open—"you start bleeding from the eyeball"—his hand went for the button—"and in a matter of seconds, you're practically blind."

He grabbed the zipper and I blurted, "Keep the toothpicks."

His hands stalled and his gaze collided with mine. "Aren't you scared?"

And how.

The sudden image of Vinnie in his skivvies had me trembling even more than the possibility of bleeding all over my favorite Christian Dior blouse and Amy Tan skirt.

I shrugged. "What's life if you can't live on the edge once in a while?"

He refastened his button and his belt. The vise gripping my insides eased.

I gathered up his weapons, shoved them into the bottom drawer of my desk, and motioned him into a client chair. A few seconds later, I settled behind my desk and handed him a clipboard with a blank profile. "Fill this out and let's see what we're up against."

TWO
♥ ♥ ♥

"**D**o you wear women's panties?" Vinnie glanced up from the clipboard I'd handed him and scowled. "What the hell kind of question is that?"

FYI—because of my primo confidence and ultra-sharp fangs, I'm not usually intimidated.

Particularly by humans.

But the SOBs were the best of the best. Specially trained to scope out the weaknesses of Others and exploit them. Skilled in the art of killing. Vinnie already had four hundred and ninety-nine born-vamp kills under his belt. Translation: He was one bad mother. Despite the fact that I'd temporarily defused the situation and bought myself some time, I was still scared shitless.

But while I knew that, I wasn't about to clue him in.

I gathered my courage, ignored the alarm bells ringing between my ears, and gave him my most benevolent smile. "Vincent, Vincent, *Vincent*. It's this exact question—and a dozen others like it—that is going to help me find you the perfect woman." I reached across the desk and plucked the clipboard from his meaty hands. I stared at the answers he'd already filled in. "It says here that you love blue." He nodded and I added, "You wouldn't want me to hook you up with someone who hated blue, now would you?" I scanned the list. "Or someone who despised cannoli. Or monster trucks. Or the Yankees. Or someone who thought *The Godfather* reeked."

"Al Pacino is the shit."

"You know that and I know that." I'd never actually seen the movie myself, but who was I to quibble with a man who made his living shish-kebabing vamps? "But what if I matched you with a clueless woman who thought Al sucked?" Vinnie's expression darkened and my heart paused. "Not that I would ever do such a thing," I hurried on, "but if I'd never asked you the question in the first place, then I wouldn't know it was a deal breaker. A good matchmaker makes it her business to know *everything* about her client. That way there are no ugly skeletons dangling in the closet."

He shifted uncomfortably in his seat, and my vamp instincts kicked into high gear.

"Don't tell me you have an actual skeleton hanging in your closet."

"Fuck no. What kind of guy do you take me for?"

Relief rushed through me.

"It's in my sock drawer."

"Now about the—*what*?"

He shrugged. "And it's not the entire thing. Just a femur and a few rib bones from my last were kill." His mouth crooked into a grin. "I broke the standing were record with that one. Talk about a tough little sucker. I chased him a full two weeks before I managed to pump a couple of silver bullets into him. Dropped just like that. He was too big to fit into the trunk of the car—we're talking were-*bear*—so I chopped him up and—"

"As fascinating as this is," I cut in, eager to ignore the preview of *Pooh Meets Jason* that played in my head, "I'd really like to get back to the, um"—I swallowed past the sudden lump in my throat (we're talking sweet, cuddly Winnie)—"questions."

"All right, but just so you know, I'm not used to being asked shit like that."

"I totally understand. Not all of the questions on this profile pertain to everyone. When you get to something that's too far out, feel free to write *non-applicable*. I'll just jot that down right here and we can move on—"

"I wouldn't be too hasty."

"Excuse me?"

"A pink rhinestone thong with glitter appliqué," he blurted. He must have noticed my surprise, because he added, "If I want this to work, I gotta be honest, right? Besides, it isn't something I do every day. Only on Fridays. That's the official SOB wear-what-you-want day. Monday through Thursday, it's regulation boxers. White. Loose. While I stuff 'em in once a week, the boys are big and rowdy. They like to run free most days."

"I'll, um, make a note of that." I scribbled a few quick words in the margin (no, one of them wasn't *freak,* but I was sorely tempted) before handing back the clipboard. "Just be as honest as you can."

He grunted and shifted his attention back to the profile while I turned to busy myself with the stack of mail Evie had left on the corner of my desk.

At least the goal was to look busy and unassuming while Vinnie finished filling out his information. The last thing I needed was for him to change his mind and decide to off me right now.

I rifled through the stack and separated everything into two piles—urgent and not-so-urgent.

Electricity bill due in two weeks—not so urgent.

Office space rent due in three weeks—not so urgent.

Visa bill due in three days—not so urgent. (Hey, a lot could happen in three days. Brad Pitt could dump Angelina, walk into my office, demand my primo hook-up package, *and* offer to pay me a rush charge and a big fat tip. My parents could waltz in and tell me that I don't have to settle down with a born male vamp and squeeze out several dozen grandchildren in order to get my trust fund. I could even win the lottery.)

The fall catalog from Banana Republic—urgent.

Register to win a year's supply of MAC bronzers— *way* urgent.

I tackled the registration card first, then flipped through the catalog. The bills I stashed in my top desk drawer with yesterday's not-so-urgents—telephone, Internet, water. My night had already gotten off to a bad start. I wasn't going to make myself even more miserable by paying my bills.

Not that I couldn't, of course. While I wasn't anywhere close to eHarmony fame, I was holding my own. It's just that every time I started to write out a check for something like, say, the light bill, I started to think about all the other things I could buy with my money—like, say, this totally cute Banana Republic hobo satchel with matching cellphone case—*if* the Founding Fathers had been the least bit intuitive and gone with "life, liberty, *electricity,* and the pursuit of happiness" instead.

Get over it, already.

I gave the satchel another once-over, folded the corner (in case I had an extra five hundred bucks laying around *after* I paid this month's utilities), and turned to my computer.

I'd just logged on to my database to work on a few existing clients when Vinnie slapped the clipboard down on my desk and declared, "Done. Now what?"

"Well." I reached for the clipboard. "Now you leave to do whatever snipers do on a Thursday night. I'll input your data and run a search for possible matches. Once I have those, I set you up on a few dates and we see what happens." I smiled. "The whole process takes about two to four weeks."

"You've got seventy-two hours."

My smile died. "That's really fast."

"I'm in a hurry." He pushed to his feet. "My mama's birthday is next Tuesday. I figure if you find me a date in a couple of days, that gives me time to take her out a few times and get to know her before I bring her home on Tuesday. We can announce our engagement at Mama's party. I've already got it all planned. My Aunt Cecille is making the pasta. We're going to have lots of balloons and presents. And my Uncle Morty is going to play the guitar. I ordered a cake from Giovanni's. Italian Crème. Mama's favorite. She's going to be the happiest woman in Jersey."

Okay, while I know Vinnie's a killer and everything, there was just something really sweet (if you overlooked the whole creepy Oedipus factor) about a guy going to so much trouble to give his mom a great birthday.

"I'll do my best."

"You'll do more than that," he said. "Find me a woman"—the Ray-Bans zeroed in on me and I found myself staring at my own stark complexion—"or I'll turn you into a popsicle." The sweet quickly faded into the demented as he snatched up my letter opener and tossed it at the wall behind me.

The blade sailed past my head, nailed the Sheet-rock, and I flinched.

"Seventy-two hours." He bit out the words, turned on his heel, and walked toward the door.

"I-I'm on it," I called after him once I managed to find my voice. "Really. It's no problem. No problem at all."

The door slammed and I contemplated using the letter opener on myself and beating Vinnie to the punch. For about an eighth of a second. I'd been around too long to give up that easily. Besides, if I did kick the bucket, I was doing it in something besides an outfit from last season (I hadn't had a chance to make it to the cleaners yet and I *so* didn't do laundry). No, I was going out in style. Chanel. Dolce & Gabbana. At the very least a pair of studded Rock & Republic jeans.

I snatched the opener out of the wall and shoved it into the nearest drawer. Then I spent the next five minutes doing some deep breathing exercises I'd seen on *Dr. Phil.*

Crazy, right? I'm a born vampire. Which meant the breathing wasn't going to do anything but waste precious time I didn't have. At the same time, it did help the cobwebs to clear.

Work. That was the only thing that was going to get me out of this mess. That, and maybe a valium. But since I didn't have any drugs on hand, I put my fingers on the keyboard and started to type in Vinnie's information.

After a few minutes, my anxiety slipped away. I mean, really. He *was* just a guy, and I'd hooked up dozens of them since opening my door six months ago.

In fact, I preferred male clients because they were, for the most part, easier to please than women. Sure, they had their ideals, which they shared in great detail in the *Ideal Woman* section. But when it came down to the *Absolute Must-Haves,* the only real requirement was usually a vagina. The rest was negotiable.

My gaze zeroed in on Vinnie's *Absolute* section, which overflowed the allotted line and continued on the back.

Blond hair.
Blue eyes.

I flipped the paper over and kept going.

Great ass.
Big tits.
Small waist.
Nice teeth.
No bunions.
No hammertoes.
Vagina (what'd I tell ya?).
Never misses confession.

I was *so* dead.

The realization hit me as I reread the list. Then I did what any born vamp on the verge of total annihilation would do (at least any born vamp with a zest for life and an addiction to pink)—I panicked.

A full-fledged I-can-feel-the-stake-sliding-between-my-rib-cage *panic*. Which was the only explanation for what happened next.

The phone rang and I snatched it up *without* checking the caller ID.

Three

♥ ♥ ♥

"Dead End Dating," I said as I picked up the receiver. "If you've got the money—that includes check, Visa or MasterCard—we've got the time." I know. It reeked as far as catchy jingles went, but I'd just been threatened by a bona fide vampire killer. Gimme a break. "Lil Marchette," I added. "How can I help you?"

"You can call me back once in a while." Jacqueline Marchette's familiar voice carried over the line. "I've left six messages. But then that's how it goes. You shed blood, sweat, and tears to give afterlife to three beautiful, healthy children, and how do they repay you? They ignore your phone calls when you're this close to picking up a gun and ending it all."

"You don't own a gun, Ma."

"Maybe not, but your father bought a paintball Uzi to use on Viola."

Viola was an ultrastylish werewolf who lived next door to my parents. She was president of the Connecticut chapter of the Naked and Unashamed Nudist Sisterhood (a group of female werewolves that met weekly at her Fairfield estate) and a Democrat. *And* the recently court-ordered owner of the controversial patch of azalea bushes that sat on the property line between the two estates.

My father was still pissed over the ruling. That, and the fact that his prized chain saw (which he'd used to chop down said azaleas time and time again) had mysteriously fallen into Viola's possession (it's a *long* story).

"The thing looks real," my mother went on, "and it causes the most painful-looking bruises."

"Don't tell me he really shot her?"

"Actually, he shot himself in the foot when he was trying to load the blasted thing. He's lucky there were only five balls in the barrel, otherwise he might have put out an eye and bled all over my Berber rug."

"Is he okay?"

"He's a vampire, dear. Of course he's okay. In fact, he's already healed. He's cocked and loaded as we speak, and skulking around the backyard. Viola's having one of her get-togethers tonight and he's got this absurd notion that he's going to cause a diversion by peppering her yard statues with paint. While she and her guests are on the back patio examining the damage, he'll sneak onto her property and steal back that bloody chain saw. Or at least that's the plan at the moment."

"Isn't that against the law?"

"That's what I told him, but he says since it's his in the first place, he's not breaking the law if he takes it back."

"What if he can't find it?"

"He moves on to Plan B."

"Which is?"

"Hiring someone named Fast Hands Freddie to do it for him. The man specializes in organized-crime hits, but he's good with burglaries, as well. Your father found him in the phone book under *Hands-on Business Consultants,* and all of this is beside the point. I deserve, at the very least, a phone call, don't you think?" She went silent for a long moment and I shifted in my seat.

In addition to the standard superpowers, all born vamps possess a special power unique to each of them. My oldest brother Max could summon a thunderstorm. My middle brother Rob could redirect the wind. My youngest brother Jack could command a burst of fire. I could sniff out a sale within a five-mile radius. My mother? She could heap on the guilt with nothing more than a moment of calculated silence.

My panic quickly fled, swamped by a wave of self-loathing.

"Geez, Ma. I've been with a client since I walked in the door and I haven't even had time to check my messages—"

"Not you. Your brother."

"Max? But he always calls you." Max was the hot and hunky kiss-ass.

"Your other brother."

"Rob?" Also hot and hunky, but instead of kissing ass, he simply kept to himself. "He calls every week." Unless he was too preoccupied with a certain daughter of born-vamp hotelier Victor Lancaster. I'd hooked up Rob with Nina One, the blond half of my best friend duo The Ninas (Nina Two lived in Jersey with her own commitment mate, courtesy of yours truly), and they'd been getting pretty serious over the past few weeks. I smiled at the prospect, but then my mother sighed and the expression died. "Maybe he's been extra busy at Moe's. Isn't it spring inventory?"

"Yes, and I'm not referring to Robert. The *other* one."

Meaning my youngest brother Jack. Once-upon-a-time jerk turned semi-decent vamp who'd recently married the woman of his dreams. The *human* woman. A fact that still didn't sit well with my mother, who'd done her best to break them up. She'd even gone so far as to hire me to find him a more suitable mate. True love had prevailed (with a little help from *moi*, of course), and they'd gotten married anyway. My mother had kept her mouth shut during the ceremony (my brother had threatened to break off all contact with her), but she'd yet to accept that her baby boy would willingly betray his heritage and give up his chance to breed baby vamps.

"Jack's in Rio on his honeymoon," I pointed out. "He doesn't get back until next week."

"So? Is there some unspoken rule that says a man can't phone his mother while in a foreign country on his honeymoon?"

"Well, yeah, Ma. It's his *honeymoon*."

"Has he called you?"

"I'm his sister. That's rule number two."

A moment of silence ticked by. "I hope he's all right."

"I'm sure he's fine."

"Then why hasn't he called?"

Duh. "Maybe he's busy having fun."

"With that human? What sort of fun could they be having? It's not like they're having sex. What's the point?"

Because they're two committed souls who want to express their devotion not just emotionally, but physically, as well. I caught the response before it could slip past my lips.

First off, I wasn't in the habit of contradicting my mother (see her special talent above) and second, she's my *mother*.

"He could be partying or sightseeing or biting unsuspecting tourists."

She brightened at the last prospect. "Do you really think so?"

"Does a vampire suck blood?"

"I suppose you're right. Jack *is* a born *vampere*. It's not like he can turn his back on his very nature. Not forever. Sooner or later, he'll grow tired of that human, and then he'll realize what a wonderful existence he had. He'll get rid of her and everything will be back to normal."

"Most definitely." *Not.* As much of a player as Jack had been, he truly had changed. I'd seen the love in his eyes when he'd pledged his love to Mandy. He wasn't morphing back into Jerk Vamp anytime in the next eternity, no matter how much my mother wanted him to.

At least, I hoped not.

"Since we're on the subject of superior born male vamps—"

"We are? I thought we were talking about Jack."

"Exactly."

Oh.

"I happen to know a superior born male vamp who's very excited about seeing you again." Just like that, my mother changed the subject and I was back in her crosshairs.

"Listen, Ma, I know I said I would go out with Remy, but we've already been out a dozen times. I'm just not attracted to him."

Remy Tremaine was the chief of the Fairfield Police Department and my mother's prime son-in-law candidate. He was good-looking, filthy rich (thanks to the private security service he ran in addition to being one of Fairfield's finest) and he had an astronomical fertility rating. He was also the son of one of my mother's oldest and dearest friends (they'd grown up together, playing paper dolls, yapping about boys, and terrorizing small villages).

While I liked Remy (we'd also grown up together, minus the dolls and boys and small villages, of course), I didn't *like* Remy.

At least, I hadn't thought so until a few months ago. We'd had a few. *ka-pow* moments (n: used to describe instantaneous, tummy-tingling chemistry) and now I wasn't one hundred percent sure he wasn't all that.

At the same time, I wasn't one hundred percent sure that I wanted to find out.

Because you like Ty.

I ignored the voice. "I'll think about it."

"Think fast because I want to invite him to the hunt. You two could leave early and spend some time alone getting to know each other. You could talk about your impressive orgasm quotient and he could talk about his fertility rating." Excitement infused her voice. "I don't want to spoil the surprise and tell you the number Estelle mentioned, but let me just say that I think you'll be more than evenly matched."

"I already know, Ma. You told me last week. And the week before that. And the week before that."

"Well, then. It's all settled. I'll call Estelle. She and I both are pushing for an April commitment ceremony. We can have it at the Huntress club and—"

"It's just dinner, Ma, and I haven't even said yes."

She ignored the second part. "First dinner, then the next thing you know, you're giving birth to little *Jacqueline Marie du Champagne Genoise Tremaine.*"

"I gotta go, Ma." I slid the phone into the receiver and tried to calm the sudden pounding of my heart.

Not because I didn't want to squeeze out a baby vamp one day. I did. Hence my recent no dead-end relationship policy. But I *so* wasn't naming it after my mother. My own name didn't even fit on a Master-Card application. No way was I dooming my child to a similar fate.

I'd rather go for something short and sweet and *now*.

Maybe Shiloh.

Or Violet.

Or Magenta.

The notion calmed me down all of five seconds and even drew a tiny smile.

One that quickly died, however, when I shifted my attention back to Vinnie's application. I keyed in a few of his *must-haves* and ran a search of my database.

Zilch.

Which meant I had to go above and beyond my preexisting clients.

Way, way up I decided after several minutes of deep thought. I pushed to my feet and grabbed my purse.

A quick swipe of lip gloss and I headed for—where else?—the nearest church.

Four
❤ ❤ ❤

I didn't actually go to church.

Despite my soft spot for MasterCard commercials, I *am* a vampire. Not that I'm liable to start smoking or burst into a ball of flames or anything that clichéd. But I do get this very uncomfortable case of hives.

My father says it's because we're born and bred in darkness, vessels of evil, minions of Satan (Yeah, I know. Overinflated ego fueled by way too many reruns of *Dark Shadows*).

My mother—just as much ego, but with an edge of practicality—says I'm allergic to the chemicals used in the stained glass (my great, great, great aunt Michelle has a similar problem. She fed on a clergy member during a tour of Canterbury Cathedral a few years back and swelled up like a Weeble). That, and I'm allergic to the accumulated holiness.

My POV? It's the overabundance of guilt.

Which was why I bypassed the sanctuary of St. Michael's Cathedral and headed for the recreation hall situated in the rear. It was Thursday—ladies' night—which meant plenty of bingo and beer. The place was packed.

I paid my donation, picked up a Corona and a game card, and went in search of an empty chair. After winding my way around several tables filled with retired couples, I wedged myself between two thirty-ish blondes.

The one on my right had blue eyes (yeah, baby), a nice complexion, a decent figure (at least from the waist up) and a passion for bingo. She had seventeen cards spread on the table before her and the look of a woman on a mission.

"Hi," I said. "I'm Lil. Lil Marchette. I own Dead End—"

"Ssshhh." She flashed me a glare before directing her attention to the old woman who stood at the front of the room pulling balls out of a spinning wire cage. "What did she just say?"

"B5," I said. "I think." She gave me another glare and I took the opportunity to use my super vamp skills to peek into her thoughts. Allison Martin. Paralegal from Queens. Single mother of two. Celibate since her last boyfriend six months ago (unless you count Buddy the Boner, an extra-large vibrator she'd purchased last month). She was desperate to win tonight's pot because her youngest needed a commu-

nion dress and she herself needed a new stash of bat-
teries.

Maybe.

Vinnie hadn't mentioned kids on his *Must-Have*
list, but he hadn't listed them in the *No Friggin' Way*
section either. No, the only thing he'd written there
had been NO PLASTIC SURGERY. Because Vinnie wanted
a real woman.

With big breasts.

And a nice butt.

And great feet.

And—

I bailed from the mental list before it could lead me
straight into a murky pit of hopelessness. Pulling out
a business card, I slid it near her beer bottle. Then I
turned to blonde number two.

"Hi," I started, but quickly clamped my lips shut
when she turned a frown on me.

Cecilia Dehart. Computer programmer. Three cats,
one dog, and a hamster named Monique. She liked
rollerblading and shopping (atta girl) and cuddling
with her animals. Major talk-show junkie whose five
minutes consisted of running into Jerry Springer at a
Hard Rock Cafe and spilling the sordid details of her
last breakup. She hadn't made it onto the show—
"My Boyfriend's a Cross-dressing Bisexual and I'm
Having His Twins"—but she had landed a ticket to
be in the studio audience. She was eager to win
tonight's pot because she wanted to send her babies—
Laffy, Taffy and Daffy—to Fur-Sace, the new elite pet
spa that had just opened up in the Village.

Hmmm . . . My own cat—which I owned completely by default, NOT because I was lonely—was overdue for a makeover. I made a mental note to make an appointment for Killer (complete with ultra-deluxe deodorant package), stashed one of my cards next to Cecilia's Diet Coke, and turned my attention to the half-dozen other people at the table.

Three of them were women. A widow who'd just celebrated her eightieth birthday. A middle-aged nurse who worked nights at Bellevue. And a recent high school graduate headed to Columbia.

"Hi," I announced, and received a collective "Ssshhh," followed by a muttered, "Talk about a nervy bitch."

This wasn't working quite as well as I'd anticipated. Since I was looking for a woman, the power of suggestion wasn't going to work (I can only wow the opposite sex). I needed an actual conversation to get them to see how lonely and pointless their lives really were without a significant other. Case in point: it was a beautiful, moonlit night in the most vibrant, happening city in the world and they were playing bingo. Alone. Talk about depressing.

I blinked against the sudden burning in my eyes. Not that I was actually crying because I realized how lonely and pointless my *own* life was without a significant other. Or because I missed Ty. Or because I was contemplating letting my mother fix me up.

Remy was prime material when it came to born vamps. While I knew we had no romantic connection, I had no qualms about getting together as friends.

Especially if it got my mother off my back.

On top of that, I had great hair, a kick-ass wardrobe, and a thriving matchmaking service.

Sure, I was playing bingo, alone, on a beautiful, moonlit night, but I wasn't enjoying it. It was purely in the interest of self-preservation.

"N32," the loud speaker crackled.

I glanced down at my own game card, saw the square, and a tiny thrill went through me.

So maybe I was enjoying it a *little*. It wasn't as if I had anything better to do until the game ended and I could network.

Fifteen minutes later, I was a mere I27 away from victory when an elderly woman with a flowered hat let out a "Whoop! Whoop!"

"Looks like we have a winner, folks," the game caller announced, and several four-letter words echoed around the room, a few courtesy of yours truly. "We'll take a ten-minute intermission to check the winning card. In the meantime, enjoy the food and beverages, and don't forget to donate for the annual spring jubilee. The proceeds go to help our missionaries in Costa Rica."

Tamping down my disappointment (we're talking a five-hundred-dollar pot), I poised myself and reached for my business cards.

I was about to open my mouth when the collective sound of chairs being pushed back grated across my eardrums. Just like that, I found myself alone except for eighty-year-old Clara.

While she wasn't even close to Vinnie's type, I wasn't about to pass up an opportunity to add one more eligible single to the Dead End Dating family.

"I own a local dating service and would love the opportunity to help you find the perfect man to share your golden years," I blurted as she struggled to her feet and reached for her walker. "Maybe we can chat—"

"Sorry, dear, but if I don't get to the concession stand, they'll run out of nachos and the popcorn gives me gas." She swung her walker around and waddled away.

This *so* wasn't working like I'd anticipated.

I sat back in my chair to regroup and plot my next move. Since I wasn't stupid enough to try to compete with a bag of chips or a Snickers bar, I wasn't going near the snack bar line. Nor was I moving on to Bunko night over at St. Andrew's or "Name That Reality Show" over at St. Mary the Virgin, not when I'd already wasted a good twenty minutes—and come *this* close to five hundred bucks myself—right here.

Seventy-one hours, twenty-eight minutes and counting . . .

Panic bolted through me and jump-started my brain cells. Genius struck and I pushed to my feet to head for the one area in the church sure to be brimming with desperate, available women—the restroom.

Out in the hallway, my gaze snagged on the line stretching out the door and down the hall. I sent up a desperate thank-you to the Big Vamp Up High, pulled a handful of cards from my favorite Dior box purse, and went to work.

By the time I'd schmoozed my way down the line, I'd met a total of zero possibilities. The single women were either (a) brunette, (b) old, (c) flat-chested, (d) bitchy (we're talking a *long* line), or (e) all of the above.

Ugh. Where was Catholic Barbie when you *really* needed her?

The question nagged at me as intermission ended and I watched everyone file back into the main room.

I was about to head back in myself and snag a few extra game cards (what?) when I heard a door open. I watched as a fairly attractive woman (tall, curvy, blond) headed for the far end of the hallway. Platform wedges thumped the laminate as she rounded the corner and disappeared.

I glided across the floor after her in time to see her walk through a doorway on the left marked STORAGE. I stepped into the small room just as she climbed halfway up a six-rung ladder propped against a wall of shelves. She reached up, stretching her arms toward a gallon-size can of nacho cheese sauce on the top shelf.

"Shit," she muttered, followed by a "Sorry," as she crossed herself and tackled another rung. The ladder wobbled and she grasped at the edge of a shelf. A can of jalapeños fell to the floor and rolled toward the corner.

The door clicked shut behind me and she let out a startled "Oh." She threw a glance over her shoulder, followed by a relieved smile. "Thank God somebody's here. Can you hold the ladder while I see if I can reach this?"

"No problem." I set my purse on a nearby box of Styrofoam cups. My hands closed over the ladder supports and Barbie tackled the next rung. Then another. Until she reached the top.

"Darn it." She shook her head. "I still can't reach the stupid thing." She started to climb down. "I'll have to go find Earl—"

"Oh, I bet we can get it."

"But my arms are too short."

"Maybe you just needed to loosen up. Now that you've stretched, you're more pliant. Give it another try."

"That's ridiculous," she said, but she climbed back up again.

"There you go. You're so limber. I bet you'll have no trouble."

"Yeah, right." She shook her head. "Here goes nothing." She stretched.

I summoned my ultra-BV strength and lifted the ladder as if it were made of Lincoln Logs. Her fingers snagged the can and crawled around the side.

"I've got it," she declared. "I've really got it." She pulled the can down into her arms. "You were right."

By the time she glanced down, the ladder was back on the floor. She looked victorious a full second before she did a double take.

The ladder, the shelf. Ladder. Shelf. Confusion clouded her baby blues.

"That's weird. It looks farther away—"

"I don't think we've met," I cut in, giving her my most brilliant smile. "I'm Lil Marchette." I stepped back as she climbed down. "I own the dating service a few blocks over."

"Carmen," she offered, hefting the cheese onto her left hip.

Carmen Gianno to be more exact. Fourth-generation Italian and the only one of nine kids who'd yet to tie the knot. She'd been close. But then her partner of eight years had left her and she'd sworn off relationships for a while. Since she'd been flying solo for so long—two years to be exact—she wasn't sure how to get back in the game, especially since she was so busy. She volunteered for a local KEEP NEW YORK CLEAN project on the weekends and ran the church daycare during the week. She'd started working the snack bar on Thursday nights in the hopes of meeting a man—specifically a straight guy who wouldn't cheat on her with a stockbroker named Dean. She loved kids and cookbooks. Her ultimate dream was to have a traditional Catholic wedding, move to New Jersey, and have a family of her own. That, or pledge her loyalty to the church and enter the convent. She'd made up her mind that if Prince Charming didn't show up in the next six months, she was giving up her Levis and buying a penguin suit.

I swept a gaze from her head to her toes. Pink-tipped toes peeked out at me from the wedges. Long legs clad in modest but nice-fitting jeans. Tiny waist cinched with a dynamite Brighton knock-off belt. Decent chest covered in a white peasant's blouse—

My gaze fixed on the deep cleavage peeking over the top button. "Are those your real boobs?"

"What?"

Yeah, *what*?

"I'm, uh, just wondering," I rushed on, "because I've thought about having some work done myself." It wasn't like I could blurt out the truth—that I was scoping her out as the potential Mrs. Balducci. Not yet. She needed to meet Vinnie first. To get to know the man beneath the rough exterior (and panty fetish). "Whoever did yours is a genius."

She smiled. "Thanks, but the only one who gets credit for these is the Big Guy himself. And a pricey Wonderbra with gel cups."

"Fabulous."

I spent the next five minutes giving Carmen the low-down on Dead End Dating and how I could help her find the love of her life if she was, you know, interested. (Which of course, she was. We're talking two *years*.)

Since she was up to her armpits in nacho cheese and couldn't abandon Marge the concessions manager on the busiest night of the week, I made an appointment to meet with her the following evening at DED. She could fill out her profile, I would work my magic, and *bam*—three potential matches (Vinnie, Vinnie, and did I say Vinnie?). And all for the rock-bottom price of—drumroll, please—zero dollars (on account of I was running a special for au naturel

Catholic blondes who actively served the community).

"It's just my way of giving back," I told Carmen as I helped her carry the cheese and three giant bags of tortilla chips back to the concession stand.

By the time I left (after slipping Marge a DED card of her own), I was feeling pretty confident that I would still be around for the début of Barney's new spring collection (six weeks and counting). Not only had I just saved my butt, but I'd done it with seventy-plus hours to spare. It was just after nine p.m., and I had plenty of time to head back to the office and get some work done for my paying clients.

I hit the nearest exit and stepped out onto the sidewalk. My footsteps echoed on the pavement as I headed around the side of the church toward the front to catch a cab. I was five steps shy of the corner when a door crashed open behind me.

And just like that, my evening went from fantabulous to freakin' scary.

Five
❤ ❤ ❤

A growl vibrated my eardrums a split second before a man plowed into me from behind. I stumbled, despite my ultrafast reflexes (this guy was *hea-vy*). My ankle twisted, pain zapped up my calf, and I pitched sideways.

Forget the "Are you okay, miss?"

Or a "Sorry, I didn't see you."

Not even a "Watch where you're standing, bee-yotch."

No, the guy kept running. He hauled it toward the corner, leaving me flat on my ass, my left Zac Posen bootie completely ruined . . .

My screaming ankle pain shushed to a steady whine as I stared down at the chunky black heel that had broken in two. My stomach pitched and my chest constricted.

No way. No friggin' *way*.

I'd sat on a waiting list for six months for these booties. Spent an entire month's salary. Searched days for just the right outfit to wear with them. And for what? So that some bozo could send them to couture heaven on their first night out?

Not.

I bolted to my feet.

In a split second, I caught the guy by the back of the neck and put on the brakes. I lifted him until he was a good six inches off the ground, his legs and arms flailing. "I think you owe me for some booties, chick."

His entire body went rigid as he turned to stare over his right shoulder. But then his head kept going all by itself, twisting on his torso until he faced me.

No, really.

Glowing yellow eyes met mine and he opened his mouth. A chorus of moaning and wailing burst past his lips, along with a rush of putrid breath. A glob of slimy green foam spewed down his chin and plopped onto the hand gripping the back of his collar.

My hand.

I snatched my fingers away (I know, right?) and dropped him. He stumbled forward (or would that be backward, considering his head had done a one-eighty on his body?). His feet hit a pothole since he wasn't looking where he was going, and he pitched forward (or backward). He hit the ground and struggled to his feet. Nearby, another door crashed open.

I whirled, ready to kick butt again, and slammed into a hard, blatantly male body.

The male body that had fueled the occasional Ty-dumped-me-so-I'm-going-to-show-him-and-have-fantabulous-rebound-sex fantasy.

Ash Prince.

Tall, dark, and *oh, baby.*

He wore a black leather bomber jacket, faded jeans, and a brown henley shirt. His black hair was cut short and cropped close to the head without a hint of product. Stubble darkened his jaw, circled his sensuous mouth, and crept down his throat. He had the blackest eyes I'd ever seen fringed with long, thick lashes. He was a demon (or so I'd guessed) and one of New York's finest. He'd helped during Ty's disappearance the previous month and I'd been lusting after him ever since.

Not willingly, of course. See, Ash wasn't any old demon. He oozed sex appeal (rather than green slime) and women couldn't seem to resist him. Nix your ordinary *Exorcist* variety. This guy was a bona fide incubus.

Which meant that said fantasies were totally NOT my fault. An incubus doesn't just reek of S-E-X, he inspires it.

Still, let's say for the sake of argument that I *had* been thinking about him—so what? It wasn't like Ty and I had an actual relationship. I hadn't seen or talked to him in a month. No phone calls. No e-mails. No text messages. Not even a measly comment on

MySpace or Facebook. Nothing since our goodbye-sex marathon.

I had absolutely no reason to feel like an über-slut because my heart was pounding and I was thinking that Ash had really terrific pecs. And kissable lips. And a gaze that promised the most wicked things.

It wasn't like I was committed to anyone, or even going steady.

Rather, I was a single, vivacious vampire having a normal reaction to a member of the opposite sex.

"What are you doing here?" Ash asked me.

"It's bingo night." He grinned and heat flooded my cheeks and a few other places, as well. "Not that I'm here because I have nothing better to do than play a half-dozen cards on a Thursday night. Hardly. I'm here for work." I sighed. "I need a hot Catholic girl."

"Don't we all." His eyes glittered hot and bright.

Suddenly, I couldn't think of anything to say. My heart pounded and my hormones chanted that old Rick James song, "Give It to Me Baby."

I know, right? Rick James is way over, but I wasn't exactly thinking clearly.

Truth be known, I wasn't thinking at all.

It was funny how the brain worked in times of extreme stress. How it was able to shut out all the self-doubt and second thoughts and send a great big *just-do-it* to the rest of the body. Just like that, anything seemed possible.

A man could climb a fifty-foot tree to escape a charging bull. A woman could lift a three-thousand-pound car to save her crushed child. And die-hard romantic *moi*? I could slide my arms around Ash's neck and hump his brains out without an iota of remorse or a single, solitary thought for Ty.

I *could*. If I'd wanted to.

"If you're looking for a woman," I heard myself say as my body chanted *me, me, me!*, "I would be more than happy to hook you up with someone. Catholic. Hare Krishna. Born vamp. You name it." I waved a DED card. "All you have to do is come in for a profile, hand over your credit card, and Auntie Lil will do the rest."

"Nice try, but I can find my own date."

"I hate to point this out, but it's a beautiful night in *the* hottest city around, and you're at *bingo*."

"I'm not here scoping out women. I'm on a take-down."

Which explained the two men (Ash's scrumptious brothers) wrestling with the slime machine a few feet away.

"Nice job, by the way," he told me.

I shrugged. "You know me. I live to kick ass."

"I thought you lived to shop."

"When I'm not kicking ass." I glanced down at my hand. The slime had dried to a sticky mess. "You wouldn't happen to have a Kleenex or a wet wipe on you?"

He patted the back pockets of his ultra-tight jeans. "Sorry. Look, you weren't planning on sticking around here, were you?"

"Maybe. Why?" Even as I asked the question, my mind raced with possibilities.

"Because I was thinking that since you're here and I'm here, maybe we could share a bingo card. And go for a drink afterward. And get to know each other. And do some primo mattress dancing."

"Because you're in the way."

"I'd love to—" The words stumbled to a halt and the smile died on my face. "Excuse me?"

His lips went from full and kissable to drawn and tight. His gaze hardened. "You compromised this apprehension."

"Hello? I helped stop a slobbering criminal."

"You gave him a way out." He glanced past me as his brothers hauled Foamy to his feet. "You're just damned lucky he didn't take it."

"What are you talking about?" The stench of spoiled, rotten meat pinched my nose as the trio scooted past us toward the back door. The sound of gnashing teeth grated across my eardrums and a coldness prickled my skin.

I stiffened and Ash's gaze hardened even more. "You shouldn't have gone after him. You put yourself in a shitload of danger."

"In case you haven't heard, I'm not exactly helpless." I stiffened against a sudden wave of fear. I know, right? I'm a *vampire*. Invincible. Ballsy. Bitchy. *Brave*. The scared-shitless chromosome hadn't made it into my DNA cocktail. I flashed a little fang to emphasize this point to Ash. "I can totally hold my own."

"Against another vampire."

"Or a were," I added. My gaze collided with his and I arched an eyebrow. "Or a demon. In fact, I think I'll stick around and pass out a few more cards." I could handle anything, even if I had led sort of a sheltered life before opening my dating service.

Basically, I'd lived at home with my parents and spent the majority of my time with other born vamps. While I'd learned about Others—everything from made vamps to weres, demons to Big Foot—I'd never actually met any of them face-to-face until recently.

Ty had popped my cherry in the made vamp category. Viola had been my up-close-and-personal with a were. And Ash had been my first demon.

While the jury was still out on Big Foot, I felt certain I could do damage in the other three categories.

My hand itched and I remembered the glob of slime running over my fingers, dribbling down my palm.

I swallowed. "That is, I would love to stick around and pass out more cards *if* I didn't have a ton of work waiting back at the office." All right, already. My aversion to blood also extended to bodily fluids. "I can see you've got the situation totally under control now, so I'll just leave you to wrap things up."

That is, unless you wanna, you know . . .

"Later."

Guess not.

I turned and so did Ash. I limped a few steps before I heard the door rock shut behind me. I was just about to whistle for a cab when my super-deluxe ears perked and I heard the creak of hinges.

My pulse leaped and a zing of excitement went through me, followed by a needle poke to the chest (a feeling I might have mistaken for guilt had I had anything to feel guilty about—which I so did NOT).

I turned, fully expecting Ash to pull me into his arms and lay one on me. Or, at the very least, stare down into my eyes and ask me out for a cup of coffee. Instead, I found myself staring at a head full of snow white hair.

My attention fell to a pair of clear blue eyes surrounded by a million tiny crow's feet staring up at me.

"Are you Miss Lil?" He was a short, stout old man wearing gray overalls and black loafers. He had a tool belt cinched around his waist. A walkie-talkie sat on one hip while a giant key ring dangled from the other. "Lil Marchette?"

"Last time I checked."

Relief filled his pale eyes. "You left this in one of our storage closets." He held up my purse, and the past half hour rolled through my mind.

Schmoozing the bathroom line. Following Carmen into the storage closet. Helping Carmen in the storage closet.

I'd set my purse aside and completely forgotten about it.

Way to go, dumbass.

"I hope you don't mind that I opened up your wallet," he went on, "but I needed to see your ID to know who it belonged to. Mighty nice picture, by the way."

"Thank you." The realization of what had almost happened hit me and relief rushed full-force through me. Forget my wallet. I'd almost lost my makeup bag, complete with the new Hot Toddy Terrific lip gloss I'd bought just yesterday.

"It's all present and accounted for," the old man went on. "Three bucks, fifty-two cents, and nineteen credit cards."

"Actually, it's twenty, but I left my Barney's at home." I'd reached my limit and couldn't use it until my next payment. "Thank you so much." My hand plunged into the bag. My fingers closed around the tube and I smiled. "You're a lifesaver."

"Glad to be of service." He grinned. His blue eyes twinkled and his stats flashed like the marquee in Times Square.

Earl Hubert Stanley. Father of four grown daughters—one of whom was a pediatrician in Rockaway Beach. Husband of fifty-two years to Emmaline Louise Stanley, who'd passed away last spring. He'd been the custodian at St. Michael's for the past twenty-eight years. He'd meant to retire last year (he and Emmaline were going to buy an RV and head for Branson and Dollywood on account of Emma was a huge Dolly Parton fan). But then Em had died and he hadn't been able to watch a rerun of *Best Little Whorehouse in Texas* since.

His oldest girl had been after him to join a bridge

club or a senior golfers group or *something*. She said he needed to get out more and meet people. Maybe a nice woman to share dinner with once in a while, instead of eating TV dinners all by his lonesome. He kept telling Susie he didn't need a dad-burned dinner date and that he liked Hungry-Mans. Particularly the fried chicken. Sure, he thought it might be nice to have company once in a while, but he couldn't quite accept the thought of breaking bread with any other woman besides his beloved Emmaline.

Awwww . . .

"You take care now, Miss Lil, and don't talk to strangers. The city can be mighty unforgiving at night." He started to turn.

"Wait." I touched his arm. "I'd really like to repay your kindness."

"Oh, no." He waved me off. "I couldn't take any money. It wouldn't seem right."

I was liking this guy more and more. "What about a date?" I handed him a DED card.

He studied the white vellum for a long moment before he shook his head. "It's mighty kind of you, but I don't think so."

"I could help you find your soul mate."

"Already found her."

My chest hitched and an image of Ty popped into my head. Not that he's my soul mate or anything. Or that we have a connection that goes beyond the physical. He's a made vamp and I'm a born vamp (oil and water), and the mental connection is simply a by-product of my drinking from him and him drinking from me. It doesn't mean anything, certainly not that we're destined to be together or forever linked or anything silly like that.

Fughedaboudit.

"What about a companion?" I asked, eager to ignore the depressing thought. "I could help you find someone to spend your free time with. Someone who likes the same things that you like." I handed back the card, along with a mental *You should call me because Emmaline wouldn't want you to be lonely. She would want you to have fun and make the most of the years you have left. Really.*

He seemed to think. "But it wouldn't be a date, right? I'm not looking for romance."

"We're talking companionship only."

He gave the card another once-over. "She has to like chicken. And golfing. And poker. I've been playing online, but my dream is to go to Atlantic City and break the bank."

"No problem."

"And *Reader's Digest*. I love the funnies—" The loud crackle of his walkie-talkie drowned out the rest of his words.

"Earl? You there, buddy?"

He grabbed the receiver and pressed the button. "Right here."

"We need you in the sanctuary ASAP. And bring the mop."

"Don't tell me," I said when he clipped the radio back onto his belt and stuffed my card into his pocket. "Clean up on aisle nine?"

"It's a tough job"—he shrugged—"but somebody's gotta do it."

I thought of Dead End Dating, Vinnie's detailed list, and the all-important fact that I could very well be *this* close to kissing my afterlife goodbye. I stiffened. "Tell me about it."

Six
❤ ❤ ❤

I hopped a cab back to the office and headed straight for the bathroom and a bottle of antibacterial soap. Clean and barefoot (I stashed the booties until I could get them repaired), I spent the next few hours entering profiles, setting up various client dates, and dodging phone calls from my mother.

Despite having my afterlife threatened and getting slimed by a stinky demon, it turned out to be just another typical work night. So much so, that by the time I powered off my computer and killed the lights, I'd stopped worrying altogether.

Everything would work out.

Carmen would fall madly in love with Vinnie and his mother. Remy would turn out to be gay and my mother would give up trying to fix me up. Barney's would extend my credit line. Ty would show up with an engagement ring the size of a third-world country. Brad would come to his senses, dump Ang, reunite with Jen, and they would live happily ever after.

Hey, it could happen.

I locked up, let myself out the back door into the alley, and closed my eyes. A little concentration and I started to feel weightless. The flutter of wings echoed in my ears and just like that, I went from fantabulously dressed matchmaker to megalicious pink bat (I wasn't hitting the pavement in my bare tootsies any more than I absolutely had to).

By cab, my apartment was about ten minutes away in a renovated duplex on the east side of Manhattan. Via bloodsucking creature of the night, I made it in a minute flat.

I flapped my way around the side and landed behind a large green dumpster. The smell of cat litter (my neighbor Mrs. Janske was a widow with about a zillion cats) and old newspapers (the accountant down the hall from me had an addiction to the *Wall Street Journal*) burned my nostrils.

A tingling swept over me and the rhythmic *whap whap whap* faded into the beat of my own heart. The cold of the ground seeped into my feet and something wet and sticky squished between my toes (I *so* needed to work on my landing skills).

I ignored the urge to look down and proceeded around the side of the building. Climbing the front steps, I keyed in the security code and slipped inside.

If apartments were retailers, my place would be a dollar store in the burglar-bar section of Brooklyn.

Obviously a huge step down from the flagship Neiman Marcus—aka my parents' Park Avenue penthouse—where I'd crashed prior to asserting my independence, but still the best move I'd ever made.

Having my own digs was primo. I could prance around in my thong, drink my dinner straight from the bottle, and leave my lingerie hanging all over the bathroom. There was no one telling me what time to be home or how to decorate or what pretentious born vamp I should boff (all right, already, so my ma was still doing this, but she did it via nagging cellphone messages rather than live and in color).

Still, in all fairness, living with my folks hadn't been a *total* nightmare. There had been a teensy, tiny sliver of sunshine in an otherwise overcast sky.

Two words. *Maid service.*

I ignored a faint niggle of regret and took the stairs toward the fifth floor. I was halfway down the hallway, humming the latest Fergie tune, when I spotted the small gift-wrapped box sitting on my LIFE IS A BEACH PARTY mat.

My heart stalled and I froze. My gaze zeroed in on the trademark Tiffany blue box.

Ty.

It was the first thought that popped into my head.

All right, already. My first thought was *holy shit*, but Ty followed right on its heels.

A notion that was too ridiculous even to contemplate, of course. I was an ultra-hot born vamp. Jessica Simpson and Carmen Electra and Jenna Jameson all rolled into one. We're talking sexy, seductive, *irresistible*.

I thought of all the cab drivers and newsstand attendants and Starbucks clerks I'd smiled at over the years.

And then I thought of the average salary of a cabbie/newsstand attendant/Starbucks clerk.

Okay, so maybe Ty wasn't that far out of the realm of possibility. Capturing criminals was dangerous work. Surely it paid megabucks.

My heart started beating again, shifting into overdrive as I knelt and retrieved the box sitting on my faded palm tree.

Excitement zipped up and down my spine, along with a rush of pure joy. I was definitely tipping the scales toward *crazy*. It wasn't like this was *it*. The right guy. The right time. The beginning of the rest of my afterlife as a committed vamp.

Sure, I'd given up dead-end relationships because I was ready to settle down, but not with Ty. We were all wrong for each other. I knew it. He knew it. That's why we put on the brakes after monumental, fantabulous sex and a crystal-clear connection even Sprint couldn't screw up. We weren't going anywhere.

Except maybe the Guinness Book of World Records for the most orgasms in a twenty-four-hour period. Fantabulous orgasms. The kind that made your toes curl and your skin tingle and your knees go weak and . . . *oh, baby.*

My cheeks heated up (along with a few other

places) and I gave myself a mental shake. We had no future together.

Made.

Born.

Comprende?

Whatever waited in the box—even if it was the gargantuan marquise with the side baguettes and platinum setting I'd been lusting after *forever*—was going straight back to the store.

Not happening.

Forget it.

No thank you.

And so there was no reason to torture myself by looking, right? I should simply call Ty, tell him that what we had was beautiful, but strictly superficial. It was over and I was terribly sorry if I misled him.

At the same time, he'd probably gone to a ridiculous amount of trouble to pick out just the right thing. He'd probably spent days, maybe even weeks, searching for the perfect thing to wow me. What kind of person would I be if I didn't at least take a quick peek and admire his selection?

I tore off the bow and gripped the lid.

Easy. My conscience went from preachy to reasonable. *It might not be platinum. It might be silver. Or gold. It might not even be a marquise. It might be a princess cut. Or a solitaire. Hell, it might not even be a ring at all. It might be a diamond necklace. Or one of those divine filigree bracelets. Or a pair of bloody fangs—*

My mind went numb and my stomach dropped to

my ankles as I stared at the surprise nestled on a bed of white satin.

After several heart-pounding moments, I snapped the lid shut as quickly as I'd opened it. I stood there doing more of the heavy-duty stress-reducing breathing I'd seen on *Dr. Phil*. The frantic in and out of oxygen only made my pulse beat that much faster. The panic mounted. Cold horror slid through me and I became quickly aware of the dark, ominous hallway that lurked around me.

I forgot all about the key in my purse, twisted the knob on my door, and pushed. Hinges strained. Wood cracked and splintered and I rushed inside. I slammed the door shut behind me, stuffed the nearest chair I could find under the doorknob (on account of I'd just taken out the dead bolt and a good chunk of wood), and went in search of coping mechanism number two—alcohol.

Since I'm more of a social drinker (Cosmos with The Ninas, appletinis after work with Evie, Jell-O shots while helping my human sister-in-law pick out an atrocious wedding dress), the best I could come up with was a travel-sized bottle of Crystal left over from a cruise I'd taken with my family ages ago in celebration of Moe's going national.

The cork popped, the opening gasped, and I downed the entire bottle in one long, desperate gulp. By the time I finished, I felt loads better.

Okay, so *loads* was stretching things a bit, but I felt calm enough to evaluate the past few minutes rationally.

Who? What? When? Why?

The questions raced through my brain, none of which could be answered unless I grew some big ones, opened the box again, and gave the contents another look. Just to make sure, you know, that the ghoulish things weren't some stress-induced figment of my imagination.

I had been threatened and slimed, and all in the same night. That was enough to wig anyone out and send them off to the Land of the Loony.

I braced myself and reached for the box.

The good news was that I wasn't a hallucinating nutcase. The bad news was that they were still there.

Gleaming white enamel. Razor sharp ends. Bloody stumps.

My chest tightened and a lump worked its way up my throat.

Like I know crying is useless and weak and yada yada, but sometimes it feels like the right thing to do, even for a badass vampire like yours truly. Especially when I noticed the small white card tucked into the lid of the box. I pried the paper loose and unfolded it.

Just a little reminder of what I'm going to do to you if you don't find me a woman . . . V.

The reality of what I was up against hit me. I sank down onto the edge of my sofa and started to bawl.

For myself.

For the poor schlump who'd lost his fangs.

For myself. Because I was going to be the next poor

schlump if I didn't find Vinnie's soul mate in time for Mama Balducci's birthday.

My vision blurred. I was sniffling like crazy when I felt a brush of warmth against my ankle, followed by a soft *meow*.

I wiped at my cheeks and blinked frantically. Killer's image came into focus.

He wasn't the most attractive cat (I'd rescued him from an alley and certain death at the hands of a rat the size of King Kong). He was brown and white, and still a little on the thin side, but I'd spruced him up with a silver collar and a white rhinestone tee that read THE KING HAS ENTERED THE BUILDING.

Instantly, my fear multiplied when I thought of Vinnie planting the box outside my door with Killer mere inches away. If the guy could dismember a were bear and rip the teeth off a vampire without one iota of conscience, imagine what he could do to a poor, helpless kitty.

Killer narrowed his bright green eyes, his message loud and clear. *Enough with the blubbering, already. I'd like to eat sometime before global warming ends and we plunge into the next ice age.*

Make that a snotty, pretentious, smart-ass kitty.

"I'm this close to losing my fangs. I could use a little compassion, here."

Compassion's for wussies. What you need is a baseball bat. Or better yet, a Glock. Cap a few in his ass and you're home free.

Yeah, right. I *so* didn't do death and destruction all that well. A gun was definitely out.

As for the bat . . .

I made a mental note to hit the local sporting goods store first thing next afternoon. In the meantime, I pushed to my feet and stashed the Tiffany box in the back of my closet until I could give it a proper burial.

A few minutes later (after searching the apartment for more body parts and double-checking the chair in front of the door), detoured off the panic highway and U-turned back to normal.

Alicia Keys drifted from my iPod docking station. The scent of my favorite Bundt Cake candle sweetened the air. I changed into pink Juicy sweats and headed for the pantry.

I'd just reached for a can of Kitty Cuisine when a strange sense of awareness crawled through me. I knew then, even before I heard the slow creak of wood and the tremble of hinges, that someone was trying to get into my apartment.

And with the sucky way my night was going, I felt pretty damned certain that it wasn't Colin Farrel.

Seven

♥ ♥ ♥

Every muscle in my body went tight. My heart stalled and my survival instincts fired to life (I had poor, defenseless Killer to protect, not to mention a closetful of designer couture).

In the blink of an eye, I morphed into killer-bitch mode and rounded the corner, fangs bared. The living room appeared empty, but the door stood wide open. The chair sat off to the side. My mind raced back to the present that had been sitting on my doorstep.

"You don't have to leave me any more surprises," I called out. "I get it. You're the biggest, baddest SOB in New York."

"Nice to see you, too."

The deep, familiar voice rumbled through my head and relief washed through me, followed by a wave of anger. I shifted from killer bitch to irritated bitch and turned on the made vampire who stood directly behind me.

I gave him my best glare.

At least, I meant to glare. But then Ty Bonner came into my line of vision and suddenly the only thing I could do was gaze.

While I'd thought about him more than once over the past several weeks since our night of goodbye sex, I hadn't actually seen him in the flesh.

He looked even better than I remembered.

Wilder. Sexier. And *très* macho.

Long dark hair fell to his shoulders. Stubble covered his strong square jaw. His blue eyes gleamed with a neon-like intensity that made my tummy tingle and my nipples pebble. He was dressed classic-cowboy in a black leather duster, black jeans, and black boots. A Stetson sat low on his forehead, shadowing the top half of his face and obscuring the tiny scar that bisected one of his eyebrows.

But I didn't need to see the tiny pucker of skin to know that it was there. I'd felt it with my hands. I'd even tasted it with my lips and licked it with my tongue. In fact, I'd licked my way down the smooth column of his neck, over the dip in his clavicle, around his nipples, his belly button, his—

Sheesh.

And they said men were obsessed with sex?

I gave myself a great big mental kick in the ass and summoned my most pissed-off expression. "You scared the crap out of me. Haven't you ever heard of knocking?"

He gave me that odd look that said he couldn't quite believe I was for real, and then he shrugged. "Knocking's overrated. You lose the element of surprise."

"And you needed to surprise me because?"

"You tell me." He stared into my eyes, his blue gaze pushing deep, probing. "Lil?"

"Yes?"

"What's your full name?" he asked, still not convinced.

"Are you kidding me? You know my name."

"But do you?"

I narrowed my gaze at him. "Have you been drinking?"

"I've been working. Now answer the question."

I shook my head and contemplated pinching myself. I had to be stuck smack-dab in the middle of a nightmare. Yeah, a nightmare would be good. That would mean Vinnie and the bloody fangs were all a very vivid product of my overstressed imagination. I'd been burning the proverbial candle at both ends, trying to build up my business and pay off the credit cards I'd used to get DED off the ground, and it was finally catching up to me.

Talk about the perfect excuse, except for one slight problem—other than the occasional beach fantasy, I didn't dream. I slept the sleep of the undead— pitch-black and consuming—and so, *it ain't happenin', sister.*

Forget the nightmare. I latched onto the next explanation that jumped into my head. "Am I being punked?"

"Is that show even on anymore?"

I didn't have a clue because I didn't actually watch much TV. Evie (she TiVo'd *everything*) usually filled me in. "*Candid Camera?*"

"No."

"*What Not to Wear?*" I frowned. "Because if that's the case, you can get Stacey and Clinton to take a hike back to the studio because I *so* don't need their help. They can take their free shopping spree and give it to some clueless woman wearing a polyester pantsuit and beat-up clogs . . ."

Wait a second. What the hell was I *saying*? We're talking the words *shopping* and *free* in the same sentence.

"I have clogs," I blurted, my mind doing a quick mental calculator of all the belts and shoes and fab bags I could afford with a complimentary 5K. "Vintage seventies. Big, bulky, *white*," I admitted. "Hideous. I should have thrown them out ages ago."

A grin tugged at the corner of his mouth for the space of two heartbeats before his frown deepened. "This isn't about clogs." His hands closed over my shoulders, his fingers strong and firm and compelling. "Stop stalling and tell me your name."

"Countess Lilliana Arrabella Guinevere du Marchette," I blurted.

He didn't look relieved. (Not that I blamed him. Saying it was bad enough. Hearing it had to be just as painful.)

His eyebrows drew together. "Favorite color?"

"Pink."

"Favorite blood type?"

"O positive."

"Occcupation?"

"Matchmaker."

"Favorite pastime?"

"Shopping."

"Wrong."

"Excuse me?"

"You like to talk," he announced with a flourish.

"True, but not as much as I like to spend money. Or plastic. Or gift cards." Which he knew full well since he'd harbored a fugitive (me) a few months back when I'd been wanted for murder.

"Hometown?" he persisted.

"A small but filthy rich village in the south of France."

"First bite?"

"The son of a nearby peasant farmer. Pierre. He had killer abs."

"Biggest weakness?"

"MAC lip gloss and Brad Pitt." *And you.* The thought rushed through my mind before I could stop it and, sure enough, Ty's gaze deepened as if I'd come through in hi-def.

Duh.

Despite our mutual agreement to end our sexual relationship, we were still mentally linked since we'd shared both sex and blood (*not* at the same time— otherwise I'd be even more into him than I was).

Since I still hadn't learned how to consciously block him the way he blocked me, he read me loud and clear. Meanwhile, I rarely got so much as a signal from him unless he wanted me to.

"You're still into me, huh?"

Like now.

"I said *was*," I told him, averting my gaze. "Meaning past tense." I shook my head and rushed on, "What's with the twenty questions anyway?"

"I ran into Ash tonight. He mentioned that you got caught in the middle of one of his takedowns over at St. Michael's. Something about a rogue demon trying to escape during an exorcism. You stopped him."

"And?"

"We're talking a *demon*. Straight from the bowels of Hell."

My brain cells clicked. "That explains it. I don't think I've smelled anything that bad since Killer swiped one of Mrs. Janske's goldfish and hid it in the laundry hamper." I shook my head. "But I still don't get why you're grilling me."

"The demon got away. One minute they were about to exorcise him and send him back to Hell, and the next he up and disappeared."

"And?" I arched an eyebrow.

"The only way for a demon to escape one body is to possess another. Since he came into direct contact with you, it's possible that he ditched the poor bastard he was in and slid into you when you touched him."

"Me? Possessed by a demon?"

"It's possible."

"Says you. There's nothing possessing me." Except maybe a smidgen of vanity. And a healthy dose of lust. "I mean, I would know, right? I would feel it?"

"Without a doubt. It's an all-out war. You versus the demon. It can get pretty ugly." He glanced behind him. "When I saw the door, I thought the mental battle had turned physical."

"I just had a little trouble with my key." I did a nanosecond of soul-searching and came up with *nada* for ugly, slimy demons. Then my attention snagged on Ty again and I couldn't help but smile. "You came over here because you were worried about me."

"That, and there's a pretty big bounty at stake."

My expression, along with my ego, died. "You really know how to burst a girl's bubble."

He grinned. "Hey, it's all about business."

Yeah, right.

He knew as well as I did that there was no use admitting that he was more worried about me than losing out on a few grand. Even if we hadn't been from opposite sides of the vamp spectrum, Ty had his own issues. Namely, a vengeful, sadistic sire who refused to let him have even a moment of happiness.

Ty knew Logan (said sadistic sire) was watching, and so he refused to get involved with me for fear that I might get caught in the cross fire between the past and the present.

Too sweet.

That was just one of many strikes against us, and so there was absolutely no reason for Ty to acknowledge his concern or for me to feel even the least bit touched by it. I should take him at his word and toss him into the pot with all the other cold, emotionless, money-grubbing vampires out there.

"How much is the bounty?" I couldn't help myself.

"A lot."

"Translate that into dollars and cents."

"A lotta dollars and an equal amount of cents."

"You don't know, do you?" Which meant it hadn't been all about the moola when he'd rushed over. "I'm about to pour a glass of blood," I heard myself say. "I've got plenty. Want to join me?"

"You don't really think that's a good idea, do you?"

Yes. "No." I tamped down a rush of disappointment. "You probably should get back to work."

"Probably."

"There's a demon out there with your name on it, after all."

"There is." He looked none too happy about it, either.

I forced a smile. "Make sure you wear gloves. I can still feel the slime."

He gave me a serious look. "You sure you're okay? You don't feel any different?"

Actually, I felt a lot different. Warmer in certain places. Desperate in others. "I'm fine. Tired, but fine. Speaking of which, you have all of a half hour to get where you're going because I doubt you brought sunscreen."

He winked. "I just happen to have some SPF 2000 right here in my pocket."

"And here I thought you were just glad to see me." Okay, so I was flirting. But we're talking harmless words. It wasn't like I was going to hoist him over my shoulder, throw him on my king-sized bed, and rip off his clothes.

Unless he asked me to.

"I'd better go," he blurted, his knowing gaze burning into mine. "You'd better get that door fixed."

"First thing tomorrow," I promised.

He nodded. A flash of black and then he was gone. My stomach hollowed out and I had the sudden urge to rush forward and catch one last glimpse of him before he disappeared down the stairwell. Or out the nearest window.

"I know, I know," I told Killer when he blinked up at me as if to say *looo-zer.* "I'm pathetic, right?"

And slow as hell. I've been waiting on dinner for a full fifteen minutes now. He added an irritated *meow* to drive his point home.

"Don't get your doggie tee in a twist. I'm getting it."

Make it quick, otherwise those fangs aren't the last little surprise you'll be getting tonight.

"I should have left you in that alley."

Yeah, yeah. And I should have shredded your favorite silk blouse. We all have regrets. Get over it.

Ty's image popped into my head and my ears prickled for the sound of footsteps or the flutter of wings. Not because I, like, *liked* him or anything. He'd been my first since jumping off the Meaningless-Sex bandwagon several years ago and climbing onto the I'm-Saving-Myself-for-My-Eternity-Mate express. He'd simply reminded me of all the fun I'd been missing.

But the fun was over now, and I was NOT going back to my old ways. I intended to find my eternity mate, settle down, and pop out a baby Shiloh or Violet or Magenta. Someday.

If my femur or humerus didn't wind up in Vinnie Balducci's sock drawer.

On that sobering thought, I moved the door back into place, wedged the chair under the knob, scooped up Killer, and headed into the kitchen.

The clock was ticking.

Eight
♥ ♥ ♥

Later that afternoon, I walked into Dead End Dating a half hour ahead of schedule. I'd put the whole fang incident in its proper perspective. It had been a warning of things to come if I didn't hook Vinnie up, which I totally intended to do. And so there was no reason to panic yet. It was only Friday, meaning I still had five days until Mama B's birthday.

If it had been Monday, well, that would have been a completely different story.

At least that's what I'd been telling myself since I'd crawled out of bed. Add a grande house brew with four shots of espresso on top of the mental pep talk, and I was jacked up on enough caffeine and optimism to match up even Vinnie.

"You brought Starbucks." Evie's eyes lit up as if I

were dangling a tube of MAC's newest lip gloss—
Cherry Buzz—right in front of her.

Evie had been with me since I'd first opened my
doors to Manhattan's rich and clueless. Simultane-
ously, she could man the phones, run a computer, and
wield a mascara wand without taking out an eye.
Like *moi*, she'd been raised with a 24-karat spoon in
her mouth. Unlike *moi*, hers had been replaced with a
plastic spork because her financial guru father had
made some poor investments.

"Have I told you how wonderful you are?" She
took the mocha latte I handed her with both hands,
closed her eyes, and took a deep whiff. "You're
the kindest"—she sipped—"prettiest"—another sip—
"most thoughtful boss"—sip, sip—"a girl could
have." Another sip and she eyeballed my sequined
Chilli Couture tank. "Nice."

"You, too."

For someone now paying her own way on a modest yet respectable salary (minus the health and dental, but I'm still looking) she always managed to pull
off office fab.

Today, she wore a Forth & Towne silk polka-dot
dress, an Anne Klein bangle watch, suede lace-up sandals, and a haggard expression.

"Tough day?"

"Tough fifteen minutes." She motioned to the storage closet, aka interview room A. "DED's newest
client and definitely the most challenging."

I followed her gaze. "Did he pay cash?"

"Is that all you think about?" When I smiled, she shook her head. "Of course, that's all you think about." She handed me several bills and checks paper-clipped together. "He paid cash, along with two other new clients. The other three wrote checks."

"Five newbies?"

"Actually, we'll have six. You have an appointment this evening with a"—she hit a key on her computer and brought up today's schedule—"Mia van Horowitz. Local business owner who doesn't have much time to date. Said she wants the super-deluxe package, so I scheduled her with you." She turned and retrieved a stack of messages. "Also, your mother called about this weekend, Nina One called about this weekend, someone named Mr. Lowe called about a private matter, your mother called again, and someone named Carmen called to confirm an afternoon appoinment." She paused and shifted her gaze to the screen. "I couldn't find her on your schedule."

"Actually, she's not an official client. I'm hooking her up with a friend totally out of the goodness of my own heart." I so wasn't going to involve Evie in the fight for my life, even if I did have the sudden urge to spill my guts to someone and share my angst. There was no reason to start some drama when everything was going to work out.

Carmen was perfect. Vinnie and his mother would love her. She would love him (hopefully). *Perfect.*

She arched an eyebrow. "Since when do you hook up anybody for free?"

"I gave you a free profile," I pointed out.

"Because we only had one other person in our database at the time—you—and you needed every entry you could get." She eyeballed me. "What's really going on?"

"Nothing." I was not going to cave. No matter how much she stared at me. "He's a friend of a friend of a friend and he's lonely. You know I'm a sucker for lonely."

"You're also a sucker for cold, hard cash."

"Maybe he doesn't have any. Maybe he works at a low-paying job helping poor people at a shelter or something and he can't afford our services. Maybe I'm being benevolent, despite my affection for cash."

"Does he?"

"Does he what?"

"Work at a low-paying job? Because last time I looked, wiseguys raked in a pretty hefty amount of money."

"He's fallen on hard times—wait a second. Did you just say *wiseguy*?"

She nodded. "Wiseguy, as in a mafia-loving, spaghetti-eating bulldog who pops people for a living." It was my turn to arch an eyebrow, and she shrugged. "My dad used to have a couple of them who worked special assignments for him. Daddy would get pissed if someone fudged on an investment, and Guido and Lou would pay the fudger a little visit. They either came back with the money, or a few bloody fingers. So why is this guy after you? What did you do?"

"Nothing. He saw me on *Manhattan's Most*

Wanted, he needs a date for his mother's birthday party, and so I'm stuck with the job." Which was, for the most part, the truth. Minus a few details—such as Vinnie being the biggest SOB in Jersey who liked to play dentist to the rich and fanged.

"You could call the police and tell them you're being threatened. They'll keep an eye on you."

"They're busy. They can't watch me 24/7." I shook my head. "It would piss Vinnie off and I've gotten attached to all of my fingers." I stiffened and summoned my courage. "Besides, there's no reason to bring the cops in at this point because I've already found him someone."

"Carmen?"

"Bingo." I took the stack of messages and mail that she handed me and shifted my attention to the closed door of room A. "Tell me about the last fifteen minutes."

She took a long gulp of her latte as if drawing strength. "You know me. I firmly believe there's someone for everyone—except my bastard of an ex who deserves to rot in hell all by his lonesome. But otherwise, we all have that perfect someone out there somewhere."

Have I mentioned that Evie and I were identical twins in a past life?

"Except in this case," she went on. She took another sip and then wrinkled her nose. "This guy is something else."

"Unattractive?"

"Obnoxious." She handed over his profile. "Do

you know what he listed under 'Special Talents'? Farting the national anthem. Not only did he write it down, but he actually demonstrated. I don't think we'll ever get the smell out."

"At least he's not shy."

"Duh. He propositioned me eight times already. Very graphically. Complete with hand gestures. I swear, if I have to go in there one more time, I'm going to give him a few gestures of my own."

"Never fear, Lil is here." Armed and ready to save the singles of the world from the cold, dark, bottomless pit of loneliness. (Did I mention I gulped down a Rockstar while waiting in line at the Starbucks?) "I'm sure DED's latest and greatest has some redeeming quality that can make him attractive to the opposite sex." I scanned the first page.

Favorite movie? *Saw I-IV*.
Favorite music? Anything by Marilyn Manson.
Favorite actor? Howard Stern.
Favorite pastime? Jacking off.

Okay, maybe not.

I shook my head. "So he's got a few hang-ups? If he were perfect, he wouldn't need us." Atta girl. It was all about being optimistic and confident. At least that's what I'd been telling myself since I'd crawled out of bed that evening, after a sleepless night worrying about Vinnie and my possible death and dismemberment.

"I'm sure we can find *something*," I went on.

"Maybe he likes to cook. Or maybe he's an animal lover."

"Funny you should mention that. Page three details a very interesting threesome with a duck and a pig. Exactly," Evie added when I made a face. "I'm telling you—lost cause."

"There has to be at least one appealing trait."

"I'd settle for a trait that doesn't make him a prime candidate for Riker's Island."

Me, too.

I was just about to flip to the second page to see what I could come up with when my attention snagged on the name scribbled at the top.

Earl Hubert Stanley.

Recognition struck and my already frantic brain cells started to buzz. My mind raced back to the previous night and the church.

"The janitor?"

"He's a janitor?" Evie grabbed the profile and flipped to the personal info section. "Great. Now we're really screwed. Nobody in Manhattan wants to date a vulgar, socially deranged, serial-killer obsessed, sexually deviant *janitor.*" She shrugged. "Then again, I just described my last four boyfriends, so what do I know?"

I scanned the profile for any mention of a dear departed Emmaline or Dolly Parton or even a measly Hungry-Man. Nothing.

Because it's not him.

This was New York City. Out of several million people, there had to be more than just one Earl Hubert Stanley. Unfortunately, the slimiest of them all had waltzed into my matchmaking service.

I *knew* it.

At the same time, my vamp senses had kicked into overdrive and I had this strange tickling in the pit of my stomach. A reaction that told me something was off.

Handing the profile back to Evie, I turned and was about to step toward room A—to have a little look-see myself—when the door behind me swished open. A blast of hot summer air rushed at me as Carmen Gianno walked in.

I forgot all about my gut feeling in favor of saving my ass. "Carmen!" I reached her in a nanosecond, my hand extended, my smile firmly in place. "I'm so glad you're here. I've already got the most perfect dating prospects lined up."

"But I haven't even filled out a profile."

"A mere formality. It's obvious you're a smart, sophisticated, attractive woman—the ideal of any and every man in the Dead End Dating database. I've already got several choice picks just for you."

"You do?" she asked.

"We do?" Evie joined in.

"You bet." I flashed Evie a please-play-along-and-beef-up-the-DED-reputation-if-you-value-your-life glance. "We have the biggest selection of prime bachelors in the city."

"We do?" Evie repeated herself. Another glare and she stiffened. "I mean, of course we do." She nodded profusely. "Biggest selection of Grade-A beefcake in the Big Apple. In the state, too, for that matter. Maybe even the country."

"I wouldn't go so far as to say the *entire* country." Okay, so maybe I would. "More like the entire continent. We have a vast database of men from all over the world." All's fair in love and the fight for one's afterlife.

"That's great, but if I do this, I would really like someone local. I had a long-distance relationship with a guy I met on MySpace once. It didn't last. He was from California."

"Too far away?"

"That, and too many lies. His profile said he was six foot three with black hair and green eyes and an engineering degree. He was really four foot eleven, bald, with glasses."

"What about the engineering degree?"

"He still had that, which was why I kept up the e-mail relationship. But a job loses its importance when you can't see eye to eye on anything. Especially when you see eye to chest."

"I met this guy on-line once," Evie chimed in, "who said he was a professional wrestler. He was, only it turned out he wasn't a member of the WWF. Instead he did transvestite pool wrestling at county fairs. He was actually a pretty decent catch—good-looking, nice, funny—but I just couldn't see myself spending my free time watching my boyfriend roll around in a bustier with another guy in a bustier."

"I hear ya." I nodded. "The good ones are always

transvestite pool wrestlers. Except here at Dead End Dating," I rushed on.

Carmen didn't look convinced. "I'm actually feeling a little nervous about this. I don't know if it's such a good idea. I wouldn't want to get stuck with another weirdo."

"You won't find any weirdos here, that's for sure."

At that moment, I heard a frantic *pop, pop, pop* that bore an odd resemblance to the opening beats of "America the Beautiful." My attention shifted to interview room A.

"What was that?" Carmen's gaze followed mine.

"Hot water heater," I blurted. "It's been acting up lately. Isn't that right, Evie?" I motioned with my eyes. "Why don't you go see if you can do something to take care of the noise? Bop it with a wrench or something."

"Why don't you bop it while I get Miss Gianno, here, started on her profile." Evie smiled innocently and reached for the paperwork.

"Actually"—I snatched the sheets from her hand—"I've already made some notes online. All I need is to ask her a few questions and we'll be all set." I smiled at Carmen. "I know you're busy and I didn't want to waste any time on the preliminaries." I winked. "It's all about getting to the good stuff." I shifted the sweet smile to Evie. "There's no need to make her go back over the same old information when I already know most of what I need to." *My fingers need you,* I mouthed when Evie didn't look any more willing.

"Fine." She finally shrugged. "I'll bop the stupid

hot water heater." She retrieved a bottle of Lysol from under her desk and pushed to her feet.

"Let's go into my office." I motioned Carmen forward.

"Oops." Evie's voice drew me back around in time to see her, hand paused on the doorknob of room A. "I forgot to tell you. Your mom's holding on line one."

I watched Carmen disappear into my office and threw a frantic "Tell her I'll call her back" over my shoulder.

"Sorry." She smiled and held up the can. "Busy."

"Please—" I started, but she hauled open the door and was quickly swallowed up by a cloud of thick, smelly air.

My stomach dropped to my ankles.

I know, I know.

I'm a denizen of the darkness. A ruthless, bloodthirsty creature of the night. I could so do my own dirty work, including telling my mother I would call her back at *my* convenience.

But Jacqueline Marchette hadn't worked her way up the corporate ladder at Guilt, Inc. by being the most understanding woman.

"I don't mind waiting if you need to get that." Carmen indicated the phone and the frantically blinking red light.

I gathered my courage, snatched up the phone, and blurted in the most Evie-like voice, "Lil Marchette is indisposed at the moment. You'll have to call back." *Plunk.* "Now." I opened up a new file on my com-

puter, keyed in Carmen's name, and shifted my attention back to her. "Let's talk about what you're looking for in a man." I sent up a silent prayer for ruthless
and mother-whipped.

"Well"—she seemed to think—"I'd really like
someone I can connect with on all levels."

I smiled and typed *Vinnie* under the *must-have* section. "When you say all levels, what exactly are you
referring to? Do you want someone you can relate to
physically? Emotionally? Morally?"

"Yes, yes and yes. I want an attractive man who's
nice and sweet."

"And Italian?"

"Italian would be good."

My smile widened as my fingers flew across the
keyboard. *Balducci.*

"I want someone who's compassionate, too."

"When you say compassionate, you're referring to
a man who's considerate, yes? A man who, say, cares
about other people? Like, for instance, his mother?"

"Of course."

I keyed in *mother-loving Italian.*

"But he shouldn't care about her more than me. I
don't want a mama's boy."

I keyed in *you are so screwed.*

I abandoned the computer screen and reached for a
blank profile. "I think I get what you're looking for.
Why don't you just fill out the personal info on this
first page—address, date of birth, that sort of thing—
and I'll play around with what I've already got and
see what I can come up with."

Carmen turned her attention to the profile and I turned my attention to the computer screen. I did a quick check on compassionate men in my database. Twenty-three came up as listing that quality as one of their biggest attributes.

Vinnie, obviously, wasn't one of them.

I ignored the professional inside of me that whispered I was going against all tried-and-true methods (and the big-mouthed romantic that screamed what a selfish bitch I was), pasted on my biggest smile, and declared, "Here we go. *The* perfect man."

"Really?" Hope blossomed in her eyes and I squelched a niggle of guilt.

I mean, really, who was I to say at this point that Vinnie *wasn't* the perfect man? Sure, all evidence pointed to the contrary. But love *was* blind. And maybe, if I was extremely lucky, deaf and dumb as well.

Vinnie might very well turn out to be the star of Carmen's hottest fantasy. Her soul mate. Her be-all and end-all when it came to the opposite sex. He would be eternally grateful to me and I would never have to worry about being an SOB target ever again.

I held tight to the slim possibility and smiled. "How would you like to meet him later tonight?"

Nine
♥ ♥ ♥

I spent the next half hour giving Carmen a few dating dos and don'ts and battling my own conscience.

I know, right?

Super vamps didn't usually get caught in the sticky details of right versus wrong. We're creatures of greed and lust and instant gratification. What can I say? I was cursed at birth. I kept picturing Little Red Riding Hood (or in Carmen's case, Little Blond Riding Hood with natural boobs and a wholesome spirit) getting dismembered by the Big Bad SOB.

All thanks to *moi*.

At the same time, there was always a chance (however teeny tiny) that they could fall madly, passionately in love. And who was I to stand in the way of true love? As a matchmaker, I'd pledged my afterlife to helping lost lonely souls find their One and Only (for a fee, of course, but that's beside the point). I would never be able to sleep during the day if I deprived even one individual—vamp, human or Other— at a chance at happily-ever-after.

Besides, Vinnie was a Sniper of *Otherworldly* Beings, meaning his handiwork was limited to Others, and so I felt certain that Carmen wasn't in any physical danger.

I made a mental note to look up the SOB handbook online—dontcha just love the Internet?—just to make sure there was a little rule in there about the non-dismemberment of humans. In the meantime, I fished a can of Mace from my bottom drawer (Evie had bought us both cans of the stuff after watching an *America's Most Wanted* episode that featured a serial rapist from Manhattan) and handed it to Carmen.

"What's this for?"

"Some businesses give out matchbooks, we give out Mace. Just in case someone grabs you in an alley, or a cab driver turns out to be a crazed kidnapper, or Mr. Right morphs into Mr. Slice-and-Dice. Not that any of that is going to happen," I rushed on. "It's strictly a promo item."

She eyed the silver can. "But there's no DED written anywhere on here."

"True, but it's the thought that counts. When you whip that baby out, you'll think about how much DED cares about you."

That, or what a lunatic I was.

While Carmen gave me an odd look and pocketed the Mace, I made a reservation at Pollo Loco, the hottest, trendiest, *busiest* restaurant in SoHo. The plan? For Carmen to meet Vinnie in an hour for drinks and appetizers and, hopefully, some major fireworks when she looked at him and he looked at her and . . . well, you know.

I crossed my fingers, gave Carmen cab fare and a reassuring smile, and watched her leave. After sending up a silent prayer to the BVU (Big Vamp Upstairs), I walked into the outer office to beg Evie's forgiveness for sticking her with Earl.

She wasn't at her desk. Her computer was off, her paperwork cleared. The door to room A stood wide open and empty.

Apparently, she and Earl had bailed while I'd been with Carmen.

The smell, unfortunately, hadn't.

Thankfully Evie bought bulk for the small votive holders we had situated around the office. I unearthed a box of candles and spread them throughout the room. I'd just finished lighting number twenty when the bell on the door trembled and my next appointment walked in.

She had long, jet black hair, pitch-black eye shadow and bright red lips. She wore a black leather tank top, ripped jeans, and black biker boots. The sharp smell of rubbing alcohol and ink clung to her. Understandable. With the exception of her face, there wasn't a visible area of her body that wasn't tattooed.

She had a purple snake that started just under her jawline and curled down around her neck. A bright pink flamingo wrapped around her right bicep. A black and white shaded portrait of Janis Joplin hugged the other. A leopard print dotted her right arm from elbow to wrist, while Betty Boop perched on the left. Hearts dotted the tops of her knuckles. Tweety Bird peeked up over the neckline of her tank and the tail of a dragon curled from under her shirt and encircled her belly button.

She eyed the candles and arched one black brow. "Human sacrifice?"

"That was last night."

"Bummer." She glanced around and held out her arms. "So where are the dudes? Your assistant said you had over one hundred eligible guys for me to pick from."

"In our database. We don't actually keep them here on display."

"Oh." She shifted from one foot to the other and I could tell she felt way out of her element. She was obviously used to being the one in control rather than the one asking for help.

One glance into her heavily rimmed eyes and I could see why. Mia van Horowitz had been on her own since sixteen, when she'd snuck away to Atlantic City to get her first tattoo.

It had been right before her younger brother's bar mitzvah, and her parents had been so outraged (by the tattoo and the fact that she'd dyed her strawberry blond hair a bright, vivid blue) they'd kicked her out of the house. A Jewish princess didn't have blue hair and a purple snake wrapped around her neck. She had a tasteful bob and a four-carat diamond wedding band wrapped around her finger. Her parents had disowned her and she hadn't been welcome at family functions since.

I quickly envisioned myself showing up at the next hunt with blue hair and a snake winding around my neck.

Nah. My cousin Jeanine had blue hair and a real live snake (a pet named Buddha) that she wore to the annual Marchette family reunion, and no one batted an eye.

"So how do we do this?" Mia asked me.

"Well, first you fill out a profile. Then we'll talk a little bit about what you're looking for and your pre-ferred dating package. The super-deluxe is my per-sonal favorite." And the most expensive—which, of course, was why it rated *numero uno* with yours truly. "You get six months in our database and ten guaranteed prospects. Plus we pay for your first date." I motioned Mia into my office and settled be-hind my desk. I pulled up her appointment informa-tion on the computer. "It says here you're a tattoo artist?" As if I didn't already know.

"I own my own shop down in the Village. I started small about ten years ago as a one-woman show. Now I've got eight other artists working for me. I re-cently bought the storefront next door and doubled

my space to accommodate more clients. Scribble—
that's my place—does everybody who's anybody in
New York. I've worked on the lead singer of Nickelback, the fashion editor from *Vogue,* even Mr.
Weather."

Mr. Weather was the local celebrity bachelor who
had been featured on *MMW* last season. He was also
the one I'd scared the shit out of during a wild carriage ride through Central Park.

"You're kidding, right?" The only thing I'd seen
painted on Mr. Weather had been an overdone tan.
He was vain and self-centered and overly obsessed
with his hair, and I just couldn't picture him doing
anything to alter what he considered a perfect body.
"Are you sure it was him?" I added. "The meteorolo-
gist from Channel 5?"

She nodded. "Did a self-portrait on his left pec. I
wanted to do the shoulder blade, but he wanted to be
able to see himself without looking in a mirror."

That was Mr. Weather, all right.

"I work at least fourteen hours a day and do anywhere from two to ten tattoos during that time." She
pulled a knife out of her pocket, slid the blade free,
and started to clean under her thumbnail.

I *know.*

"That doesn't leave much time to date," I told Mia.

"My social life doesn't suck because of lack of
time. Time I can make. It's lack of patience." She
waved the knife. "I hate playing games. I have certain
things I want from a guy and I'm not shy about telling

them. Most men are intimidated by that, which is why I don't get asked out much."

That, and the fact that she looked freakin' scary.

"So what is it you actually want? Compassion? Understanding? Someone to unclog the toilet?"

"Sex." She folded the gonzo knife and stuffed it back into her pocket (thankyouthankyou*thankyou*). "I need it all the time. At least three, four times a day. I should have the guys lining up, right?" She shook her head. "While I like sex, I'm not into meaningless affairs. I've had enough of that. I want one guy—with a clean bill of health—that I can share myself with again and again."

"And again."

"Exactly. Most of the guys who like to do it a lot are players. I thought Buck, my last boyfriend, was the exception. No VD or HIV. The guy was as clean as a whistle. He lasted for about eight months, but then he had to bail. Left me a note saying he just couldn't keep up and that he was checking himself into Hoboken Rest and Rehabilitation because he had a strained penis. He said I was a freak and I needed Sexaholics Anonymous." A glimmer of sadness lit her eyes and my chest hitched. "The thing is, I've tried SA three times and it just doesn't work for me on account of I *really* like doing the nasty."

Amen.

"Maybe I am a freak," she went on, "but what's the harm? It's not like I'm lazing around all day just getting after it. I'm a productive citizen. I pay taxes. I have a job. Sure, I take a few more breaks than most people, but it's not like I'm puffing away in the alley and killing my lungs, or gulping down a bottle of whiskey and pickling my liver. I'm working my muscles and building stamina. Sex is healthy."

"Extremely." I nodded.

"So instead of trying to get rid of a healthy lifestyle, I'm thinking I just need to find a decent guy who can give it to me as often as I need it. If that means paying for ten prospects, or even twenty, I'm there."

I multiplied the super-deluxe package by two and smiled. "You've definitely come to the right place."

Once Mia had filled out her profile and written me a sizable check, she left to make a late-night appointment with some high-society Park Avenue princess who wanted the latest cover of *GQ* (featuring Russell Crowe) immortalized on her lower back.

I spent the next thirty minutes running searches for possible matches. I came up with a whopping one when it came to common interests—Mia liked sharp objects, New Age Goth music, and deadly reptiles. Unfortunately, the one possibility turned out to be Evie's cousin, Word.

Word Dalton was a twenty-something horndog who loved heavy metal Goth bands and had a sexual fetish for small, furry creatures. I knew this because he'd installed a speaker system at DED a few months back and I'd actually set him up on a few dates in lieu of payment for services rendered. Word was human, but that hadn't stopped me from fixing him up with a were squirrel. A match made in heaven, right? Wrong. It turned out that the were wasn't full-blooded (do NOT ask), and so Word had quickly lost interest. He was back to being a head-banging, animal-lusting loser.

While he gave new meaning to the word horny, he hadn't had enough actual experience to fill a plastic Coke cap. No way could he satisfy a woman like Mia.

I was definitely going to have to go outside the DED family for this one. I started brainstorming, jotting down any and all possible hot spots to find Mia's type. I'd managed to come up with three when the phone rang.

My heart started to pound as my gaze shifted to the caller ID.

UNAVAILABLE stared back and relief rushed through me. Like all born vamps, my mother kept up with the times, changing and blending. At least when it came to clothes and shoes and kick-ass hairstyles. What she hadn't kept up with were the advances in technology. Namely, she still didn't know how to work her answering machine and she'd yet to figure out how to set up voice mail on her cell. Punching in a code to hide her phone number was completely out of the question.

I picked up the phone. "Thank you for calling Dead End Dating, where love is always in the air." Along with a few other things, courtesy of Earl Hubert Stanley. "This is Lil. What can I do for you?"

"You can overnight me an extra-large bottle of valium. I can't get any here, at least not legally, and I haven't worked up my nerve to try the street version. A few more days in *paradise*, however, and I just might change my mind."

"Who is this?"

"Mrs. Jack Bertrand Pierre Phillipe du Marchette." Translation, Dr. Mandy Dupree, the human forensic pathologist who'd married my brother Jack in a beautiful moonlit ceremony at the Waldorf Astoria.

I'd been the maid of honor, much to my mother's horror, and my brother Max had been best man. My mother had written Max's decision off as the usual boys-will-be-boys, while mine had rated my-traitorous-daughter-is-driving-a-stake-through-my-heart. (Have I mentioned that in addition to being the CEO of Guilt, Inc., my mother was president of Double Standards?)

"Boy," Mandy went on, "I never realized that would be such a mouthful. It's a good thing I didn't hyphenate. Then again, that's the least of my problems right now."

If my brother had boffed one of the cabana girls or nailed the night maid, I was *so* going to fly down to Rio and kick his ass myself. "What did Jack do?"

"Nothing. He's wonderful. The perfect man, er, I mean vampire." Her voice trembled. "It's Mother Marchette."

"Mother who?"

"*Marchette*. She told me to call her Jacqueline, but that seems so disrespectful. My mother likes Mother

Dupree, so I figured if it worked for mine, it would work for yours."

"Uh, yeah." *Not.* "What did she do?"

"She won't stop calling. The first time, we figured she just wanted to see if we'd made the flight okay. That was two and a half weeks ago. She's called every day since."

"But she said she hadn't talked to Jack."

"She hasn't. We've been taking the phone off the hook, so she's been calling the front desk. She's talked to everyone in the hotel. She's also bribed them, so we aren't getting a moment's peace. Concierge is constantly checking on us. Maid service shows up unannounced. Room service is forever bringing wine or champagne or *something*. Even the hotel manager pays us a nightly visit. We've complained and threatened to switch hotels, but it's the busy season here and there isn't another decent suite available at any of the other resorts. Besides, your mother would just do the same thing if we switched hotels. You know, Lil"—worry crept into her voice—"I'm starting to think that she's not all that thrilled with the marriage."

Ya think?

"Nonsense," I heard myself say. "You're a wonderful woman. Any born vampire would be lucky to have you for a daughter-in-law."

"That's what you think. But what about your mother?"

"Does it really matter what some pompous, closed-minded, irrational third party with decent taste in shoes thinks or does? You're happy and Jack's happy. That's what's important. The two of you *are* happy, right?"

"Extremely."

"Then forget about my mother."

"That's a little hard to do when you have the *policia* walking in on you while you're buck naked and bent over a hibiscus plant."

I was *not* going to ask.

"Apparently, your mother knows every vampire in the free world over the age of five hundred," Mandy went on. "General Guerrero, the chief here, used to be General Genoise about eight hundred years ago. He and your mother are old, *old* friends and he was more than happy to check up on us for her. He even brought a fruit basket."

"That's sweet."

"The fruit basket was for me. He brought two hookers for Jack."

"I'm sorry."

"You and me both. The fruit we could toss, the hookers wanted to hang around and watch cable on account of they'd never actually seen a real television because they were from a really poor area of the city. Jack and I felt so bad for them that we even let them order pay-per-view." A pleading note crept into her voice. "We only have three days left and we haven't had so much as two solid hours without some sort of interruption. You have to help us."

"What can I do?"

"Talk to Mother Marchette."

"I was thinking more along the lines of another fruit basket. Maybe a nice bottle of wine." Because talking to Jacqueline was useless. I'd found that out firsthand at the age of five, when I'd threatened to hold my breath until she agreed to let me go to Mass with Sister Wilhemina, my au pair at the time.

In other words . . . *get the fuck out.*

"Jack would talk to her, but he feels bad enough avoiding her. He's afraid he'll buckle if he hears her voice and feels the guilt firsthand."

"Tell me about it."

"I'm begging you," Mandy added. "You're our last hope."

Nuh, uh. Not happenin' sistah.

"*Please.*"

"Okay," I blurted. Come on, she said *please.*

"Really?"

"Stop worrying and have fun. Drink a few margaritas for me and tell Jack he owes me big time."

"You're the best sister-in-law in the entire universe."

I smiled as I slid the phone into place.

Then the expression faded as I realized what I was going to have to do next.

"I've thought about it," I heard myself say after I dialed my mom's number and she picked up. "I'll do it. I'll go out with Remy. An official date."

"You will?" She sounded surprised for about an

eighth of a second. "But of course you will. How could you not? He's absolutely perfect. Handsome. Wealthy. Well-endowed, at least according to his mother, who told me that his—"

"One date," I cut in. "That's all I'm agreeing to."

"Right now. But once you see his—"

"*One*," I cut in, despite the sudden curiosity that bubbled through me. I couldn't surrender completely to the dark side, otherwise she wouldn't have to go to any trouble—*time-consuming* trouble—to convince me that Remy was the One. "We'll talk, have a few drinks and see what happens."

"Sex," she concluded. Before I could protest, she rushed on. "I have to call Estelle. She'll be so happy you've finally come to your senses. She'll need to let her mother know, of course. And her grandmother. And her great, great grandmother. And her great, great, great grandmother. They're all still in France and it'll take a few weeks for them to make arrangements to fly over for the commitment ceremony, which we can easily do at the club in the next few weeks—"

"It's just one date, Ma." I slid the receiver into place, ignored the tiny tremor of panic in my gut (commitment ceremony, two weeks, tons of relatives), and focused on a surge of victory. "Am I a total genius or what?"

"I'm voting for number two." The deep, familiar voice echoed in my ears.

I glanced up to find Ash Prince standing in my office doorway. He looked as hot and yummy as ever and my legs trembled.

But then I took one look at his face, serious and slightly homicidal, and my excitement drained into full-blown irritation.

Ten

❤ ❤ ❤

"I've already been through this with Ty," I told Ash as he walked into my office, his two hunkalicious brothers right behind him. "I AM NOT possessed by a demon."

I'd barely gotten the last words out when I found myself snatched out of my chair and shoved up against the nearest wall, my arms behind me.

A hard male body pressed up against my back. Mo or Zee, I wasn't sure. I only knew Ash stood just to my right, his dark gaze drilling into me.

"Pat her down," he told the man holding me.

A strong male hand plunged under my hair and felt its way down my neck, over my shoulders, down the length of each arm.

"I'm not," I insisted. "Now let me go." Hands slid around my rib cage and my heart started to pound. I became increasingly aware that I'd worn a silver lamé halter minus a bra or even pasties. My nipples pebbled. The air grew hot and thick and my throat went dry. I summoned my most threatening voice. "Don't make me get all vampy on your ass." Meanwhile my hormones chanted *lower, lower, lo-wer!*

The hands quickly obliged. Fingers spanned my waist, played over my hips, my buttocks, my thighs . . .

Wait! my hormones screamed as the strong, purposeful touching moved down toward my knees. *Come back!*

"I mean it," I warned again. "I'm getting pissed."

"You're lying." Ash's warm breath ruffled the hair near my right ear. "You were the last person to make contact with him. It *has* to be you."

"Says you." The hands reached my feet, which were clad in a pair of leather Casadei animal print peep-toe stilettos. Fingertips circled my ankles and grazed my arches, and I fought down the laughter that bubbled in my throat. "Stop." A smile tugged at my lips. "Please."

So I'm a vampire and I'm ticklish? Get over it.

"She's clean," a deep voice announced, the search-and-destroy over as quickly as it had started. "You want to go ahead and chop off her head now?"

What?

I barely heard Ash's voice through the sudden thunder of my own heart. "Let her go."

I was free all of two seconds before Ash caught me from behind and whirled me around.

He loomed over me, his hunky brothers flanking

him. "You can't run," he told me, his dark gaze firing a bright liquid gold. My tummy hollowed out.

"I have no intention of running," I managed. "Or letting you cut my head off. Because I'm NOT the demon."

"Then who is?" Ash asked.

I gave my hormones a great big mental bitch-slap and gathered my control. "Your brothers?" I arched an eyebrow. "If I recall, *they* were the last ones to make physical contact with Slimey. They dragged him back inside the church, remember?" I motioned to both men. "If I were you, I would seriously be considering these two."

"It's not them."

"How do you know?" I eyeballed Mo and Zee. "They both look pretty demonic to me." And pretty damned hot.

I gave the old hormones another great big slap.

"They can't be possessed by a demon."

"Why not?"

Because they're demons themselves, dummy.

Ultra-hot, über-sexy demons with perfect, kissable lips and really great hands—*slap*.

"You already know what we are," Ash pointed out.

"True, but you never actually said it out loud." Or whispered it in my ear. Or murmured it against my cleavage.

Slap. Slap.

"I need confirmation," I went on. "So far, I've been assuming based on pure instinct. That and the fact that every woman within a mile radius starts panting like a dog in heat whenever you guys walk into a room." Or thinking crazy thoughts like how good we would all look naked and rolling around on the floor together.

Slap. Slap. Slap!

He grinned and my insides quivered. "You *are* a demon, right?"

"You're getting off the subject."

"No I'm not. We're talking about the big D. You're one. And so are your bros, here." I arched an eyebrow. *"Right?"* I pressed.

They both glanced at Ash, who continued to stare at me. "You know you're not getting away," he told me. "Not this time. We *will* catch you."

And do wicked bad things to my body?

Okay, so obviously the mental slapping was doing more harm than good. My sadistic hormones were still racing ninety-to-nothing for Smutsville.

I gathered my self-control and fought against the sensations ripping through my body courtesy of not one, but three sexual dynamos—

My thoughts came to a staggering halt as a realization struck and Mia's image popped into my head.

I smiled. I was definitely one hundred percent, certifiable *G-E-N-I-U-S.*

"Gentlemen." I pushed past all three men and motioned them into chairs. "Make yourselves comfortable and let's talk."

"We'd rather stand," Ash declared, his gaze still suspicious.

"Suit yourself." I perched on the corner of my desk and put on my most persuasive you-want-to-do-everything-I-want-you-to-do expression. "You know, guys, we've never really taken the time to get to know one another." I zeroed in on Mo. "Tell me about yourself. Do you have a special talent? A hobby?" I glanced at Mia's profile spread out across my desk and beamed. "Perhaps a knife or dangerous reptile fetish?"

"Uh, no." He seemed caught off guard by my sudden shift from threatening and defensive to sexy and determined. "Not really. I mean, I know how to use a knife, but—"

"Forget it," Ash cut in. "She's clean. Let's get out of here."

"Wait a second." I was right on their heels as they walked into the outer office. "You're leaving? But why?"

"You're not possessed."

"But five seconds ago, you said I was."

"I changed my mind."

"Why?"

He turned on me. "Demons are tricky, but not a one of them likes to play matchmaker." He seemed to pause, as if noticing something. He sniffed at the air and wrinkled his nose.

"We had a gassy client," I explained.

"I can tell." His eyes fired their brilliant yellow as he drank in the scent for a long, silent moment.

Ugh. To think I actually considered jumping his bones less than two minutes ago.

"Keep your eyes open," he finally told me when he stopped sniffing (yay) and his gaze cooled to an impenetrable black. "If you notice anything strange, call me right away."

His words sank in for a startling moment and I swallowed. "You really think he's been *here*? A real demon?"

He nodded and I thought of Mia. Appearance-wise, she certainly looked the part. But I couldn't forget the flash of hurt in her gaze when she'd mentioned her ex-boyfriend. That, and I hadn't heard any wheezing or moaning. Nor had she slimed me even once.

"If it isn't you," Ash went on, "it's someone. Someone who's been in the vicinity." He glanced around, his scrutiny bouncing from wall to wall before shifting back to me. "You have my cell number." I nodded and he motioned to his brothers. "Let's roll."

"Wait!" The word burst out of my mouth as I remembered Mia's check and my futile database search. Panic rushed through me. "I know there's a dangerous rogue demon on the loose, but what happens once you catch him?"

Ash paused, his hand on the door. "First off, we don't want to lose him again, so we have to cut off the head of the person he's possessing. Then we chop the body into pieces and burn it. Then we take the ashes back to Hell, where they belong."

I swallowed the sudden bad taste in my mouth. "And after that?" I pressed.

"We move on to the next case."

"What about down time? Don't you guys ever take a break? Maybe toss down a few beers at the local bar or watch a football game, or *something* that qualifies as social?"

"We have sex," Mo offered.

"Lots and lots of sex," Zee added.

I smiled again. "Perfect. Now if I could just get a little more information—"

"Forget it." Ash shook his head. "We don't need a dating service to get women."

"What about a quality woman? Someone who's got it going on personally and professionally? Someone you can take home to mom and dad?" Or, in Mia's case, someone to boff in the storage room of a really hip tattoo shop.

"We don't take women home. Too dangerous." He grinned. "But thanks for the offer."

A dozen questions crowded my brain, bumping and kicking to get down the neural pathway and out of my mouth first.

The one that made it out was "Huh?"

"*Anything strange,*" Ash reminded me as I stood there still trying to process the "dangerous" comment. His grin faded into a serious expression that sent a sliver of dread down my spine as he pushed open the door. "Call me ASAP."

"Thanks so much for babysitting," I told Mrs. Janske a half hour before sunup when I stopped at her apartment to pick up Killer.

While I'd come to the conclusion that Vinnie

wasn't going to rip out my fangs just yet, I wasn't taking any chances that he might come back and decide to do a little nip and tuck on Killer. Just in case I didn't get the message the first time.

"Just don't go making a habit of it. I got better things to do with my time than chase after a crazy cat all night long."

Like chasing after a dozen crazy cats.

My gaze slid past her and riveted on the smorgasbord of felines parked throughout her living room. There were white cats. Orange cats. Black cats. Spotted cats. Tiny cats. Fat cats. Cats with lots of hair. Cats with no hair.

"Besides," Mrs. Janske went on, "Wonder Woman and Whiskers don't like this one," she said, holding up Killer. "He keeps trying to play hide-the-Vienna-sausage with them."

"Killer?" I glanced at my cat, who wore a who-you-gonna-believe-me-or-some-old-biddy? expression.

"I don't cotton to that sort of lewd behavior in my house," she added.

"I'll have a talk with him." I took the cat from Mrs. Janske's outstretched hands. One of his claws grazed my forearm and I winced.

"What was that for?" I asked him once we were on our way up to the fifth floor.

That's for leaving me with Baby Jane back there. I'm definitely peeing on your favorite Chanel suit when we get home.

"She's grouchy, I know, but it's just a cover. Deep down she's extremely lonely."

Deep down she's as crazy as Britney and Lindsay rolled into one certifiable package. She talks to her cats.

"I talk to you."

But you can hear me because you're a vampire. She's just a lunatic lady who talks to a bunch of lunatic cats that don't talk back to her. Two of which are oversexed pussies who almost ate me alive.

I grinned. "I thought you were the one getting fresh?"

Pu-lease. I've got standards, you know. We're talking a hairless job and one who's been eating too many cans of Gourmet Kitty. Bald and fat are NOT my style.

"That's not very nice."

Yeah, well you wouldn't be very nice either if you'd come this close to being raped and violated. If you ever leave me with that old bat, I'm running away from home.

We reached my apartment in a matter of seconds. Thankfully, there were no little surprises waiting on the doorstep.

"I was just trying to protect you," I told Killer as I locked and bolted the door behind us (I'd reported the broken one to my landlord, who'd obviously fixed it while I was getting felt up at the office). "But if you would rather stay in the apartment and get sliced and diced, so be it. Maybe Vinnie will make a necklace out of your claws."

Killer blinked up at me as I set him on the Berber rug the Ninas had bought me as a housewarming present. *The hairless one was sort of cute, if you go for the whole Mrs. Clean look. And, of course, I've always enjoyed a female with a little meat on her bones. More cush to the push, if you know what I mean.*

I arched an eyebrow. "And my suit?"

I would never desecrate the sacred name of Chanel.

"That's what I thought." I turned and headed into the kitchen.

But your shoes . . . Killer's thoughts followed me. *Those are a completely different story.*

Eleven

♥ ♥ ♥

"**S**he's perfect," Vinnie declared.

"Really?" It was early Saturday evening and I was on my way to work. I rounded the corner near Lexington and Seventy-fifth, a black coffee with a double shot of espresso in one hand and a studded silver Foley + Corinna bag in the other.

On the surface I was biker chic in a black leather puff-sleeve jacket, white ruffled blouse, black pencil skirt, and a pair of B & D Python heels.

Inside, I was majorly tripping after a nearly sleepless day tossing and turning and worrying about Vinnie and Carmen's date.

"Damn straight," Vinnie went on. "She's Catholic and really stacked, *and* she can cook a mean lasagna. What more could a full-blooded Italian man ask for?" Before I could answer, he rushed on, "Mama's going to love her."

"So you're happy?"

"Does a werewolf shit in the woods?"

I thought of Viola and her mega-room mansion. "Don't they use toilets like everyone else?"

"It's an expression, for Chrissake."

"An inaccurate expression. Werewolves are responsible, civil members of society." That is, when there's no full moon. Or raw meat. Or really hot alpha males nearby.

"Says who?"

"Me."

"A bloodthirsty, murdering born vampire?"

"For the record, I *am* thirsty, but I can totally nosh on the cup of coffee in my hand rather than biting some poor, defenseless schmoe."

"Yeah, right."

"Aren't we getting a little off the subject? I thought we were talking about Carmen and how wonderful she was."

"She's the shit."

Relief swamped me, followed by a rush of *hell, yeah!*

I'd done it. I'd saved my ass—and my fangs—and matched up Vinnie Balducci. I was *so* going down in the Matchmaking Hall of Fame for this one.

That is, as long as the feeling went both ways.

The doubt wiggled its way into my head and I heard myself ask, "So, um, do you think she liked you, too?"

"Are you kidding? She winked at me every chance she got, and she even tried to play footsies with me under the table. It was all I could do to keep her from ripping my clothes off right there in the friggin' restaurant."

Hey, you couldn't argue with footsies.

"I want to see her again," Vinnie went on.

"No problem." I rounded another corner and dodged a puddle of water. "I'll give her a call and set something up. How about lunch? Tomorrow?"

"Dinner. Tonight."

I glanced at my silver bangle watch and coffee dribbled down my arm. "But it's already seven o'clock." I juggled the cup to my opposite hand and shook away the warm liquid. "What if she's already busy—" *Click*.

"Vinnie?"

"If you'd like to make a call, please hang up and dial . . ."

Great. Just great.

I hit the OFF button. Dread firebombed my stomach and my heart started to pound. I had no clue if Carmen was even home right now, much less if she wanted to do dinner like, *now.*

Then again, if things had gone that well, she was undoubtedly as anxious to see Vinnie as he was to see her. She could be sitting by the phone at that very second, just waiting for it to ring.

I searched for her number on my cell and hit TALK. Sure enough, she picked up during the first ring.

"Hey, Carm, it's Lil." I grinned. "A little birdie told me all about last night."

"You mean the absolute worst two hours of my entire life?"

"Vinnie wants," I started, but then her question registered and my words stalled. *Absolute? Worst? Entire life?*

"But I thought you guys hit it off?" I asked when I finally found my voice. I dodged another puddle of water, a homeless person, and then a fire hydrant. "Vinnie said you were winking at him."

"My contact was folded."

"What about the footsies?"

"I was wearing flip-flops. They kept slipping off and I had to chase them around under the table with my foot." She blew out an exasperated breath. "I've never had a date that bad in my entire life."

Don't panic, I told myself. *Do. Not. Panic.*

It couldn't have been all bad, right?

"You know," I used my most professional Auntie-Lil-knows-what's-best voice, "there are a lot of other factors that go into a date—other than the actual daters—that can ruin an otherwise wonderful experience."

"You think?"

I stopped at a crosswalk. "I see it all the time. Vinnie might have been the perfect guy, but you just couldn't recognize it because the overall dating experience wasn't up to par. Maybe if we dissect last night piece by piece, we can figure out the real problem. First off, how was the food?"

"It was great, but Vinnie burping his appreciation wasn't. That man is the crudest person I've ever met."

"Good food." I ignored the "that man" comment and pushed on. "What about the atmosphere?"

"We had candles and soft music. Overall, it was very romantic, except when Vinnie almost punched out the waiter for pouring water into his empty tea glass."

"Nice atmosphere." The light turned green and I crossed the street. "What about the service?"

"Other than the water-in-the-tea-glass incident, it was really good. We only had to wait three minutes to get a table. Our food came right away. Of course, nothing was fast enough for *him*. He kept glancing at his watch and motioning for everyone to hurry up."

"Conversation?" I stepped up onto the curb and started down the sidewalk.

"Well, I did everything you said. I asked him lots of questions about himself and tried to get him to talk, which he did. He told me all about his love of mob movies with lots of blood and gore, and how he enjoyed kicking ass whenever someone pissed him off and that he hated cats."

Oh, no he didn't.

"And dogs," Carmen went on, "and most every animal in the universe with the exception of a tank full of fish he has at his apartment."

I fought down my hatred (while Killer and I had a hate/hate relationship, I still had a soft spot for the cuddly little guy) and searched for some silver lining.

"Does he have goldfish? Guppies? Some of those cute Nemo look-alikes?"

"Piranha." She blew out an exasperated breath. "It just didn't work. We're too opposite. I idolize Mother Teresa and read poetry and watch the ballet. Guess who Vinnie idolizes?"

I crossed my fingers. "Gandhi?"

"Jimmy Hoffa. He also reads the obituaries and watches WWF." She sighed. "If we were concession candy, I'd be a Three Musketeers and he'd be a giant Jawbreaker. The guy has no feelings. There was a woman walking around with roses and I hinted that I would really like to have one. Do you know what he said? He said flowers were for funerals and that when I kicked the bucket, he'd be happy to send me a whole truckload."

"At least he's not cheap."

"He's morbid. And crude *and* obnoxious, and I don't think he has a compassionate bone in his body."

"You know, Carmen"—I summoned my most convincing voice—"that's a little hard to believe. Vinnie is actually one of our most sought-after clients."

"He is?"

"Of course." *Not.* "I mean, I know he doesn't make the best first impression, but he does have other good qualities."

"Like what?"

"Nice hair," I blurted after a long, contemplative moment. "He's got very nicely groomed hair."

"Would that be the hair on his head, or his back?

Because he took his shirt off to flex for me before I climbed into the cab. He was so furry that I couldn't tell if I was looking at his pecs or his shoulder blades."

Definitely too much info.

"Talk about poster boy material for a heavy-duty wax job," she went on. "As for the hair on his head, I swear he uses an entire bottle of Dippity-do. Even a tornado couldn't do any damage."

"I know he's a little fifties when it comes to the hair, but retro is in"—I thought of Vinnie's Gucci jacket—"and back hair aside, he does know how to dress."

"He wore all black. I felt like I was talking to a funeral director."

"Don't be silly." I summoned a laugh. "Vinnie's not a funeral director." *Although he does contribute heavily to the industry.* "He's in the, um, cleanup business."

"Does he recycle?" She sounded hopeful.

I thought of the bones in his sock drawer. "Sort of." While I wasn't sure that he was using them for anything other than souvenirs, at least he wasn't cluttering up the local landfill. "He's definitely into conservation." Before she could say anything, I rushed on. "Why don't you give him another chance? Maybe you two just got off on the wrong foot last night. He's a little rough around the edges, true, but beneath the surface, he's a sweet guy."

"Really?"

"A marshmallow," I assured her. "You just have to get past the hard shell."

"He picked his teeth with a razor blade."

"You can't blame a guy for good hygiene. Come on, give it one more try. I promise you won't regret it."

"And if I do?" She sounded hesitant.

"I'll reimburse your profile fee."

"I didn't pay a profile fee."

Oh, yeah. "A free spa trip," I blurted, thinking of my monthly spray tan appointment with Dirkst (next Wednesday, six p.m.). The man had the fastest gun in New York. He also had a twin brother. "Two full hours with the one and only Devin. He gives the most magnificent Swedish massage."

"A massage?"

"Not just any massage. A Devin massage. You know what they say about a man with big hands?"

"That he has a big penis?"

That, too. Those thin white spa pants left little to the imagination.

I shook away the sudden image. "I'm talking about his grasp. Guys with big hands usually have strong fingers. They can go after those deep muscles like nobody's business."

"I *have* been under a lot of stress lately," she said after a long silence. "A massage might be just the thing to take the edge off."

I rotated my head and listened to the *snap, crackle* and *pop* of my own muscles. Maybe I needed a visit with Devin and his gonzo feelers myself.

"So you'll give Vinnie another chance?" I persisted.

"Did I mention the hair on his shoulders?"

"I'll throw in a pedicure."

"One more date, but that's it."

"Monday night," I told her. "I'll call with the details."

Twelve

❤ ❤ ❤

After I hung up with Carmen, I headed up Lexington and quickly outlined a plan of action before I dialed *casa di Balducci*.

"Just tell me where and when," he said when he picked up the phone on the second ring. "And I'm there."

"Dead End Dating. One hour."

I know, I know. I was definitely digging my own grave by not setting up the date for tonight, but if I wanted to make this work, I couldn't send Vinnie back into play without softening him up a bit first.

A few minutes and another coffee spill later, I pushed through the front door of DED to find Evie sitting behind her desk.

While I didn't require her to work on Saturdays, she usually stopped by in the afternoons to get organized for the upcoming Monday. That, and for the occasional client who couldn't spare the time to stop by during the week.

"New client?" I set the paper cup on the corner of her desk. Shoving my hand deep into my bag, I retrieved a wet wipe to mop at my coffee-drizzled skin.

"Just lining up a few matches for Monday. Is that for me?" She snatched up the coffee before I could say *"No, it's for me. I didn't know you would be here,"* and downed half the scalding liquid in one swallow. "Man, I fucking needed that."

Time. *Out.*

Since when did Evie go around using the f-word? Sure, I did it myself, but only in extreme circumstances—when I burned myself with the curling iron or someone cut in front of me at the Starbucks or when Killer took a dump inside my favorite suede boot.

But in normal, everyday conversation? Try never.

I eyed her and noted her pale complexion. "Is everything okay?"

"You bet." She downed the other half of the coffee, wadded up the cup, and slam-dunked it into the nearest trash can before turning back to her computer.

The hair on the back of my neck prickled and something niggled at my gut.

I know, I know. She was a grown woman. If she wanted to say *f-this* and *f-that,* who was I to say anything about it? I terrorized poor, unsuspecting humans and drank their blood for Damien's sake.

All right, so I bought the stuff already bottled from my favorite deli. The point was, I wasn't one to be waving my finger at someone else.

I cleaned my hand, tossed the used wipe, and shifted my attention to the task at hand. "Do you think it's too late to get a hot wax kit?"

"I could probably pick one up at the pharmacy around the corner. They're open until eight on weekends." She grabbed a stack of manila folders, pushed up from her desk, and started toward the file cabinet. "Just let me put these away and I'll head over."

As usual, she looked office fab in a flowing white silk top, gray slacks, and worn camouflage Crocs—

Wait a sec.

I blinked, but they were still there. Still worn. Still camouflage. Still *Crocs.*

I tried for a nonchalant voice. "Those new?"

Evie shoved the folders into the top drawer and glanced down. Her eyes widened as if seeing the shoes for the first time. "They, um, belong to my maintenance man. He leaves them by the front door every night."

"Okay, I'll bite." Not literally, of course. While Evie and I shared everything from fashion tips to man troubles (she thought Ty was as megalicious as I did), I'd yet to come out of the coffin. Not because I didn't trust her. Rather, I'd disappointed my parents enough by snubbing my nose at the family business—in particular the closet full of beige Dockers and lime green polo shirts also known as Moe's trademark uniform.

I wasn't going to break the number one born-vamp commandment—Thou Shalt Keep a Low Profile—and add another black mark to my already tarnished record. "Why exactly are you wearing your maintenance man's shoes?"

She looked as puzzled as I felt. "I don't really know." She shrugged and closed the cabinet with a loud *thunk*. "I guess I was in a hurry and just grabbed the first pair I saw." She walked back around her desk, opened the bottom drawer, and traded the Crocs for a pair of rhinestone ballet slippers she kept on hand for aching toes.

"One hot wax kit," she said once all was right with the fashion universe again. "Coming up." She reached for her purse.

At least, I thought it was her purse. One of those new box types from Chanel that were all the rage in Paris.

Only I'd never seen a Chanel box bag with MANNY'S CHINESE TAKEOUT printed in bright red letters on the side.

Evie took one look at the take-out carton and her hands started to tremble. Her face went even whiter and her bottom lip quivered. "What's wrong with me?" she finally asked, the question so soft and vulnerable that my chest tightened.

"PMS?" I asked hopefully.

"My period was last week."

"Post-PMS?"

She gave me an odd look. "Funny."

"Just trying to keep the situation light." Not. Thanks to my DNA, I've never actually had a monthly visitor (tampons so didn't fit with the gorgeous and glam born-vamp image). "Maybe you're out of sorts"—*and crazy as a loon*—"because you've got the flu."

She shifted her desperate gaze to me. "You think so?" I nodded and she tugged at the collar of her blouse. "I do feel a little flushed. And the room is sort of spinning."

"Why don't you call it a night and head home?"

She sank into her chair and blinked several times as if trying to shake off a dizzy spell. "But I haven't finished my matches for Monday. I need to make reservations and notify the parties involved and—"

"I can do it." I ignored the ridiculous urge to hug her. Born vamps didn't hug. They sneered and looked down their noses and behaved like typical pompous asses.

Then again, BVs were all about the almighty dollar. Since Evie was my ultra-faithful employee, any "mothering" on my part would fall into the category of good asset management.

I gathered her things and pulled her to her feet. Sliding an arm around her, I steered her outside.

A few seconds later, I loaded her into the backseat of a waiting cab, gave the driver a twenty, Evie's address, and a mental command: *Get her home safely or I'll hunt you down and use you for a chew toy.*

"Take a bath, put on your sweats and veg in front of the TV," I told Evie before I shut the door. "You'll be as good as new after a few *CSI* reruns." FYI—in addition to having great taste in clothes, my assistant had a thing for David Caruso and the entire Miami gang.

I stood there until the cab disappeared up the street. Turning, I tried to shake off the feeling that something wasn't right. It was the flu. Or some other nasty virus that humans were so susceptible to. End of story.

That's what I told myself. Evie had a bug and I had a date with Vinnie and his back hair. I headed around the corner to the pharmacy and tried to decide on the best way to broach the makeover with Vinnie. Instead, I found myself thinking about Evie and how strange she'd acted.

How different.

"If it isn't you," Ash's voice echoed in my head, *"it's someone. Someone who's been in the vicinity."*

Someone like Evie.

But why? How? Where? When?

The questions rushed through my head, pairing up with the slim amount of information that I actually knew.

Why had me completely stumped.

How? She had to have touched the demon, or someone possessed by the demon.

Where? According to Ash, the demon had been

right here at DED, or nearby. Maybe the alley out back. The walkway out front. The coffee shop around the corner.

When? I didn't know that either. I only knew that she'd been her old self last night when she'd waltzed into room A to deal with Earl.

A completely different man from the one I'd met at the church. The one who'd been summoned on his walkie-talkie to report to the sanctuary right away for a cleanup.

My fingers itched. I could still feel the green slime courtesy of Ash's Most Wanted.

Had Earl been cleaning up after Slimey and accidentally touched him? Had he inadvertently soaked the little bugger up and brought him here to DED?

There was only one way to find out.

I left the wax kit on Evie's desk and rifled through the cabinet until I'd unearthed his file.

Walking into my office, I sank down into my chair. Flipping through his information, I found the phone number and punched it in.

"Earl Hubert Stanley?" I asked when a man's familiar voice carried over the line and dread settled in my stomach. "The Earl Hubert Stanley who works at St. Michael's?"

"That would be me. Who is this?"

"United States Census Bureau. We're doing a, um, telephone poll for our latest statistics and you're next on my list."

"Okay. Let me just turn down the TV and I'm all

yours." I heard some moving around and the groan of an easy chair, and then Earl said, "Shoot."

"Let's see . . ." I did a little speed-reading through Earl's profile. "First off, can you verify your address?" He repeated the exact information scribbled on the form. "Date of birth?" Ditto. "Children?"

"Four daughters."

It was him, all right.

"Have you recently visited a dating service?"

"Can't say as I have. Met a lady who owned one not too long ago, but haven't worked up my nerve to call yet."

"So you didn't fill out a profile at one beautiful, gracious, fantabulously well-dressed woman's dating service—Dead End Dating, I believe the name is—just last night?"

"Course not. I was as sick as a dog last night. Been that way for the past two days."

Since that night at the church.

"I called in and spent the whole evening catching up on sleep. I feel loads better today."

Because he was no longer possessed by green-and-slimey. The demon had expelled himself in a cloud of foul-smelling flatulence and traded late-model Earl for a newer, flashier Evie.

"Thank you, sir."

"That's it? Don't you census folks usually ask a lot more questions?"

"Did I say census? Silly me. This is the United States *Dating* Bureau. We're only concerned with your social life, or lack thereof. Since you don't have one, I don't have any more questions for you." I disconnected and sat there trying to come to terms with the truth.

Evie. Possessed.

EVIE. POSSESSED.

EVIE. POSSESSED.

Anxiety swamped me, followed by full-blown panic. My body trembled and I bolted to my feet. I had to *do* something.

I had to call Ash. He would know how to handle the situation.

Uh, yeah. He would show up with his brothers and drag Evie straight to Hell.

I couldn't let that happen. I owed her. She'd put in months of loyal service without medical or dental or even a paid vacation. She was as committed as I was to the success of Dead End Dating.

No, I had to figure out a way to expel the demon and save Evie before the Prince brothers figured out that she was their Most Wanted.

And cut off her head.

And chopped her up into itty-bitty, teeny, tiny pieces.

And chucked the whole lot into a blazing inferno—

The bell on the front door jingled and pulled me off the Morbid Express.

I stiffened and gave myself a great big mental kick. There was no sense dwelling on what *could* happen, because it wasn't going to happen. I wouldn't let it. Somehow, someway, I would get rid of the demon and save Evie before Ash Prince could blink his incredibly sexy eyes, much less figure out the truth.

The soft pad of leather soles echoed in the outer office and the smell of garlic and Dippity-do burned my nostrils.

But first things first—I had to deal with an SOB.

Thirteen

❤ ❤ ❤

"**A**re you sure you didn't have a bad connection?" Vinnie sat in my office, an impatient look on his face. He glanced at his watch. "Maybe she said I was a hot stud with a really cute butt."

"No." I swallowed and summoned my courage. *Again.* "She definitely said you were a big dud and she hated your guts."

Silence stretched between us as the news settled in. His gaze narrowed and his mouth thinned. He leaned forward, clasping his hands together, his knuckles white. I had a sudden vision of myself tacked up to the nearest wall, a bull's-eye painted mid-chest, while Vinnie selected a weapon for his record-breaking BV kill.

I slid a discreet hand across the top of my desk (I had a feeling Vinnie had a low tolerance for sudden moves) and retrieved the letter opener that lay near my stack of bills. I scooped it into my top drawer, followed by every visible pencil and pen. The corkscrew I kept on hand for the bottle of AB negative in my minifridge. A container of paper clips and some folder brads.

There. I tried to relax. Short of carrying his own weapons arsenal, he wasn't—oh, wait. He *did* carry his own weapons arsenal.

My stomach hollowed out.

"That's the bad news." I smiled, trying not to act the least bit unnerved by the sudden tension in the air or the all-important fact that I was SO screwed. "The good news is she definitely wants to see you again."

He looked about as happy as a born vampire during an IRS audit. "I'm through playing games." He pushed to his feet. "I gave you a chance and you blew it." His hand disappeared inside his jacket and he pulled out a long, lethal-looking stake that made my letter opener look like a dental pick.

"I didn't blow it," I blurted, at the same time mentally surveying my available options. I could (a) use my BV strength to kick Vinnie's ass and hope his aim was as bad as his hair or (b) make a run for it. Even in stilettos, I had no doubt I could get away (it's a bird, it's a plane, it's Super Vamp).

It was the inevitable trip back to my apartment for my clothes and Killer that scared the crapola out of me. Vinnie was sure to be waiting with a pair of gonzo pliers. Being the first toothless matchmaker in

Manhattan was about as appealing as sinking my fangs into Rush Limbaugh.

"You want Carmen and she wants you," I rushed on. "That smacks of success."

"But you just said she hated me."

"She hated the wrapping." I gestured from his head to his toes and back up again. "But she's willing to stick around to see what's inside the package."

He grinned at the last word. "I knew it. She wants me to bone her."

"She does not want you to bone her." *Men.* "Not yet, that is. Carmen is a sensitive woman who needs a sensitive man. A man who isn't afraid to show his true feelings. A man," I added, "who's completely in touch with his feminine side."

"In other words, she wants a pansy."

"No, she wants a man who isn't afraid of his inner pansy." Where did I come up with this stuff? "See, every man has a soft, compassionate nature, also known as the inner pansy. Some men have no problem flaunting their inner pansy."

"My cousin Paulie showed up at the last family reunion wearing a taffeta dress and a goddamned tiara."

The fact that Vinnie could distinguish taffeta from the vast number of fabrics stirred a tiny bubble of hope that maybe—just maybe—Vinnie wasn't as one hundred percent macho as he appeared. "Paulie is obviously in touch with his inner pansy."

"And his outer pansy. The boy's as gay as a three-dollar bill." He shook his head. "You're barking up the wrong tree if you think I'm jumping the man ship and diving into the fruity Pacific."

"Being soft and sensitive isn't about changing your sexual orientation. Vinnie, Vinnie, Vinnie." I shook my head. "All men, not just the gay ones, have a feminine side. For some men like Paulie, it's close to the surface. For others like you, it's six feet under. But regardless, it's still there." I tapped my chest for effect. "Inside."

"Says you." He didn't seem the least bit convinced. Still, he shoved the stake back into his pocket, hiked up his pants legs, and sat back down. "I'm telling you right now, there ain't no inner pansy in a man like me." I arched an eyebrow, so he added, "Wearing women's panties every now and then don't mean shit. Arnold Schwarzenegger wears a Speedo, which is practically the same thing, and there ain't nothing fruity about him."

"A man doesn't stay married as long as Arnold without getting up-close-and-personal with his inner pansy. Which brings us to you." I eyeballed him. "You want to settle down, right?"

"Damn straight."

"And you want to do it with Carmen?"

He nodded. "She's everything my Mama's ever wanted in a daughter-in-law."

"Then you have to open up and let it all hang out. Show Carmen you're not afraid to be sensitive. Stop being so gruff and dangerous. Wear a pink shirt once in a while. Cry during a sappy movie. Watch a re-run of *How to Look Good Naked*."

He shifted uneasily and my vamp instincts kicked into full gear. A grin tugged at my lips. "Get. *Out.* You watch *How to Look Good Naked*?"

"Only 'cause my buddy Harry—he's an SOB out of Rhode Island—said they show the occasional boob shot. Fuckin' idiot. I seen every episode and I ain't never caught a full boob. Sure, they hint at boobage and even a little trim, but there's always a bra and some fancy-schmantzy panties in the way of the really good stuff."

"A pink shirt?" I asked hopefully.

"I'd sooner have cement blocks tied to my ankles."

"A sappy movie?"

"I'd rather take a bullet to the brain."

"So sayeth the outer you. I'm sure the inner you is just dying for a *Steel Magnolias* sequel." I pushed to my feet. "See, Vinnie, people are like onions. They're made up of many different layers." I walked around my desk and grabbed the white paper sack that I'd picked up at the pharmacy. "Once we peel back all the machismo, I have no doubt we'll find a man who's kind and caring and compassionate." I pulled out the wax kit.

Vinnie's eyebrows shot up above his Ray-Bans. "What's that for?"

I gave him my most reassuring smile. "The first layer we're peeling away is the hair."

"See? I told you there was an inner pansy inside of you just waiting to break free." I handed Vinnie another Kleenex and watched him blow his nose. His eyes were red and puffy, his face wet with tears. "Of course, I didn't think we'd get to it in just one layer."

He sat straddling a small chair, his arms folded and propped on the back.

At least that was his current position. For the past hour he'd been as rigid as if rigor mortis had set in, his muscles tight, his body braced as he'd dug his hands into the back of the chair during each painful *rrrrrrrip!*

"It looks great by the way," I added as I eyed his bright pink back and shoulders. "No bleeding at all." I glanced at a particularly raw-looking patch on his right shoulder. "At least nothing that won't stop fairly soon." I pulled off the gloves that had come with the kit. "I think we'd better call it a night." Otherwise I'd be calling 911.

He mopped at his eyes and sobbed something that sounded like *Thank you.*

Then again, judging from the pained look on his face as he un-straddled the chair and the Jersey salute he gave me, I could have been a few letters off.

"Th-this had better be worth it," he finally rasped after he'd managed to shrug on his shirt. "B-because if it isn't, I'm not just going after your f-fangs. I'm going to s-skin you alive f-first."

My hands stalled on my Rolodex, and the triumph I'd felt at finally cracking Vinnie faded into a wave of panic.

"You really know how to ruin a moment."

"Just don't jerk me around."

"I'm trying to help you."

He stared at me long and hard, the Ray-Bans drilling into me for several heart-pounding moments before he finally shrugged. The action made him wince and he sucked in a breath.

My chest hitched.

What can I say? I'm totally in touch with my own inner pansy.

"Put this on your back and it'll ease the pain." I handed him an extra-large tube of Neosporin. "Every hour on the hour."

"And call you in the morning?"

"Actually, I want you to call me tonight. On the hour, every hour. It's part of our next exercise." I scribbled down an address and handed it to him. "I want you to park it in front of this building and keep an eye on the tenant in 3B."

"Surveillance? What the hell does that have to do with my inner pansy?"

"It's an exercise in control of the outer asshole. Why do you usually park it in front of someone's residence?"

"Because I'm going to kill them."

"Exactly. See, outer is used to stalking someone for a purpose—to pull out their fangs or chop them up."

"Or skin them," he added, reminding me of his earlier comment.

"You never just sit back and watch, right?" He nodded and I went on. "This time the goal is to resist the urge to slice and dice and simply keep an eye on the woman in 3B."

"Were? Vamp?"

"Human."

He looked disappointed. "What's the fun in that?"

"The fun is to be had when you announce your upcoming wedding to your mama. Now, if this woman—we'll call her Slimey—goes anywhere, I want you to follow. But under no circumstances do you make contact with her. You hang back, take notes, and report back to me."

"For how long?"

"Until we meet back here tomorrow afternoon."

"But that's all night and all day?"

"Stop whining. This isn't a sweatshop. You get the required fifteen minute breaks and a full thirty for lunch."

"That's still a helluva long time to sit and watch some broad for no fucking reason—"

"Forget it then. I'm sure I can find you a nice Presbyterian to take to your mother's birthday party."

"Don't get your panties in a wad. I'll do it. But you'd better know what you're doing."

"I'm a professional, Vinnie. I always know what I'm doing."

"I don't know what the hell I'm doing," I told Nina Two when I called her the moment Vinnie left. I explained the situation with Evie and swore her to secrecy. "So what do you think I should do?"

"Give it to me from behind," Nina said, her voice breathless and excited.

Reality dawned and a burst of ego shot through me, followed by a sliver of dread as I realized what I had to do. "Nina." I chose my words carefully. "You know you're one of my oldest and dearest friends, but I just don't like you like that. I know, I know," I rushed on when she started to speak. "You can't help yourself. It's understandable. I *am* pretty hot. But you can't do this. You're already committed to a wonderful—albeit slightly boring—vampire. I know you. You would never be able to live with yourself if you cheated on him."

"Not you," she told me. "I was talking to Wilson. We've decided to start having children and this is night one in our Baby Quest." Her voice went slightly muffled as if she'd cupped her hand over the receiver. "Honey, try it this way." I heard the squeak of bedsprings and the distinct slap of bare skin. "Just . . . like . . . *that*."

"Why don't I call you back later?"

"Yes."

"Yes, you want me to call back? Or yes, honey, give it to me again?"

"Both," she breathed.

I hung up and tried Nina One.

"What do you know about demons?" I asked when she finally answered her cell.

"They sparkle and they're definitely a vamp's best friend."

"That's diamonds. I said *demons*."

"Oh," she giggled. "Let's see . . . Lots of hair. Major BO. Noisy, especially when the moon is full."

"That's a werewolf."

"Cold, cynical, and only interested in sex?"

"Made vampire." That, or half the single men in Manhattan.

"Tall and hairy?"

"Big Foot."

"Short and stumpy?"

"A troll."

"Oops." She giggled. "You'll have to forgive me. I'm a little out of sorts." More giggling, and I distinctly heard the baritone of a man's voice. "Rob's here and you'll never guess what I'm holding in my hand at this very moment."

Uh-oh.

Panic rushed through me and I had the sudden urge to cover my ears.

Crazy, right? Sex was natural. In fact, it was the end-all and be-all of the entire born-vamp culture. Our civilization centered around the Deed. We were conceived via sex. We stopped aging when we lost our virginity. We then spent the rest of eternity getting jiggy and making babies.

Every *other* born vamp, that is.

I, on the other hand, was too busy matching up SOBs, saving my loyal assistant from the flames of Hell, and fantasizing about a certain bounty hunter to procreate. I so didn't need to hear anything that reminded me of sex, which reminded me of my lack thereof.

That, and the fact that we're talking about my *brother*.

"It's big," she went on, "and very impressive and—"

"You're really creeping me out," I cut in.

"Not *that*. Not right now anyway. It's a snakeskin Ferragamo belt with a rhinestone buckle."

"*The* snakeskin belt with the aqua rhinestone buckle? From the new spring collection?"

"That's the one."

"But there's a waiting list for those."

"I don't know how he pulled it off, but he did."

"Anything for you, babe." My brother's familiar voice sounded in the background.

Awww . . .

"It's a bribe," Nina went on. "To get me to move in with him."

My panic morphed into shock. "You and Rob? *Living together?*"

"I guess so." She laughed and Rob let out an enthusiastic *"Hell, yeah!"*

"That's terrific," I said once I'd found my voice. "Really fab." Or it would have been if I wasn't suddenly feeling like the only one who didn't get invited to the hottest party of the year.

Vinnie was one layer closer to wedded bliss.

Nina Two was happily committed and had just embarked on the Baby Quest.

Nina One was moving in with my brother.

And here I was sitting all by my lonesome, doing research on Satan's minions.

To save your friend's life, my conscience reminded me. A task that was oodles nobler than boffing my brains out with a certain hot, hunky bounty hunter.

Sure, it wasn't much fun, but sometimes a vampire had to take the high road.

Or, in my case, Sexless Avenue.

"We're going to tell everyone at the hunt tomorrow night. You'll be there, right?"

I thought of my mother's reaction (shock, outrage, and the inevitable dive straight into a double martini) and my depression lifted. "Are you kidding? A pack of rabid werewolves couldn't keep me away."

Fourteen
♥ ♥ ♥

After I hung up with Nina, I dialed Vinnie's number.

"Are you in position?"

"Are you friggin' kidding me? I just left your place about five minutes ago. I'm stopping off at Marciano's to take a whiz and pick up a double pepperoni with anchovies. Then I'm on my way."

"Call me when you get there."

"I'm not so sure I'm going to make it. I still think this whole assignment is for shit."

"You can quit if you want. It's totally your choice." I hummed the opening *dum-dum-de-dum* of the wedding march, and then said, "Besides, Presbyterians aren't *that* bad."

"I'll call when I get there." *Click.*

I spent the next few minutes going through my bills. (Was I desperate for a distraction or what?)

After writing several checks that left me with all of twenty-three dollars and eighty-seven cents in my bank account, I closed up shop and headed home early. I stopped off at a nearby Blockbuster (which left a whopping seven dollars and fifty-nine cents) and then headed home for a DVD marathon with Killer.

"You might not want to watch this," I warned as I popped in *The Exorcist* and settled on the sofa with a glass of nuked blood. "I wouldn't want you to have nightmares."

Are you kidding me? Eat, sleep, and poop. That's it for us felines.

"I wouldn't be too sure." I took a sip and the warm liquid sizzled down my throat. My stomach clenched, begging for more. I swallowed against the urge to gobble up the contents and took another small, controlled sip. "This movie is supposed to be really scary."

Maybe you're the one who shouldn't watch.

"I'm a vampire. We invented scary."

By the time THE END flashed and the credits started to roll, I'd checked the closets twice (I'd kinda sorta heard some really weird noises that could easily have been a skanky demon rather than the hot water heater) and flipped on every light in my microscopic apartment.

I'd just checked the locks on the front door for the

umpteenth time when I turned to find Killer staring up at me, a what'd-I-tell-ya? gleam in his eyes.

"This is New York," I blurted. "Crime capital of the world. You can never be too safe."

Wimp.

After five movies—including *The Exorcism of Emily Rose, The Omen* and all three *Exorcist* movies—several updates from Vinnie, and a measly three hours of sleep, the only thing I wanted to do when Sunday afternoon rolled around was bury my head beneath the pillow. I'd come up with the bare bones of a plan to save Evie, but in order to fill in the details, I needed to rest.

And be the first to break three hundred years of Marchette tradition by missing the weekly hunt?

Yeah, right.

I'd given my word to Mandy and the go-ahead to my mom. What's more, Nina and Rob were making their big announcement.

I hauled my tired but fabulous ass out of bed and into a hot shower, and tried not to think about the upcoming date with Remy. And the all-important fact that, despite my objections, he really was the perfect born vampire for me.

First off, he didn't reek of bread pudding or cheesecake or cherry chocolate brownies. He smelled of subtle cologne and virile manliness, thanks to a special pill designed by top vampire scientists to mask his natural scent (all born-vamps reeked of sweet and yummy) and give him an edge when sneaking up on dangerous criminals. Hence, he didn't clash with my eau de cotton candy.

Second, he was good-looking and wealthy and he had a phenomenal fertility rating.

On top of all *that,* he actually liked me. I knew as much because he'd helped me out of several jams in the past and even offered his house up so that I could host a baby shower for Viola and the other Connecticut NUNS.

He liked me, all right.

And I liked him.

Sort of.

It's just that we'd grown up together. I'd seen him stick marbles up his nose, and so every time I tried to picture us in the classic let's-get-it-on fantasy, I only managed half the equation because—let's face it—there wasn't anything remotely sexy about a man with a marble lodged in his nostril.

Sure, I always started out with a nice mental picture of Fairfield's finest, but then raw, primal lust took over. My heart pounded. My body trembled. My hormones started a frenzied bump and grind. At that point, my brain did a cut and paste and, *voilà,* no Remy.

Instead, I ended up with something like this . . .

I stretched out on the cushy pillow top mattress and opened my arms to the vampire standing nearby. He raked a piercing neon-blue stare from my head to the tips of my toes and back up again. I purred my encouragement. He growled his excitement. The bed dipped and his strong, muscular body covered mine. I touched my lips to the tiny scar that bisected his eyebrow and closed my eyes to the rough feel of his callused fingertips on my—

"Don't you wish your girlfriend was hot like me?" Ahh. "Don't you wish your girlfriend was a freak like me?" Ahh. "Don't you . . ." My favorite Pussycat Dolls ringtone blared from my cell and yanked me back to reality.

Disappointment niggled at me as I grabbed my phone and flipped it open.

"I'm this close to passing out," Vinnie declared before I could so much as say hi. "And I have to take a dump. Too many anchovies."

"How goes it with Slimey?"

"Other than ordering takeout—everything from burgers to Thai—she's staying put. And I"—a victorious note in his voice—"haven't so much as knocked on her door. No breaking her ankles or cracking her skull with a hammer or stuffing her into my trunk. Not that she would fit. I've still got that three-hundred-pound werewolf I offed last week stashed on top of my spare."

"You mean to tell me you went on the date with Carmen with a dead werewolf in your trunk?"

"What? It's not like you could smell anything. Not then." I heard the *click* of a glove compartment and then the *shhhhhh* of an aerosol can. "So do I pass the assignment or what?"

"Not yet. Stay in position for the next few hours and then meet me at my office at midnight."

"But I need to sleep."

"You can sleep when you're dead."

"Yeah." A menacing note crept into his voice. "And so can you."

"Thirty minutes in the backseat," I blurted. "Forty-five at most. But then you're back to peeling away the next layer."

"This layer crap had better work," he warned again before he disconnected.

I ignored the urge to pack the nearest bag, snatch up Killer, and head for a remote tropical paradise. Granted, I'd get to keep my fangs for a little while longer, but where would that leave Evie?

Pushing aside my fear, I went about my usual afternoon. I drank my breakfast, put on some makeup and flat-ironed my hair. Pulling on a silver Rock & Republic tunic and short black leggings, I topped off the outfit with a pair of silver Armani flats and worked my favorite supermodel pose in front of the mirror.

Smokin' hot as usual, despite the demon marathon, a shitload of worry, and very little sleep.

Ah, the perks of being a card-carrying member of the undead.

After a quick exchange with Killer (he promised to behave himself if I promised to buy him a Hello Kitty scratching post) I dropped him off at Mrs. Janske's and climbed into a cab bound for Connecticut.

As we left the city behind, I decided to ignore the dread churning in my stomach and the cab driver ogling me in the rearview mirror.

Time to look on the bright side.

Sure, I was stuck with the usual Sunday routine—hiding out in the pool house while the rest of my family battled it out for extra vacation days from Moe's. But maybe I wouldn't have to go through with the post-hunt date with Remy. I mean, really. My mother had fresher blood to drink, right? One of her precious sons was actually trading in his confirmed bachelor status to move in with—gasp—a *female*. And after just a measly five weeks of dating. Who cared that Nina and Rob had grown up together? He was barely five hundred and fifty-five. A mere *bebe*. My mother would be so freaked when she heard the news that she would surely forget about yours truly and shift her radar to my bro.

I smiled. I was definitely off the hook.

"I thought you would never get here," my mother declared when she hauled open the massive front door. "Everyone's waiting."

Jacqueline Marchette looked as immaculate as ever in a gold Bill Blass wrap dress that accented her tall, svelte figure. She wore her long dark hair in a chic French braid. Her rich brown eyes were fringed with long, thick lashes. She had a perfect nose and high sculpted cheekbones. A shimmering cocoa gloss accented her full lips. The rich, sweet scent of cherries jubilee clung to her, along with a cloud of expensive perfume.

"*Everyone* meaning you and Dad and Max, right? Rob's not here." Otherwise she would be clutching a glass of vodka and oozing disapproval instead of staring at me as if the fate of the born-vamp nation rested solely on my shoulders.

"He's here." She motioned me in. "And Nina, too."

"But they just got here, right?" Meaning they hadn't had time to break the good news.

"No, they've been here awhile. In fact, Rob's been putting with your father for the past half hour."

"They're obviously waiting for the right moment to tell you."

"Tell me what? That they're moving in together?"

"They're moving in—wait a second. You know?"

"Of course I know, dear. Rob announced it the second he walked in."

"And?"

"And I'm sure they'll get along fabulously until the newness wears off." She waved a hand. "Then, of course, he'll break up with her and move on to the next one like he usually does because he's much too young to settle down right now." She nailed me with a gaze. "As for you and Remy . . . the two of you practically scream eternity." She smiled. "Come." She motioned me through the foyer toward the main room. "Your father and I are trying something new tonight to spice up the hunt."

My panic went on hold at the possibility of padding my padless bank account. "Dad's giving away money instead of vacation days?"

"Nonsense. Your father's much too tight for that." Excitement gleamed in her eyes. "This is much better."

"Dad volunteered to be *it*?" *It* was the one who wore the whistle and risked massive shoe damage while fleeing a handful of vacation-hungry vampires. We usually drew randomly, and I was notorious for picking the short straw. "We don't have to actually draw?"

"Nonsense. Your father hates being *it*." Excitement flashed in her gaze. "This is even better."

My heart pounded faster. "We're giving up the real thing and doing a simulated hunt on Dad's Xbox?"

"Better."

What could be better than sitting comfortably in the living room rather than traipsing through the woods in a pair of Armani flats?

"Couples hunting," she announced.

My stomach dropped to my knees. "Couples?"

She nodded. "As in your father and I as one team. Max will pair up with some human woman he brought—they met on the Internet. Rob gets Nina. And you"—her eyes twinkled—"get Remy." Her glossed lips spread into a wide smile. "Isn't it ingenious?"

"I . . ." My words got caught in the sudden lump that formed in my throat.

"Just think," she went on. "You won't have to wait until after the hunt to spend some time together. You can start right now."

Oh goody.

Fifteen

❤ ❤ ❤

"**N**ice night," Remy commented a half hour later.

We sat—or hid, rather—in the pool house, waiting for the whistle to sound. Which meant we couldn't actually see said night firsthand.

Not that it mattered.

I knew he was just trying to make conversation to fill the awkward silence that had settled around us.

"A really nice night," I added.

"A really, *really* nice night." He wore a dark gray long-sleeved henley that clung to his broad shoulders and outlined his muscular chest. Faded jeans accented his long legs. He had short, whiskey-colored hair with white-gold streaks and the greenest eyes I'd ever seen.

When we were kids, I'd envied the sun-kissed look

of his golden locks. Then he'd shoved a spider down my dress and I'd started to wish with all of my undead heart that the earth would open up and swallow him whole. That, or he'd be struck by a bolt of lightning or staked by vampire killers or guillotined by French extremists.

He'd been such a pain.

"The weather's been great," he commented.

"Really great." I strained my super-vamp ears, searching for some sign that the agony would soon end.

How long could Max and his Internet bimbo (tonight's *it* couple) actually outrun everyone? See, the *it* person took the lead and got a full minute's head start. Whoever caught him first and got close enough to blow the whistle around his neck won. Being saddled with Delicious Delilah (I swear I'm not making this up), Max wouldn't be half as fast as usual. Talk about an easy target.

While my dad wasn't half the hunter he'd once been (not that he would ever admit it), he had my mom to help out. She could definitely kick ass.

Then again, the ass in question belonged to the oldest and dearest fruit of her womb (her words, not mine). Not to mention the whole point of couples hunting was to give Remy and me some time together as a—you guessed it—couple.

My mother was undoubtedly doing her damnedest to stall.

Which left Nina and Rob. The best of the best. Rob had already won oodles of times and Nina, well, if she went after that silly whistle with the same tenacity she hunted down a Fendi original, Remy and I would be out of here in no time.

Unless Nina and Rob weren't actually hunting.

Sure, they were both bloodthirsty and extremely cunning. But they were also as horny as two werewolves during a full moon.

With my rotten luck, they were probably boffing upstairs at that very moment.

My ears prickled and, sure enough, I heard the distinct squeak of mattress springs followed by Nina's high-pitched voice: *"Who's Your Vampire?"*

"I heard it might rain this weekend." Remy's deep voice pulled me back to the pool house and the thick tension.

"Bummer."

"Not that it's a given. Those guys from Channel 5 are always getting it wrong."

"Way wrong."

The minutes ticked by and Remy went on about the weather. And unreliable meteorologists. And how the Fairfield PD required its street officers to wear rain ponchos as a preventative measure against pneumonia.

I know, right?

If he started talking about the Mets, I was *so* going to throw myself on the nearest umbrella pole.

"So how about those Giants?"

Close enough. I pushed to my feet. My gaze darted frantically for a long, pointy escape.

"It's not over, is it?" He stood and eyed the door. "Did you hear the whistle?"

If only.

My gaze went to the stack of floats that covered one wall. A pile of extra pool chairs cluttered the far corner. The tiny interior was packed with everything from the chaise lounges where we sat to a small minifridge, extra pool-cleaning equipment, a floating bar, several volleyballs, and even a spare net, but not one stinking umbrella pole.

"Look." I gave up the self-destructive thoughts and went for Plan B—spilling my guts. "I know I agreed to this date, but I only did it because my mother's bugging the hell out of Jack and Mandy and I wanted to distract her so they could finish up their honeymoon in peace. Not that I don't like you. I do. You're a great vampire." *The perfect vampire,* a small voice reminded me. "But I just don't see a future for us as anything other than good friends."

He went silent for a long moment. "Can't forget me in the tights and knickers, can you?" he finally asked, his green eyes glittering down at me.

A mental picture stirred and a smile tugged at my lips. "Actually, those were kind of cute."

"Huh?"

Yeah, huh? "Not that they weren't pretty awful back then. But in retrospect they don't seem all that horrific. Not compared to the marbles." Memories rushed at me. "I'll never forget that time you went up against Jean Michel Gustave for the record. He managed four in each nostril."

"While I did an impressive five." He shook his head. "What the hell was I thinking?"

"You weren't thinking. You were seven."

He grinned, a slash of dazzling white in the dim light. "I got into so much trouble when my mother found out. She made me clean out the stables for two solid months."

"No wonder you smelled so funny back then." Not that he smelled funny now. The faint scent of expensive cologne and virile male teased my senses and I caught myself drinking in a deep breath.

"Do you remember that time you chased me with the spider?" I blurted, suddenly eager to recount all the reasons why I didn't like Remy Tremaine. "You tried to set that skunk on fire and I threatened to tell your *maman,* and then it was all-out war."

"Ahhh, my pyro phase. Which came after the marble phase. Which came after the torture-innocent-villagers phase."

"You never tortured any innocent villagers. Did you?" I prayed for a great big *yes.* Anything to douse the sudden rush of heat skimming my bare skin.

"I wouldn't go so far as to say *torture.* Annoyed was more like it. I stole chickens and hid eggs and I even stole Madame Giselle's wooden teeth."

"You did not?!"

"I did." He shook his head. "She was so pissed, she chased me half a mile with a broom. Who knew the old woman could run that fast? Of course, that was nothing compared to the skunk. I barely got within two feet of that damned animal before he sprayed me. I haven't set anything on fire since."

I wanted to argue with him. As he stood there staring down at me with his bright green eyes, I felt a spark in the pit of my stomach, followed by a rush of warmth.

Hunger. Obviously. The hunt was taking forever and I'd only had one glass of blood before leaving the house and, well, a girl's gotta eat, right?

No wonder my heart was pounding and my skin was tingling and my nipples were quivering and—

Wait. Back the freakin' coffin up.

No way should my nipples be involved if I was *just* hungry. Heart, yes. Skin, perhaps. I might even have a few knee tremors or some lightheadedness. But nipples didn't come into play unless . . .

Nah. We're talking *Remy*.

Even as I told myself that, I did a quick inventory to assess the current state of my über-hot bod.

Pounding heart? *Check.*
Tingling skin? *Check.*
Knee tremors? *Check.*
Lightheadedness? *Check.*
Quivering nipples?

Uh-oh.

Realization struck and I did the first thing that came to mind (okay, the second thing, because I was NOT jumping his bones, no matter how much I suddenly wanted to).

I stuck both fingers into my mouth and let loose a loud, earsplitting whistle.

Game *over*.

"Where's Max?" my mother asked several minutes later when she and my dad emerged from the trees. They crossed the immaculate lawn and joined Remy and me on the veranda.

I shrugged and tried not to look guilty. "He, um, got away."

"He *what*?"

"He took off running." I pointed to the left and then sort of swept my hand in a vague circular motion. "That way."

"But he's not supposed to run once the whistle blows," my dad pointed out. "That signals that the hunt is over."

"That's right," my mother added. She glanced around, her gaze searching the surrounding landscape. "Why ever would he keep running?"

"Maybe he got into the spirit of the whole thing and his survival instincts kicked in. He didn't want to go down without a fight."

"What about his human?" my mother asked.

"She followed him, of course. They're probably deep in the woods having afterlife-affirming sex as we speak." Oops. Bad sister. But I was sort of hoping that the notion of my do-no-wrong older brother getting jiggy with a mere human would be enough to distract my mother from the questions swimming in her gaze.

"Remy?" My mother shifted her attention to the man standing next to me. "Did you see Max?"

"I sure did and, I must admit, he was something to see. When Lil went for the whistle, he put up a hell of a fight. You folks obviously trained him well."

My dad puffed out his chest. "It's all about tradition. Sure, we've got bottled this and bottled that, but what happens if the blood bottlers ever go out of business? My children won't be wasting away for lack of skill, let me tell you. Each one of them has the ability to find and conquer, no matter how cunning their prey."

"And they're obviously resilient," Remy added. "Even limping and exhausted, Max refused to concede defeat."

"We Marchettes *are* fighters," my dad offered. "We stand up for what we believe in and refuse to cower. It's a matter of principle. Of pride. Why, Viola may think she won just because the court ruled in her favor, but I'm not giving up." His gaze narrowed and he flashed his fangs. "Those are still MY bushes."

"Now, now, dear." My mother stroked his arm. "Don't get all worked up again. Those are your bushes and everyone else in Fairfield, particularly the judicial system, is simply clueless."

"I have a right to protect my property," my dad insisted.

"Of course you do, and you have the resilience to back it up. Even at eight hundred and ninety-six, you're as cunning and as virile as the day I met you."

Have I mentioned that in addition to kicking ass

my mother can do a stellar job of kissing it, as well? At least when it came to my father's.

"What about Nina and Rob?" my mother asked. "I don't see them."

"They're already in the house having a drink." At least I hoped they'd graduated to the after-sex drink. Otherwise, I would be flying solo with my mother, and I so couldn't handle that right now.

My body still tingled and certain things were still quivering and I was still doing my best to ignore the fact that Remy, of all vampires, was the one responsible.

Knickers. Marbles. Skunks.

No matter how I tried to conjure the memories, the only thing that kept registering in my head was Remy looming over me, his eyes so green and hungry and—

"I *really* need a drink." I whirled and walked as fast as my preternatural feet could carry me.

Remy followed, his strong, muscular body much too close for comfort.

"Congratulations," Nina declared when I walked into the living room to find her sitting on the couch next to Rob. "You totally deserve the vacation days."

"Thanks." I headed for an antique sidebar and a newly opened bottle of AB negative. My hands shook as I poured a glass. "But I don't work for Moe's."

"So?" Nina stared at me as if she couldn't quite put two and two together.

No wonder, with my brother's hand on her knee, his fingertips tracing lazy circles.

I had a sudden vision of my own knee and Remy's hand and how utterly brain-dead I would be if said hand worked its way up the inside and—

I shook away the thought and downed half the glass in one long gulp. Warmth slid down my throat and firebombed my stomach. My nerves eased and my vision sharpened. There. That was more like it.

"What's wrong with you?" My mother came up next to me, her narrowed gaze trained on my face. She looked so concerned that my chest hitched. I had the insane urge to throw myself into her arms and blab my lustful thoughts.

Confession *was* good for the soul.

Besides, maybe if she knew how conflicted I felt and how I really, *really* liked Ty, she would understand. She was my mom, after all. She *loved* me.

"I don't think this date with Remy is a good idea." The words popped out of my mouth before I could stop myself.

"Of course it's not a good idea."

A weight lifted off my chest. "Really?"

"It's a fabulous idea," she went on. "The best I've ever had."

The weight dropped and I downed the other half of the glass. When that didn't hit the spot, I grabbed the bottle and took a long swig.

"Raking in the vacation days makes me thirsty," I blurted when I noticed that everyone—with the exception of my father who was busy pulling out his golf clubs—was staring at me. I held up the bottle. "Anyone up for a drink?"

"Actually," my mother plucked the AB negative out of my hand and set it back down, "I arranged for you and Remy to head over to the club for drinks." She smiled as if she'd just sucked the blood out of the entire staff of Chippendales. "Just the two of you."

"I'm up for it." Remy winked at me and my stomach hollowed out. "Lil?"

I swallowed. No way was I going anywhere with Remy. Not for drinks. Or for really hot monkey sex. Or drinks *and* really hot monkey sex.

No way. Nuh, uh. Not this vampire.

"You can take my car," my mother offered.

Car was slang for my mother's coveted red V8 Porsche convertible which she never—repeat *never*—let me touch, much less drive.

Except that one time.

But then she'd gotten the bill for all the damage done by that telephone pole that had jumped out in the middle of the road—I swear—and my Porsche privileges had gone the way of the one-eyed Caribbean were crab.

I had a quick vision of myself flying down the road, stereo blaring, hair blowing in the wind, soft Italian leather surrounding me, all that power right at my fingertips . . .

A few drinks couldn't hurt, right? I mean, sure I was sort of straddling the fence when it came to control, but I could keep my hands to myself if it meant proving to my mother that she could start loaning me the Porsche every now and then.

I nodded. "Drinks would be good."

"Great." My mother smiled and reached for her keys. "Remy can drive."

Was I having shitty luck or what?

Remy went to bring the car around while I drowned my sorrows in another glass of red sustenance and tried to come up with an excuse to bail.

I was debating between "There's a nuclear weapon hidden in the subways of New York and I'm the only one who can show the police the exact location before the whole city goes up in a mushroom cloud" and "I left the iron on" when my cellphone rang.

"She's gone," Vinnie said the minute I punched TALK.

My heart stopped beating. I forgot the bottle I'd been nursing and walked to a far corner out of earshot. "What do you mean *gone*?"

"I mean *gone*, as in *poof*, the TV's still blaring and her lights are on, but she's not there."

"She has to be somewhere." She couldn't have vanished into thin air.

Or could she?

While I hadn't actually seen any disappearing tricks in any of last night's movies, I wasn't so sure it was out of the realm of possibility.

"Did you ask around? Maybe she went to the market or the laundromat."

"Who cares? The point is, she's gone and I'm going home."

Panic rushed through me. "But we have to find her."

"Finding some chick isn't part of my lesson. I was

supposed to watch her and keep my hands off. Mission accomplished. I need to sleep."

"Self-sacrifice," I blurted. "To really bring out the inner pansy, one must peel away the layers of selfishness. The only way to do that is to sacrifice. You give up sleep and you're one layer closer to Carmen."

"You're fried, lady."

"Fine. Don't listen to me. But when your mother is saying a dozen Hail Marys for her pathetic excuse of a son who can't find it in his heart to give up a few measly hours of sleep so that she can have even one grandchild—"

"All right, already." He sighed. "Jesus, have you met my mother? Because I swear you just nailed her."

"Lucky guess." And a lot of experience.

My gaze slid to my own mother, who eyeballed me and mouthed *hurry up*.

"Stay put. I'll be right there," I told Vinnie. "Dating emergency," I announced as I snatched up my purse and aimed for the front door. "I have to get back to the office." An engine purred somewhere out back and I added, "Tell Remy I'm sorry."

"But," my mother's voice followed me, "the two of you barely had a chance to get to know each other."

Maybe I wasn't having such shitty luck after all.

Sixteen
❤ ❤ ❤

I headed back to the city via the fastest means of emergency transport—life flight for the average human, the batmobile for us born vamps.

A half hour later, I stood on the front steps of Evie's building—she leased a third-floor apartment in Greenwich Village—with her downstairs neighbor and landlord, Mr. Ernest Wallace.

Seventy-five. Never been married. Met the woman of his dreams in Italy during World War II, but she was already married and so the relationship had never stood a chance. She'd stayed with her husband and Ernie had headed home to open a comic book shop on Lexington. He'd sold the store a few years back. He was now president of the Neighborhood Watch Association, since he spent most of his days sitting in his kitchen, playing cards, and staring out his window.

He'd been doing just that two hours ago when he'd heard Evie switch off her TV upstairs (he not only kept an eye on everything, but he also kept his hearing aid tuned to CHRIST THIS IS LOUD). A few seconds later, he'd heard footsteps on the stairs. The door had opened and he'd watched Evie stomp down the front stoop. She'd been wearing blue jeans, black combat boots, and an oversized flannel shirt.

If I'd had even one doubt about the whole possession thing, it went bye-bye the moment I heard the play-by-play regarding her wardrobe.

She was shacked up with a demon, all right.

"And," Ernest went on, "she had all that pretty blond hair of hers pulled back in one of those scrunchie things you gals are always wearing."

Make that Satan, himself.

The one ray of sunshine in an otherwise rain-drenched sky?

She hadn't pulled a Casper and vanished into thin air.

Rather, she'd vanished in a grimy yellow cab—license plate too dirty to read—driven by a Jamaican man.

At least Ernest thought the man was Jamaican. He could also have been Puerto Rican or Indian, or any of the other zillion nationalities floating around the Big Apple.

"Why don't you call a few of the cab companies

and give them a description? Why, I bet you'll have no trouble locating the driver that picked her up."

Um, yeah.

There were about as many foreign cab drivers in New York City as there were Hannah Montana fans in the continental U.S.

"Miss Evie ain't in any trouble, is she? Edna up in 2D says Evie's a communist on account of she's always getting those Democrat mailers, but I'm a Democrat and I ain't no communist."

"Actually, she *is* in a little trouble. Nothing political, though. This is personal."

He shook his head. "Those dad-burned drugs'll get you every time."

"No drugs."

"Debt?"

Not as much as yours truly. I shook my head. "No, nothing like that."

He wiggled his eyebrows. "A love triangle?"

"There are only two parties involved in this."

"That's a relief. Love triangles never work. Except for that young gun down in 1B. He brought home two women the other night and they didn't leave until after breakfast the next morning. I had my shotgun ready for trouble, you know, 'cause women can be mighty possessive. But these two were as friendly as clams. Nice young man, too, even if he is a little too big for his britches, if you know what I mean. Say, I could introduce you if you want. As pretty as you are, you could probably settle him down real quick."

"No thanks. Listen, I really appreciate your help."

I handed Ernest a Dead End Dating card. "Call my cell if she comes home. Or if you'd like to trade in the solitaire for couples bridge."

"Ain't never played no bridge. Played strip poker once, but I had a bad case of athlete's foot. When my turn came, I slid off the old loafers and that pretty much cleared out the room."

"You can keep your shoes on during bridge."

"All righty then." He grinned and slid the card into his pocket.

I gave Ernest a smile, an extra card for the young gun in 1B, and a mental *Forget Italy and get over it already. There are at least a dozen women out there who would love to play cards with you. And maybe even a few who wouldn't mind the athlete's foot.*

Hey, it takes all kinds.

I left the apartment building and climbed into the passenger's seat of the black Cadillac that idled at the curb.

Vinnie slumped over the wheel, his mouth wide open, his nostrils flared. A loud *zzzzzzz* drowned out the old Van Morrison song playing on the radio.

Touching a fingertip under his chin, I snapped his mouth shut. The *zzzzzzz* turned to a muffled *arghhhh*. I fastened my seat belt and debated my options all of five seconds—I had only one—before pulling out my cellphone.

Ash answered on the second ring.

"Yeah?"

"It's Lil."

"I already knew that."

"I'm fine, how are you?" I shook my head. "Haven't you ever heard of phone etiquette?"

"Did you call to test my manners or did you have something on your mind?"

"Well, since you seem to think this demon has been"—*or is*—"hanging around my office, I thought I should get a few details. Just so I know what I'm dealing with if he happens to show up again."

"What do you want to know?"

"Just the usual stuff. Favorite color. Favorite food. Where he might go if he were possessing an innocent woman addicted to TiVo." Okay, so maybe that was a little too detailed. "Not that he is," I rushed on. "I'm just speaking theoretically. If he were and he wanted to get out for a little while and stretch his legs, where exactly would he go and what might he do?"

"He'll go to his usual hangout."

"Usual for the possesser or the possessee?"

"The demon. He'll search out a familiar place and try to follow his usual MO."

"What's his MO?"

"He likes to mutilate and torture young women between the ages of twenty and thirty-five."

My heart stopped. "You're kidding, right?"

"Hardly. This particular demon was once a serial killer back in the seventies. He faced off with the cops, they won, and he took a bullet to the head. The body went six feet under and the spirit headed straight to Hell. He's been serving the Big Guy for the past couple of decades. He escaped a few weeks ago and I've been chasing him ever since."

"But he hasn't actually killed anyone since the escape, right?"

"Wrong. Once he settled into a new body—it took about a week for him to overpower the guy's spirit—he sliced up a woman from Long Island and two girls from Jersey."

"So he could be in Long Island or Jersey?" It wasn't as specific as I would have liked, but at least it narrowed things down some.

"All three bodies were found in the city. We know from the past that he doesn't like to make the actual kill too far from where he does his shopping."

"And he shops where?"

"The two Jersey girls frequented the same club in lower Manhattan. That's where he met them. The Long Island woman he picked up at a bar just around the corner. Both places were near Times Square, so we've been combing the clubs and bars in that area for some sign of him—a feeling, a smell, *something*. So far we've come up with zilch. He must be lying low."

"Or watching *CSI: Miami* reruns," the words came out before I could stop them. "Or, you know, whatever."

He went silent for a long moment before he murmured, "Is there something you're not telling me?"

"No." I was most definitely NOT holding some-*thing* back. Rather, I was holding a lot of somethings back. Guilt niggled at me and I decided to launch my own offensive as a diversion. "Is there something *you're* not telling *me*?"

"Hell, yes."

My curiosity was piqued. "Like what?"

"Don't worry about it. Just be careful and keep your eyes open. If you see anything remotely suspicious, *do not* interfere."

I crossed my fingers. "I would never do such a thing."

"Uh-huh."

"No, really."

"Keep your nose out of it."

"Your wish is my command."

He went suspiciously quiet again, as if he didn't buy my cooperation. Smart guy. "I mean it, Lil. We're talking torture and mutilation here. This demon is extremely dangerous. He's just settled into a new body, which buys us a little time before he gets homicidal. When the possession is still in the early stages, there's an internal struggle going on. The battle will keep him busy for now. But once he wins the fight, he'll start killing again. Guaranteed."

"Even if he's possessing someone who's kind and sweet and has really fantastic computer skills?"

"What?"

"What if this person has such a good spirit," I rushed on, the words tumbling out before I could stop them, "that he won't be able to take complete control and do anything really awful?" I held tight to my hope. "That could happen, right?"

"Unless we're talking a bona fide saint, the answer

is no. He'll overpower whichever human spirit he's battling right now, and then he'll kill again. And again. And he won't stop until I stop him."

"By chopping off his head and cutting him into tiny pieces?"

"The body is his vessel. His source of strength. If we destroy the body, he has no protection."

"Unless he jumps into another body, right?"

"Exactly. That's why it's important that you don't interfere. You're just as vulnerable to him as any human."

"Then why didn't he possess me when I tackled him outside the church?"

"Maybe you didn't hold on to him long enough. Touching is key in the transfer process. Anyone's fair game if they touch him, even a vampire. It's not as likely, of course, because a vampire's spirit is much stronger than the average human's and, therefore, harder to suppress. But it *has* happened. My brothers and I are the only ones not susceptible to him."

"If you guys are all that, then how come he escaped in the first place?"

"A fluke. We'd just arrived on the scene when he had the run-in with you. After that, Mo and Zee were dragging him toward the sanctuary so he would be trapped—a demon can't escape a religious dwelling or any space marked with holy water or religious symbols. That's when the maintenance man showed up. He accidentally bumped into the demon, and just like that he was gone. We didn't realize it until after the fact. By the time we realized what had happened and tracked down the maintenance guy, the demon had already body-hopped again."

Straight into Evie.

"We're retracing his steps and trying to pinpoint when and where the demon bailed," Ash went on. "We can't risk another escape. That's why my brothers and I have to be the only ones involved in the takedown. A demon can't possess another demon."

Nor could he possess anyone pure of heart (see the saint reference above). At least, that's what I'd learned during the demon marathon. That, and the average minion of Satan could levitate furniture and cuss like a sailor and do Olympic-worthy projectile vomiting.

"Can't you just cast him out of the body first and then take him back to Hell?"

"And how do you suggest I do that? A spirit is intangible. I have to have something tangible to take back."

"Why not force him into a bottle?"

"He's a demon, not a genie."

"A Ziploc baggie?" I was grasping, I knew. But I had to figure out a way to help Evie.

"He's not a peanut butter and jelly sandwich. There's only one way to take him back, and that's via a sliced and diced tangible body."

"Then how did he escape the flames of Hell in the first place?"

"A near-death experience. People don't always see the proverbial light. Sometimes, they take a right turn and end up seeing hellfire and brimstone instead. In this case, a certain bad guy doomed to Hell arrived a little too soon via a near-fatal car accident. The demon hopped a ride when the Big Boss sent the new arrival packing."

"I still don't—" I started, but Ash cut me off.

"I mean it, Lil. Don't interfere." And then he hung up.

I mulled over Ash's words for a split second and then I nudged Vinnie's arm. "Wake up." When he didn't budge, I pinched him.

He bolted upright, his disoriented gaze bouncing around the inside of the car. "What the fuck?"

"Let's go."

"Home?" He looked so hopeful (and tired) that I almost nodded. Almost.

But I'd already made up my mind to help Evie and I wasn't changing it, no matter if Ash had given me the heebie-jeebies.

I know, right? Super-vamp, invincible, yada yada. Still, my heart pounded and my stomach jumped and I felt as if I'd swallowed one of my dad's golf balls.

"Times Square," I forced the words out. "And hurry it up. We don't have much time."

Seventeen
❤ ❤ ❤

It was half past midnight and we were on our fifth club when I finally spotted Evie.

I stood just inside the doorway of Ladies Night, a popular lesbian martini bar on West Forty-third, just around the corner from the Hard Rock Cafe. It was a far cry from my favorite haunts (Butter and the Beatrice Inn), but it definitely fit with the demon's MO. The place screamed chick magnet.

Pink walls accented a mirrored bar that ran the length of one wall. A sizable dance floor dominated the far end of the room. The crowd was a mix of blue-collar and professional, the women dressed in everything from business suits to jeans and tees. The air reeked of estrogen and cigarette smoke.

My gaze sliced through the hormonal fog, to the couple at the far end of the bar.

Evie stood with a buff redhead wearing a tank top that read FOREVER FITNESS. I sent out a silent vibe and the woman glanced up.

Jean Crowder. Twenty-eight. Personal trainer and editor for *Bitch Beat,* the official newsletter for the New York chapter of Women for the Advancement of Lesbian Culture. She was actively looking for that one special woman (or two) so that she could give up the bar scene and party in the comfort of her own living room (complete with video cam). She thought the female in front of her had terrific camera potential. She wasn't too thrilled with the bad breath, but a few tic tacs and *poof,* no longer an issue.

Evie laughed and the redhead retreated a few inches.

Make that several tic tacs and a year's supply of Binaca.

"Can I get you something?" The voice drew my attention and I turned toward the six-foot-plus brunette who towered behind the bar. "Lemon martini? They're our specialty tonight."

"No, thanks."

"Aw, come on. My treat." The voice came from my right. I twisted to find a short, voluptuous Puerto Rican standing next to me. Her name was Maria. She was this month's centerfold for *Lowrider* magazine and an advocate for same-sex marriages. She spent her days signing autographs for slobbering male fans and her nights searching for Miss Right. She eyeballed me and smiled.

Clearly her search was over.

"Two, please," she told the bartender, "with two shots of lemon schnapps on the side."

"Thanks, but no thanks." My gaze shifted back to Evie. My first instinct was to rush over, grab her by the arm, and haul her outside.

Definitely a bad idea, I decided, as I watched the redhead slide a possessive arm around Evie's shoulders. There was no way I would make it two steps without a catfight.

Not that I couldn't hold my own. A little fang and some preternatural strength, and Red would most definitely back off. But drawing attention to myself by playing the vamp card was the last thing I needed. It was bad enough that Evie might start sliming Red at any moment. I wasn't adding crazed vampire to the SLOBBERING DEMON headline sure to appear in the next issue of *Bitch Beat*.

As for overzealous extremist . . . that I could deal with.

"One drink," Maria persisted.

"Sorry."

"Then at least tell me how you keep your ass looking so good?" She leaned back and eyeballed my trunk. "Butt Buster? Crotch Cruncher?"

"Mother Nature. How about you?"

She slapped her right cheek. "Glute sculptor. Bought it off the QVC. By the time you make the four easy payments, bam, you're bootylicious." She smiled. "You sure you don't want that drink?"

"Not tonight." I gave her an apologetic smile and a mental *You'll never meet someone in a place like this.*

If you really want to make a connection, you should try a dating service.

Her eyes widened as she read the thought and then her brown eyes calmed to a murky chocolate. She spaced out for the next few moments so that I could make my escape.

I slipped my card into her back pocket. Hmmm . . . that glute sculptor was definitely worth the money.

Leaving her staring into space, I headed for Evie.

"I'm Lil," I said as I waltzed up to Red and reached for her hand. I gave it an enthusiastic squeeze. "We're so happy to have you on board. I'm sure Evie has told you all about our organization and how you can join the fight to eliminate the propaganda that is poisoning our society."

"I beg your pardon?"

"You *did* tell her, didn't you?" I turned my attention to Evie and arched an eyebrow.

Desperation sparked in my loyal sidekick's gaze and I knew Evie hadn't given up the fight completely. I held tight to a sudden burst of hope as the faint glimmer faded into the glittering black nothingness of the demon's stare. "Get lost," Evie said, her voice low and guttural. "I'm busy."

"Oh." My gaze ping-ponged from Evie to Red and back. "*Oh*. Sorry. My bad." I shrugged. "I guess you haven't told her yet."

"Told me what?" Red looked puzzled.

"Who we are."

Red's gaze ping-ponged to Evie. "What is she talking about?"

I beamed. "We're with the Society for the Preservation of Heterosexual Relationships—SPHR for short. I'm the head recruiter." I turned toward Evie. "And this is our president."

"Yeah, right." Red put her back to me and focused on Evie.

So much for overzealous extremist.

My fingers were a few inches shy of closing over Evie's upper arm when I heard Vinnie's voice above the *boom, boom, boom* of the music.

"Just grab the dyke already and let's get the hell out of here."

The entire place seemed to come to a collective pause. Heads swiveled. Spines stiffened.

A heartbeat later, the three of us were being ushered toward the rear exit by a mammoth of a woman named Bertha. She had me by one hand, Evie by the other, and she was shoving us along behind Vinnie. I kept my gaze trained on my friend and prayed that her head didn't spin.

Her eyes glittered with anger, but at the same time there was a distinct flicker of relief. Evie was fighting, all right.

Atta girl.

"I'm going, I'm going," Vinnie grumbled as Bertha kept pushing us along. "Don't get your jockstrap in a wad."

A few more steps and the door opened. Bertha shoved us out into the alley.

"Heterosexual assholes," Bertha muttered. The

door slammed shut and I turned on Evie while Vinnie went to set the car.

"We can do this easy or we can do it hard. Your choice, but either way, you're coming with me."

Evie's eyes darkened to a ferocious black. "I'm going to slice you up into tiny little pieces and make you beg for mercy." The deep unearthly voice seemed so out of character coming out of Evie's mouth that I couldn't help myself.

I grinned and she frowned. "Sorry. It's just really hard to take you seriously when you're wearing lip gloss and a toe ring."

"Can it, bitch."

"Now, now." I reached for her. "Is that any way to talk to your boss?"

"Let go of me"—Tall, Dark, and Slimey struggled—"or I'll rip you to pieces."

"Looks like someone has anger management issues." I locked my grip around her upper arms and started hauling her around the side of the building.

"Let go."

"No."

"Asswipe."

"If you think calling me names is going to rattle me, forget it. I've been called *much* worse. Case in point: last week's after-hours sale at Barneys. Picture the last pink silk scarf, a half dozen salivating women, and yours truly."

"Shithead."

"Sticks and stones."

"Cunt."

"Is that the best you can do?"

"Where'd you get that skirt?" the demon spat. "Wal-Mart?"

Okay, now I was pissed.

I ducked, caught Evie in the middle with my shoulder, and flipped her over. She beat at my back and I clamped my arms tighter around her legs. A blaze of headlights bounced off the brick building as the black Cadillac appeared at the end of the alley.

Vinnie climbed out of the car and popped the trunk as we reached him.

I took one look at the pile of animal fur and shook my head.

He shrugged. "What?"

"Don't you think it might be a little crowded in there?"

"Are you shittin' me? These caddies have massive trunks. I once fit two werewolves, a made vampire, a fairy, and two were pigs in here, and I even had a few inches to spare."

"You must be so proud." Not. I carted Evie around to the backseat and folded her in. "Could you just close the trunk and drive?" I crawled in after her. She was kicking and spitting and clawing at the seats, but it did little damage other than to piss me off.

"If you don't stop," I growled, "I swear I'm going to get nasty."

"You and what legion?" she spat.

"No legion. Just me and my buddy Ash."

As if a switch had been tripped, the movements

stopped. Evie's gaze went white and her head lolled back.

Cripes, if I had known it would be that easy, I would have mentioned his name sooner.

I settled into the backseat while Vinnie climbed behind the wheel.

He glanced over his shoulder at Evie. His Ray-Bans glittered in the darkness.

"Don't ask," I told him.

"She a friend of yours?"

"She works for me. Human," I added before he could ask. "And no, she doesn't know what I am."

"A blood slave?"

"You've watched *Blade* too many times." That, or he'd been in attendance at the last Marchette family reunion. "We don't do that anymore." *We* being me, myself, and I.

"She drunk?"

"Very. That's why I'm taking her home. And no, I'm not going to take advantage of her and rip her to shreds. Despite what you think, not all vampires are bloodsuckers."

I expected a smart remark, but instead he shrugged. "Where to?"

"My place." I gave him the address.

Vinnie gunned the engine and headed for Broadway.

I turned toward Evie. She was limp and cooperative right now, but for how long? My mind replayed the conversation with Ash and I tapped Vinnie on the shoulder.

"We have to make one stop first."

* * *

"What are we doing here?" Vinnie stared through the driver's window at the massive church fifteen minutes later. The stained glass windows of St. Michael's reflected the nearby street lights and gave the place an ominous feel.

"After all those clubs, I figured a little confession was in order."

"I didn't know you were Catholic."

"Not for me, for you."

He half-turned, his arm on the seat as he eyeballed me. "The sanctuary's open, but there's no priest here at this hour."

"Then just light some candles and say a few Hail Marys"—I motioned to the thermos sitting on his dashboard—"and snag me some holy water while you're at it."

I expected a smart-ass "I don't see how this is going to bring out my inner pansy," or, at the very least, a threatening "You better not be shittin' me." But twenty-four hours without sleep seemed to have peeled away the difficult-asshole layer of Vinnie Balducci. The most he did was shrug.

Reaching for the thermos, he climbed out of the car and headed for the massive double doors.

Eighteen
❤ ❤ ❤

Once we were back at my place, I left Vinnie out front with Evie (with a strict DO NOT TOUCH policy) and headed upstairs to demon-proof my bedroom. I sprinkled holy water on the windowsills and around the outer perimeter of the room, and then I headed back downstairs for my friend.

I found her sitting in the backseat of Vinnie's Caddy, puffing away on a cigar.

I snatched the nasty thing from between her lips. "I'm not saving you from the bowels of Hell so you can get lung cancer and wind up there anyway."

"Bite me."

"Yeah, yeah." I held up my cellphone. "Why don't you tell that to Ash?"

Her eyeballs rolled back in her head again and she went limp.

What can I say? Works every time.

I hauled her out of the backseat and carted her up to my apartment. I deposited her on my bed and finished sprinkling the holy water across the threshold where I'd just entered. Once I felt certain I'd closed every entry and exit, I shut the bedroom door and headed back into the living room. I nudged Vinnie awake—he was half asleep on the couch—and sent him to Mrs. Janske's to pick up Killer.

"She said to tell you that she's filing rape charges against your boy, here," he told me when he returned a few minutes later.

"Come again?"

Vinnie held up the cat. "Said the little guy was humping everything in sight."

Killer gave an exhausted *meow* and Vinnie grinned.

I frowned. "If you two start high-fiving each other, I'm kicking the both of you out."

"Promise?" Vinnie looked so hopeful—and exhausted—that my chest hitched. "Because I don't think I can take much more. The oldest vampire in existence could be standing right in front of me and I don't think I'd have the strength to nail him, even if it meant a bonus trip to Jamaica." He set Killer down and was about to collapse on my sofa when I grabbed him by the shoulders and steered him around toward the front door.

"Out."

"Really? I get to sleep now?"

"Not exactly. Go home and watch these first." I handed him the extra three DVDs—*Pretty Woman*,

The Notebook, and the first season of *Grey's Anatomy*—I'd picked up while shopping for the demon fest. "Then get some sleep, take a shower, and meet me at DED tonight at eight."

He took one look at the movies. "I hate you."

"That's the point. If you were totally cool with all of this, then you wouldn't need my help. Just stop whining, watch the movies, and DO NOT show up with any dead bodies in the trunk."

"I *really* hate you."

"Matchmaking." I shrugged. "It's a tough gig, but somebody's gotta do it."

Once I sent Vinnie on his way, I gave Killer a can of cat food and an abstinence lecture, and then nuked myself a glass of blood. After downing the contents, I collapsed on the sofa to check my cellphone messages.

I had six. All from my mother.

The first four demanded to know why I'd bailed on Remy.

Number five reminded me that I owed my mother for seventy-two hours of labor and a lifetime of nurturing.

Number six announced that my mother's oldest and dearest friend, Louise Bastillion, was about to welcome her sixty-ninth grandchild, and meanwhile my poor mother had a big fat zero.

I tamped down a sudden rush of guilt (the woman knew her stuff) and went to check on Evie.

She lay on her side, eyes closed, face passive. If not for the thin line of green drool (I was so hitting the nearest Linens 'n Things when this was all over with) oozing from the corner of her mouth, I would never have made her for a demon.

Okay, so the drool and the smell, and the gnashing of teeth. But otherwise, she could have been any hot, happening twenty-something crashing after a night of lesbian club-hopping.

She was still Evie.

I clung tight to the hope, shut the door, and headed back to the sofa. I sat there for several moments and debated whether or not to turn on the TV. Or the radio. Or something. *Anything* to shatter the sudden isolation that wrapped around me.

I hadn't felt quite this lonesome since the time I'd been wanted for murder.

But even then, I'd had Ty to help me out, talk to, confide in. I hadn't been alone. *Lonely*.

My fingers itched and I almost snatched up the phone to call him. But Ty and Ash were buddies. Calling him would be as good as handing Evie over to Ash myself, and I had no intention of doing that.

I had to figure out a way to help her on my own.

I would, just as soon as I cleared out the cobwebs and got a decent day's rest. Sleep first, then surely genius would strike and my problems would be solved.

I stretched out on my side and dangled an arm over the edge of the couch. I snapped my fingers and made kissy noises at Killer, who sprawled on the floor a few feet away.

He lifted his head and blinked at me. *Give a guy a break, would ya? I'm exhausted.*

"Don't flatter yourself. I just thought you might want to cuddle since we have a demon in the very next room and it's common knowledge that cats are a hot commodity when it comes to demons. I figured you might need someone to watch your back." I shrugged. "But if you're not interested . . ."

You're making that up.

"Maybe, but what if I'm not?"

He blinked again before pushing to his feet. *Oh, all right. But don't think I'm making a habit of this. Demon or no demon, I'm not the cuddly type.* A few steps and he leaped up onto the sofa and settled down next to me.

"Just this once," I assured him, gathering him close. "In the interest of self-preservation."

Damn straight.

He snuggled closer and I hugged him tighter, and in a matter of seconds, we were both sound asleep.

When I woke up later that afternoon, I was no better off than when I'd first closed my eyes. Despite my high hopes, I hadn't had one stroke of genius or even a tiny dream to clue me in as to a solid plan to help my assistant. Sleep wrought nothing except a massive headache and a mouthful of cat hair.

I came up sputtering while Killer gave me a that'll-teach-you-to-cuddle-with-me look.

I checked on Evie, who lay on her back, her arms extended on either side. She hung suspended in midair approximately two feet over the mattress, her mouth open, her eyes rolled back. Her chest heaved and a loud wheeze vibrated through the air.

"Don't mind me." I tiptoed into the frigid room, retrieved a pair of Rock & Republic jeans, a rhinestone AC/DC tee, and a pair of Courtney Crawford black leather ankle straps. I was halfway to the door when her eyes opened and her head swiveled toward me. Her gaze snagged on the shoes in my hand and her mouth opened.

"You wouldn't . . ."

Her face split into an evil grin and I picked up my steps.

I ducked through the doorway and shut the door just as a glob of green goop came flying across the room. It hit the wood with a solid *splat* and reminded me that my time was running out.

Today, Evie was sliming filthy expensive, wicked hot footwear. Tomorrow? Chopping some poor woman into a zillion pieces.

I spent the next half hour ignoring my cellphone (give it up already, Ma), getting ready for work, and mapping out my next move.

By the time I dropped off Killer at Mr. Blumfield's down in 3C (I'd decided to give Mrs. Janske some time to cool off and rethink the lawsuit) and headed to work, I'd come up with a workable plan.

First on my list? Finish prepping Vinnie for tonight's date.

Then I needed to find at least one decent match for Mia and set up various dates for other clients. After that, I was going to sort mail and return phone calls and change the light bulb in the back storage room.

And, oh yeah, I was going to find someone qualified to perform an exorcism.

"Do you really think I'm ready?" Vinnie asked a few hours later as he checked his reflection for the countless time in the small oval mirror that hung on one wall of my office.

He wore beige slacks and a pale blue shirt (which I'd picked up for him on my way into work that evening). His hair was gel-free and slightly tousled.

"You look perfect."

"I look like a pansy."

"In other words, perfect." I walked up behind him and stared over his shoulder. "She'll love it. Just make sure you remember what we talked about."

He nodded. "No cursing or spitting or whacking anybody and stuffing them into the trunk."

"What about the basement?" asked a familiar female voice. "Or the crawl space under the stairs?"

I turned to find Mia standing in the office doorway. She wore a black leather vest, black leather pants, and a pair of silver-studded black knee-high dominatrix boots. Her lips were painted a bright blood-red, her complexion a ghastly white.

Vinnie looked ready to bolt for his jacket and the nuclear toothpick stuffed in the pocket when I touched a hand to his arm. "She owns a tattoo shop and she's just really artsy." In other words, she's not a card-carrying member of the undead. "Hey, Mia." I smiled at my newest client. "You're early."

"I finished up with my last customer a half hour ahead of schedule. I did this rad pic of Vincent Price on the inside of his left forearm. It turned out gnarly."

"That's great."

"You do snake tats?" Vinnie asked her, his gaze raking from her head to her toes and back up again.

"Are you kidding? I live for snake tats." She motioned to the python that wound its way around her neck. "I didn't actually do the needlework on this, but I did do the design."

"Not bad."

"Says you. It's friggin' fabulous." She smiled. "Nice outfit, dude."

His tension seemed to fade in a rush of insecurity. "Really?"

Her red lips parted in a smile. "No." She shook her head. "You look like a registered dork."

Vinnie's mouth drew into a tight line and he inched toward his jacket.

"The PC term is pansy," I said, gripping his hand just before it dipped into the coat. "Chill," I snapped. "She's human."

"You sure?"

Hello? Fangs, remember? "I know a human when I see one," I whispered to Vinnie. To Mia, I said, "Vinnie's trying to find a woman to take home to mama."

"You're a mama's boy *and* a dork?"

Mia smiled, Vinnie frowned, and I had a quick mental flash of the carnage about to take place on my very expensive Persian rug unless I did something really fast.

"Vinnie, go." I pointed toward the door. "Mia, sit." I motioned to the chair. "Come on, people. Let's *move*."

A minute later, Vinnie was on his way to a tearoom on Manhattan's Lower East Side and Mia was picking her teeth with my letter opener.

"So?" she asked when I sat down behind my desk and eyed her.

"I think I've found the perfect man." Or at least one to tide her over until Mr. Perfect materialized. "His name is Wes Johnson and he's a graffiti artist."

"Creative." She tapped the letter opener on her front tooth. "I like. Is he hung?"

"Like a horse," I replied, and Mia smiled. "He's also well rounded and very in-depth. In addition to his art, he likes listening to heavy metal music and attending thrash parties. He even has a hobby."

"Knife-throwing?" Mia asked hopefully.

"Body piercing via safety pins."

"I think I'm in love."

For now.

Until she realized that Wes wasn't half the badass in person as he was on paper. He cried during movies and never missed *Ellen,* both of which explained why I hadn't dug him up during my first database search for possible Mia matches.

He wasn't the man for her.

In fact, judging by his emotional state, I wasn't so sure he was a man, period. He'd been wearing sunglasses the one and only time I'd interviewed him, so my information was limited to what was actually written on the profile—namely, overemotional male desperate for ultra-sensitive female who wouldn't mind, occasionally, switching gender roles in the relationship.

Namely, he wanted to wear the thong every now and again while she wore the tighty-whities.

I ignored the sinking feeling in the pit of my stomach and the voice that whispered *You are so dead,* and held tight to the vision of Mia in her dominatrix boots. Hey, it smacked of gender reversal to me.

I gave Mia the details of her upcoming coffee date. Once she left, I spent a half hour matching up a few other clients—a stewardess with a high school gym coach, a financial analyst with a bungee-jumping instructor, a construction worker with a fledgling architect. After that, I poured myself a cup of coffee and started Googling local exorcists.

I'd just scribbled down the info for two possibilities—a retired Catholic priest now residing in Connecticut and one Dr. Zoombababazoom, a voodoo high priestess from Jersey (ya gotta love the Internet)—when Remy Tremaine walked into my office.

He looked as scrumptious as ever in jeans and a black Ed Hardy T-shirt.

If my heart hadn't already stalled thanks to last night and a jumble of feelings that I had no desire to examine too closely, it would have definitely skipped a few beats courtesy of Ed and my weakness for designer *everything.*

"Nice," I commented.

His gaze zeroed in on me as I sat behind my desk. While I knew I was, for the most part, hidden by lots of chrome and glass (he was a vamp, not Superman), I couldn't shake the feeling that Remy Tremaine saw much more than I wanted him to, from my blond highlights to my hot pink toenails, and everything in between.

"You're not looking so bad yourself." He stared at me a few more moments before shifting his attention to his surroundings. He swept a gaze around my office. "Nice place."

"It's not the penthouse of the Trump Tower, but it'll do." At least as far as I was concerned. "My folks think I should stop slumming it and report to the nearest Moe's."

He grinned. "My parents felt the same way when I decided to forgo the family banking business and start a security service. But they finally came around. So this is where you do your thing."

"This is it."

He sank down in the chair opposite my desk and leaned back, his casual stance belying the blatant interest in his gaze. "What exactly is it that you do?"

"Well, it all starts with one of these." I showed him the multi-page profile and went through the basic steps that clients followed to sign up to find their dream mate. "Then they write a check, I do my thing, and they live happily ever after. So, um, what brings you here?"

"I need a date." His gaze collided with mine. "See,

I had one last night, but she split before we had a chance to get to the really good stuff."

Oh, boy.

I swallowed. "About that . . ." I licked my lips and tried to ignore the way his gaze riveted on my mouth. "I'm sorry, but I really did have a life-or-death dating situation. I'm sure you can understand. You probably have emergencies all the time."

He nodded. "There are always drug deals that go wrong or robberies that turn sour or the occasional officer who needs advice on whether or not to kiss on the first date."

"Very funny."

"Actually"—he grinned—"I was going for charming and/or irresistible."

"I'll give you charming, but the irresistible needs some work."

He stared at me and I stared at him and the tension thickened.

"So," he finally said. "How about it? You up for a drink or something?"

My body trembled. Boy, was I ever. "I can't," I blurted. As physically attracted to him as I was, there was just something that kept me from ripping off my clothes and propositioning Remy right there, right then.

Something, or someone.

"I'm really busy," I rushed on. "Swamped."

The ring of the phone punctuated the sentence and I gave him a what'd-I-tell-ya? shrug.

"Dead End Dating, where your pathetic love life is

our livelihood." It wasn't even close to "Where's the Beef?" but at least I was trying.

"I heard that a certain born vampire was spotted at a certain club in Times Square where a certain demon is rumored to be hanging out," Ty's deep voice rumbled in my ear. Suddenly I forgot all about Remy Tremaine.

My heart gave a frantic double thump and the blood started to pound through my veins. My legs trembled and warmth stirred low in my belly.

"Um." I shifted in my seat and searched for a comfortable position. "Is that so?"

"You don't happen to know which born vampire I'm talking about, now would you?"

"Let's see . . . born vamp? Times Square? Lesbian nightclub? Nope, I'm afraid I'm drawing a great big blank."

"I never said it was a lesbian club."

Uh-oh. "I just assumed?"

"You're lying. Dammit, Lil. What part of 'Stay out' don't you understand?"

The sound of a throat clearing drew my attention, and my gaze collided with Remy's. He arched an eyebrow at me and I murmured, "Could you hold just a sec?" Before Ty could grumble *hell, no*, I clamped a hand over the mouthpiece. "Can I take a rain check?" I asked Mr. Tall, Blond and Perfect.

"Tomorrow night?"

I thought of Evie levitating in my bedroom. "What about next week? Or the week after that?" I held up the phone. "It's my busiest time of year, but I'm sure things will calm down soon enough."

He nodded and pushed to his feet. "I'll call you then."

"I can't wait."

"Can't wait for what?" Ty's voice drew me back to the phone in my hand.

"Nothing." I watched Remy disappear. The bell on the outer door jingled and my nerves relaxed for a nanosecond.

"Who were you talking to?"

"A client."

"Since when is Remy Tremaine one of your clients?"

"How do you know I was talking to Remy?"

"Because I'm standing across the street from your place and I just watched him walk out."

"You're spying on me?" No sooner had the question burst past my lips than I reached the front door. I stared through the glass at the vampire who lounged against the opposite building.

He was all lean lines and hard muscle, his face partially hidden beneath the brim of his black Stetson. He wore black jeans and a black leather vest with nothing else on underneath. His heavily muscled biceps gleamed in the moonlight and an excited shiver worked its way down my spine and back up again. "You *are* spying on me."

"It's not called spying. It's called watching your back, and someone has to because you sure as hell aren't covering it on your own." He frowned, his grip going white on the cellphone in his hands. "I know for a fact that you were at that bar last night."

"So what if I was?" I stared into his bluer-than-blue eyes and my tummy hollowed out. "It's a free country. Last I heard, I didn't need special permission to go drinking with my friends."

"Unless there's a dangerous demon on the loose who's hunting new victims."

"I seriously doubt he wants to hack me up. He has a history of slicing and dicing humans. As in living, breathing. I'm much too dead for him."

"Or way too stubborn."

"Either way, I'm safe."

"And what about your friends?"

"I'm perfectly capable of protecting Evie." Guilt stabbed at me as I said the words because I knew it was my fault that she was floating in midair and sliming innocent shoes. I'd sent her into room A to deal with Earl Hubert Stanley armed with nothing but a Lysol can and some attitude. Why, I'd practically hung a raw T-bone around her neck and shoved her into the lion's den.

"You're just a vampire," Ty said, as if sensing my sudden remorse. "There's only so much you can do. Any human—male or female—is fair game for this demon. Even Evie."

Especially Evie.

"Just do us all a favor," Ty went on, obviously mistaking my silence for deep thought rather than *mucho* guilt. "Go barhopping down in SoHo or Greenwich.

Hell, head for Brooklyn if you have to. Just steer clear of Times Square."

"Are you done?"

"That depends. Are you going to listen?"

"Don't I always?" I gave him a smile and a mock salute. He grinned and the slow, sexy slant made my legs quiver.

Bad legs.

"So what's with Remy?" Ty finally asked, his expression fading into a tight frown, as if he'd just remembered something. "What was he doing here?"

"He wanted a date."

"With you?"

"Does it matter?"

It did. I could see it in the sudden flare of his neon-blue eyes.

At least, I thought I saw it, but then the jealous light faded and I was left to wonder if I was reading more into Ty's feelings than what actually existed.

Maybe the reason we had no relationship wasn't because he couldn't have one, but because he didn't want one.

Maybe he didn't feel anything more for me than a great deal of lust and I was just imagining the rest.

Maybe . . .

And maybe it didn't matter one way or the other. Regardless of the hows and whys, we weren't together and we never would be, and there was no sense crying over what I couldn't have.

Right?

Right.

"I really have to go." Before he could say anything, I punched the OFF button and turned away from the doorway.

You can't get away from me that easily. His deep voice whispered through my head and I stiffened.

Just watch me. I gathered my courage and put up the biggest mental block I could summon. Granted, I couldn't permanently sever the emotional link that connected us, but I could sure as hell put a crimp in the wire.

I put all of my thought into powering off my computer, straightening my desk, and NOT thinking about Ty or how blue his eyes were or how much I really, *really* wanted to kiss him again.

Or how, even more than kissing him, I wanted to talk to him. To tell him about Evie and how I was just a teensy, tiny bit concerned (that's *concerned,* mind you, NOT scared) that I might not be able to actually save her.

I mean, really. What did I know about exorcisms?

I shook away the question and busied myself with several file folders. By the time I grabbed my purse and headed home, it was a half hour later and Ty had given up his post across the street.

Thankfully.

I had more important things to worry over than what Ty did or didn't feel for me. I realized that the moment I climbed out of a cab a few blocks over to find half my closet littering the street in front of my apartment.

I ducked as a pair of Chanel pumps sailed past my head and whacked into the concrete.

What the hell . . . ?

I twisted and caught a glimpse of Evie framed in the open window, her eyes a bright yellow, before a black patent Mary Jane nailed me smack-dab in the middle of the forehead.

And just like that, everything went black.

Nineteen
❤ ❤ ❤

I didn't actually black out.

Yes, one minute I was staring up at Evie and the next I was stranded in total darkness, but it wasn't because I'd lost consciousness.

Come on. I'm a vampire, for Damien's sake! I'm made of stronger stuff than that. I wasn't going down just by getting whacked in the head with a hot-looking shoe.

Rather, it was a hot-looking coat—wool with silk lining—that had me flat on my back, fighting to peel the stifling material off my head.

There. I stared up at the sky and drank in a deep draft of oxygen to get my bearings.

It didn't work, for obvious reasons, and I scrambled to my feet. My gaze shifted to Evie, who stood in the window ready to chunk my all-time favorite black sequined Bergdorf Goodman—*Nooooooooooo!*

It hit me square in the face. A split second later, it was raining scarves and undies and—*oh, no! Not my bras, too!*

"Nice skivvies." The comment came from a bum parked near the curb. He reeked of alcohol and bad decisions. A grin split his face and revealed several missing teeth as he held up a purple lace bra. "You fill this out with the real thing or are those fake boobies?" He motioned to my chest.

"Real." I snatched the scrap of lace from his hands and started scooping up everything she tossed. The faster I scooped, the faster she tossed until—

Enough!

I could slip on my preternatural Nikes and spare a few seconds to hightail it up five flights of stairs, down hallways, and through doorways, or I could cut the bullshit and put a stop to this right *now.*

My gaze swept my surroundings. Since I didn't have a nearby phone booth (think *Underdog*), I had to settle for crouching behind a fire hydrant.

Kapow. Shazam. Shimmy-shimmy-cocoa-pop!

Just like that, I went from pissed off vampire to determined pink bat.

"Holy shit," the bum's voice echoed in my tiny ears, but I was too far gone to worry about him at the moment.

My sight shifted from Technicolor to night-vision and I headed for the window and the red blob holding my prized Chanel boots.

The blob dangled one precious leather creation over the edge. I gave a high-pitched scream and dive-bombed through the open window. My wing hit her cheek. The frantic fluttering drove her back until she collapsed on the bed. Just like that, her body went limp and her eyes rolled back in her head, as if the effort of destroying my life had exhausted her.

Uh, yeah.

Meanwhile, I landed in a flapping heap in front of my now empty closet. I focused my gaze. My breathing slowed and my limbs grew heavy. The steady beat of wings faded into the pounding of my own heart and I was once again Lil the vivacious vamp instead of Lil the lean, mean bat machine.

My first instinct was to cry.

I glanced at the upside-down shoe boxes and empty hangers and my gaze narrowed.

All right, already. So maybe my first instinct was to kick some demon ass.

But since said ass still belonged to my loyal assistant, who was now an unconscious heap on the bed, I kept a tight rein on my temper. I forced myself into the kitchen to retrieve the spray bottle of leftover holy water.

Back in the bedroom, I latched and locked the window. Rather than squirting the stuff around the edges as I'd done before (which had still left plenty of room to unlatch the window and toss things out without vi-olating the holy barrier), I aimed for the glass itself and let loose. Water drenched the pane, running in rivulets that drip-dropped and puddled on the hardwood floor. I squirted the latch, as well.

"That ought to do it," I said, turning back to the bed. Evie had pushed herself into a sitting position, her back against the headboard. The whites of her eyes had been replaced with vicious yellow slits that fixated on me.

"You really think that will stop me?" The demonic voice slithered into my ears and a strange sense of coldness wrapped around me. "I could skin you alive if I wanted to."

"Really?" I took a step toward the bed. "Then do it." I held up the spray bottle as if I meant to use it and sure enough, Evie flinched. "Just what I thought. You're a big talker, but when it comes to backing it up, you're just a chickenshit."

The demon opened his mouth and let loose an agonized wail, followed by a rush of putrid green fog.

I debated whether or not to spritz him just once to prove my point, but I didn't want to cause Evie any more agony than she was obviously already in. Instead, I aimed the nozzle and sprayed a tight circle around the bed. I knew it was overkill since I'd already secured the room. But spraying, however futile, gave me some small sense of control.

"You won't save her," the voice followed me to the doorway. "She's already mine."

I opened my mouth to tell him where to go, how

fast to get there, and what a filthy crazed psycho he really was. But as his words sank in, my throat grew suddenly tight.

Because deep down I was starting to fear that he might actually be right.

The doubt followed me all the way back downstairs, where I gathered up what was left of my stuff—who knew a drunk could move so fast and have such good taste?—and carted it back up to my apartment.

I was not going to cry.

I was not going to cry.

I was not going to cry.

I recited the chant as I dropped several armfuls on the sofa and tried not to notice the dirty splotches and green slime that covered practically everything that was left. There were even tread marks where a passing cab had run over my ivory chenille skirt.

My eyes burned and the tears spilled over.

I spent the next half hour mourning the loss of my wardrobe while Evie cussed and spit and threw a major hissy fit in the bedroom.

Finally, after a lot of wailing and gnashing of teeth—my own, not Evie's—I managed to get myself under control and look on the bright side. No wardrobe meant nothing to wear, which meant that, extra cash or no extra cash, I *had* to go shopping.

I sniffled, wiped my face, and pushed up from the sofa. The noise in the bedroom had quieted to the occasional four-letter word.

"I'm calling Ash," I called out after one in particular, but the warning fell on deaf ears. Maybe because the demon had finally figured out that I didn't really mean it. Or, worse, he was getting more powerful, the possession nearly complete, and so Ash didn't pose as big a threat.

Either way, I knew my time was running out. I had to do something quick. I grabbed my cell and punched in one of the numbers I'd Googled earlier that evening.

"Yes," I said when someone finally answered. "I'm looking for a Father Donald Patrick. Is he in?"

"Father Patrick died last month. A heart attack."

"That's terrible. Was he in the middle of a taxing exorcism?"

"Actually, he was in the middle of an audit. He'd been misappropriating church funds and the IRS got wind of it."

"Oh. Sorry." I hung up and dialed the second number. Evie had stopped cussing, but now the bed thumped the wall here and there.

Bam.

Thunk.

Splat.

I tuned out the sounds and focused on the cell in my hand. My mind conjured visions of midnight sacrifices and naked bodies dancing around an open campfire. I could practically hear the drums beating as I dialed the second number. "May I speak to Dr. Zoombababazoom?" I asked when someone finally answered.

"She's in the kitchen right now."

Smack-dab in the middle of a poultry sacrifice, no doubt.

"Would you like to leave a message?" the voice asked.

"Yes, please. Can you tell her that I have a life-and-death situation that needs her immediate attention."

"I'm sorry," the voice replied. "She doesn't do love spells anymore. The last guy she tried one on ended up humping a water fountain in Central Park. It wasn't pretty."

"I don't need a love spell."

"She doesn't do the diet spells either. The last woman who paid for one ended up on *Dr. Phil* during a 'Can This Woman Be Saved?' episode and Doctor Z almost got sued."

"I don't need a diet either." I swallowed and gathered my courage. "I need an exorcism."

"An exorcism?" Her voice took on a strange note. "Can you hold on just a sec?" I heard muffled voices, followed by an excited "Hiya. This is Dr. Zoombababazoom. What can I do you for?"

I'd expected an ancient crackle of a voice. One that dripped wisdom and knowledge and black magic. Instead, the woman on the other end sounded like a bubbly sorority girl.

"Dr. Zoombababazoom? *The* Dr. Zoombababazoom that consulted on the exorcism of Tina Radley that was featured in *People* last year?"

"Duh. What's up?"

"My, um, name is Lil. Lil Marchette. I'm a match-maker in Manhattan and I need"—my voice lowered a notch—"an exorcism."

"Cool. So what makes you think you're possessed?"

"Not me. I'm a—" *Vampire* was there on the tip of my tongue, but I held it back and ended with *"really well-dressed matchmaker. It's my assistant who's foaming at the mouth."*

"She could have rabies."

"She's cussing in five different languages."

"So does my gardener, but he's just really well educated and really pissed off at this new line of topsoil that's supposed to make everything grow when all it really does is cost an arm and a leg more than the old stuff."

I opened the bedroom door a crack and peered inside at Evie. "She's crawling around on all fours on the ceiling and her head is on backwards."

"Now that smacks of possession."

"Can you help me get rid of the demon?"

"You bet."

You bet? I'd expected a somber *"Of course, I can, child."* Or maybe a serene *"I'll rally my spirit guides and we'll raise an army to defeat the demon and release your friend."* Or, at the very least a confident *"Let me consult with the elders and we'll see about solving your problem ASAP."*

"Where are you?" I couldn't help but ask, suddenly

desperate to prove that Dr. Z was as real as they came and I'd actually hit pay dirt.

"In the kitchen."

"And you have a knife in your hand, right?"

"Sure thing."

"And you're slicing the head off a chicken?"

"A jar of peanut butter. I'm making PB&Js."

I was not getting a good feeling about this.

"So you have a demon problem," she went on as if she were discussing a possible termite infestation. "How long?"

"A few days."

"That's good. The sooner the little buggers are detected, the better."

"So you've dealt with this before?" Sure, I'd read the article online about the Radley possession, but they'd listed Dr. Z as a consultant only. Tina's priest had done the actual exorcism. "Other than with Tina Radley?"

"Sort of."

"Which means?"

"I haven't actually gotten rid of a demon before, but I have been trained in the process."

A virgin. Just my luck.

"I know that doesn't inspire a tremendous amount of confidence in a situation like this," she went on, "but you can bet I know what I'm doing. I'm the best in Jersey."

"How many exorcists are actually in Jersey?"

"Let's see." She grew silent for a moment as if

doing a mental count. "That would be two. Doctor MacIntyre and you-know-who."

"Dr. MacIntyre? I didn't see him mentioned online when I was doing my research."

"He usually does more house-cleansing than actual physical possession, but he does take on the occasional demon. So long as it's not on a school night."

"Excuse me?"

"He's got kids. He's a very involved dad. He's out in the yard right now putting together one of those Rainbow Gyms. We're married," she added. "I know what you're thinking. Why didn't this girl hyphenate? I was going to. I mean, all of my sorority sisters did, but since my name is a zillion letters long in the first place, I just said to heck with it and kept my maiden name. At first, Kip was a little put off, but he finally came around."

"Kip? Is he your husband?"

"Wow, you're good. Are you psychic?"

"More like stupid."

"Excuse me?"

"Cupid," I blurted. "I'm more like Cupid in that my expertise involves finding love for Manhattan's lonely and desperate."

"How sweet." She giggled.

No, really.

She actually *giggled* before rushing on in her pixie-like voice, "It was love at first sight for Kip and me. We met during a seminar called 'Name That Demon' at St. Paul's Cathedral. Three years and a set of twins later, and we're still going strong. If you don't mind waiting until he finishes putting the play set together, I'm sure he can help you."

"Why don't I just call you back at a more convenient time?" *Not.*

While I needed an exorcist in the worst way, I wasn't about to put a pair of young human parents in the same room with Satan's own. We're talking *twins.*

She giggled again. "Holla."

So much for Google. I spent the next ten minutes brainstorming other alternatives.

I could cruise the local churches for an experienced priest, but I knew I wouldn't make it inside the door without breaking out into a massive case of hives. Not to mention—and this was the biggie—no Catholic priest would agree to perform an exorcism without a full-blown investigation by the Church, which was why I hadn't headed for St. Michael's in the first place.

First off, I couldn't afford the attention (denizen of the darkness, remember?). Nor did I have the time to spare for such a process. I'd already been spotted in Times Square with Evie and Vinnie. It was just a matter of time before Ash and his brothers figured out what was going on and tracked the demon back to me.

I racked my brain for other options.

I could run an ad for an exorcist in the local Wanted section, but that, too, required time I didn't have.

I could call my great Aunt Lourdes, who had a blood slave who was related to someone high up at the Vatican. The only problem with that was that Aunt Lourdes—the typical snotty, pretentious born vampire—wouldn't begin to understand why I wanted to help a human. She would most certainly narc to my parents. Which would mean another black mark next to my name.

Not that I cared, of course (okay, maybe a little, but there was nothing I could do about it, since I actually liked the person I'd become). But I wasn't going through all the drama with my folks for nothing, which was exactly what I would be doing because, in the end, no way would they help me help a human.

I could check the Yellow Pages for a listing of local saints. But, come on, this was New York. Pure and the Big Apple didn't really go together, so I had a gut feeling I would come up with a big fat zero.

Still . . .

I'd just pulled out my local phone book (hey, desperate times and all that) when a strange awareness did a fast jig up and down my spine.

My ears perked, tuning to every sound, from the soft pad of footsteps out in the hallway to the whistle of a tea kettle in some distant apartment. My nostrils flared, drinking in a swirl of scents—from the rich aroma of bottled blood to the leftover tuna Mrs. Janske had fed to her cats to the putrid stench coming from my bedroom.

A familiar tingling started in the pit of my stomach,

spreading and gaining momentum until every nerve in my body buzzed to life. My hands trembled and my heart paused.

And just like that, I knew a certain hot, hunky bounty hunter stood on my doorstep.

Twenty

♥ ♥ ♥

I heard the steady rap on the door, followed by Ty's familiar voice. "Open up. We need to talk."

A loud thud from the bedroom punctuated his request and I rushed to the door. Instead of hauling it open, I plastered myself against it to make sure it didn't budge. "Now's not a really good time," I said through the thick wood. More knocks drifted from the bedroom, followed by a gasp and a loud, wet burp.

Ugh, I was *so* docking Evie's pay when this was all over.

"Look, I know you're mad because I was spying on you," Ty went on, his deep voice echoing in my ears. The wood seemed to warm beneath my hands and my fingers tingled. "But there was no way around it."

"Mad? I mean, yeah, yeah, I'm mad." I frowned at the door. "I'm royally pissed."

"I know you and you always seem to end up in the middle of trouble." He went quiet for a long moment before he added, "I don't want anything to happen to you."

My heart gave a tiny lurch and I barely caught the smile before it tugged at my lips. "FYI—I'm perfectly capable of taking care of myself."

"Sure you are."

"What's that supposed to mean?"

"That in the past six months you've gotten yourself staked by a jealous werewolf, arrested for murder, poisoned by another jealous werewolf, and nearly decapitated by my sire. Most vampires attract the opposite sex. You? You attract trouble."

Hey, I attracted my share of the opposite sex. I ignored the tingling against my palms and frowned. "I don't need you following me all over the city, keeping tabs, asking questions." *Watching.* The last thought sent a burst of excitement through me and my toes shivered.

"Open the door," came the deep, mesmerizing voice.

"No."

"Why not?"

"Because . . ." I glanced around frantically, my gaze bouncing from the bedroom door to the leftovers of my wardrobe cluttering the couch. "Because my place is a mess."

"Since when do you care about that?"

Since never. I tried again. "I had a tough night at work and I haven't had a chance to touch up my makeup or hair."

"I like the natural look."

My heart gave another lurch. "Trust me. Medusa's got nothing on me."

"You always look great. Now open up."

Darn it. Where was a *"Thanks for the heads-up. I'm outta here."* when you really needed it?

I sent up a silent prayer that Evie would keep quiet, slid the chain into place, and then unlatched the dead bolt. I pulled open the door the mere inch that the chain allowed and peered through the crack at Ty. "Yes?"

He arched one dark eyebrow, the tiny scar kicking up a notch as he eyeballed me. "So that's how it is? You're not even going to let me inside? Just because you're pissed off?"

"I don't need a watchdog."

"Really?"

"Yes, really."

"Look me in the eyes and tell me you didn't go wandering around Times Square because of this demon."

"I didn't go wandering around Times Square because of this demon. I went because of Evie. She was, um, dying to try out this new club and I'd promised to go with her." I shrugged. "What can I say? I don't like to break my promises."

"Yeah, well neither do I, and I promised Ash I'd keep an eye on you so he wouldn't have to."

Nix the tiny sliver of hope that Ty was here because he was really and truly worried about me. It was all about business.

I stiffened. "You and Ash need to get an afterlife. Now if you'll excuse me, I've got things to do." I started to shut the door, but suddenly his hand was there.

"Like what?"

"I'm cleaning my oven," I blurted, my brain latching onto the first excuse that popped up.

"You don't clean."

"I'm watching TV."

"You never watch TV."

"I'm balancing my checkbook."

"You never balance anything. You just stash the statements in your underwear drawer and hope everything works out."

Did this vamp know me or what?

"Last chance," he went on. "Open up."

"Or what?"

"Or this." Metal popped and the chain ping-ponged and suddenly it was his arm that pushed inside. Then half his body made it in and suddenly the door was open and Ty was standing right in front of me.

His brows drew together as he stared down at me. "What's wrong with you?"

"N-nothing. I . . ." I swallowed. "What makes you think something's wrong?" *Other than the fact that I'm acting like a lunatic?* I squelched the last thought and squared my shoulders. "Nothing's wrong. Everything's fine. Really."

He tore his gaze from mine and glanced around. "Is somebody here?"

"Of course not." I summoned my best laugh. "It's just me. Yours truly. The one and only."

He started to move past me and I planted my hands on his chest before he could step over the threshold. "What are you doing?"

"I'm going to sit down so we can talk this out."

"But there's nothing to talk out. I can take care of myself, end of talk."

Suspicion sparked as he stared down at me. "You know more about this than you're letting on, and I want to know what you know." He gripped my hands and forced them to my sides.

For a made vamp, he was surprisingly strong. Then again, I hadn't had my dinner and so I was running low on super born-vamp energy at the moment.

Even so, I stood firm and blocked his entrance.

"You might as well move because I'm coming in," he warned.

"No, you're not." My hands still smarted from his grip and a thought struck. "I haven't invited you in," I added with a flourish. "So you can't come in."

He played the super-strength card again, grabbed me by the waist, picked me up, and set me off to the side. "That only works in the movies." And then he waltzed right into my apartment.

Okay so I knew that, but I'd been desperate.

"Stop," I blurted as he started for the bedroom

door. A steady *thump, thump, thump* drifted from the other side and I knew Evie had switched on my iPod docking station.

Uh-oh.

Marvin Gaye's "Sexual Healing" blared from the speakers. The music and lyrics mingled with a long low guttural moan, and Ty stiffened.

"What the hell . . . ?"

"You can't go in there." I flew around him and plastered myself against the bedroom door. "There's . . ." I searched for the words. "Someone's in there," I blurted. There was nothing left to do but spill my guts and hope my BV charm would be enough to keep Ty from calling Ash and ratting me out.

My charm, or my tears. Big wet suckers that would have him so freaked he would forget all about what sat behind Door Number One and concentrate on getting the hell out of PMS-ville.

"I was going to tell you." I blinked several times and willed the waterworks. "I just didn't know how."

"This is what I think it is, isn't it?" Ty's face darkened and his eyes fired a blinding shade of blue.

I summoned my voice. "Yes, it is."

His mouth pulled into a tight line and his brows pinched together. "Dammit, Lil."

"I can't just turn my back on someone I care about," I rushed on. "We have a history together. We're tight."

He shook his head as if he couldn't quite believe what he was hearing. "He means that much to you?"

He? I was actually referring to Evie, and not the

demon, but since Ty looked ready to rip me a new one, I wasn't going to argue semantics.

"Yes," I declared. "He does."

"I don't fucking believe this." He shook his head again before nailing me with that piercing blue stare. "So that's it? You're sleeping with Remy now, so I'm just supposed to forget everything that's happened between us, turn around and walk away?"

I nodded. "Damn straight I'm sleeping with—wait a second. Did you just say *Remy*?"

"He's here, isn't he?" He indicated the door at my back. "In there."

"He is? I mean, yeah"—I nodded vigorously—"he is." *Liar, liar,* my conscience chided. But we're talking a little white lie as opposed to a great big black one. What's more, I hadn't actually thought up the lie. Ty was the one who'd mentioned Remy. I was simply perpetuating the lie in the interest of self-preservation because, let's face it, if Ty didn't know I had Hell's Most Wanted locked in my bedroom, I sure as hell wasn't going to tell him.

I nodded vehemently. "He's in there right now. Naked," I blurted. "Locked and loaded, if you know what I mean." Marvin launched into a loud *"I'm hot just like an oven . . . I need some lovin' . . ."*

Ty looked ready to bite someone's head off. "And just where does that leave us?"

I'm sorry. That's what I meant to say. Something quick and to the point and non-engaging so that Ty would leave and all of this would be over. *I'm sorry. I never meant to hurt you. G'bye.*

But seeing the accusation in his eyes, the hurt, unleashed something inside of me—namely my own hurt, which I'd been nursing since we'd had our closure sex and he hadn't made any effort to contact me.

Closure, a voice reminded me. As in finished, done, *over*.

My head knew that, but my heart . . .

"Us?" I bristled. "Did you just say where does that leave *us*? Since when is there an *us*? There's you, who doesn't have the courtesy to call or send flowers or even e-mail me to see how I'm doing. And then there's me, who thinks it might be nice if you'd called or sent flowers or e-mailed to see how I'm doing. Hell, I would have been happy with a text message."

"Lil—"

"Don't *Lil* me. You've made it very clear you can't have a relationship and now you want to act offended because I'm not sitting around waiting for something that you've assured me is never going to happen? Talk about pompous and self-centered."

"You know I can't . . ." His words trailed off and he ran his hand over his face. "It's not safe."

"We can't be together. I know that." Boy, did I ever. "But what does that mean? That I'm supposed to sit around crying about it and never get on with my life? I like Remy." I wasn't sure when the conversation had shifted from a ruse to cover for the demon in my bedroom to my mixed-up feelings for Fairfield's police chief, but suddenly I wasn't just trying to convince Ty. Even more, I was trying to convince myself. "He's a decent vampire."

"I don't trust him."

"You don't have to because it's not your decision. You already made your decision by not calling or trying." *Or caring.* The tears came on their own this time. I blinked frantically to hold them back, but no dice.

A hot drop slid down my cheek.

Okay, make that two.

Whereas the waterworks had sounded like a good idea just a few minutes ago, now they seemed foolish. I wiped frantically at my face. "I really think you should go."

He stared down at me as if debating his next move, then his gaze slid past me to the closed door. Marvin belted out *"Baaaaaa-beeeeee, I can't wait much longer, it's getting stronger and stronger . . ."*

"This is really what you want?" Ty finally asked.

What I really wanted was a white sand beach, a margarita, and a very naked, very committed Ty, but since that was out of the question, I nodded. "I want you to leave." Sniffle. "Please."

"Liar." His deep voice echoed in my head. *"I saw the beach, sugar."*

Damn the stupid telepathic link. I stiffened and gave him a defiant stare. *"So what if I'm still hot for your body? It doesn't change the fact that I'm ready for a real relationship. I've had enough wild, meaningless sex in my life."*

"You're swearing off sex then?"

"I wouldn't go that far. But I want companionship in addition to the wild, meaningless sex."

"Then it stops being meaningless."

"Exactly. Now butt out of my business and my head. I'm busy right now." I steeled myself and pushed him out of my thoughts.

Physically, however, he didn't budge. He simply stood there, towering over me, his gaze riveted on mine. "So you *really* like him?" he asked after a long, silent moment.

Okay, so *really* was pushing it, but there was some definite *like* when it came to Remy Tremaine. I nodded and his frown deepened.

"And you think he can make you happy?"

"I'm willing to give him a chance. I'm willing to give *us* a chance, which is more than I can say for you."

I knew all the reasons why a relationship with Ty couldn't work. At the same time, that small romantic part of me wanted to say to hell with everyone—Logan, my parents, the entire snotty, pretentious born-vamp race—and go for it anyway.

Even more, I wanted Ty to *want* to go for it, as well. To be so crazy over me that he couldn't stand the thought of living an eternity without me. I wanted him to want to take the risk. To try. Even if we were doomed.

Crazy, I know, but there it was.

His gaze brightened and I had the distinct feeling he'd read some of the ridiculous thoughts racing through my head despite my mental barrier. I saw the push-pull of emotion in his gaze, but then his mouth drew tight and he turned away.

"Take care." The words slipped past my lips. Lame, I know, but it was all I could think of at the moment.

My chest suddenly hurt and my throat felt tight as I watched him walk toward the door.

The creak of wood echoed in my head, followed by a soft *thunk* that sliced through the Marvin Gaye song and made me flinch.

I stepped forward with every intention of bolting the door. Instead, my hand closed around the door-knob and I fought down the sudden urge to haul open the stupid thing and go after him. To grab him by the arm and tell him the truth.

That, and throw him on the nearest horizontal surface.

But what was the point?

As great as we were together physically, it wasn't going to happen. I knew it. He knew it.

It was time to accept it and move on.

Good riddance, I told myself. Now I could get on with my afterlife and stop wondering *what if*. I could actually give Remy a real shot and see what happened. Maybe he *was* the perfect born vamp for me and I'd just been carrying around too much Ty baggage to realize it. Maybe we would fall for each other and live eternally ever after in Fairfield and have tons of baby vamps and—

Bam! Bam! Bam!

The rap on the door shattered my train of thought—thankfully. We're talking an eternity in *Fairfield*. Ugh.

I opened the door.

Ty stood there, his hands braced on either side of the doorjamb, his muscles tight, his face set in a distinct frown. His eyes glittered a hot, bright, knowing blue and I felt a funny niggle in the pit of my stomach. "I forgot something."

His words pressed my panic button and my heart gave a frantic lurch. He'd figured it out. In the five seconds since he'd stormed out on me, he'd done the math and bingo—demon in the bedroom.

I tamped down the crazy thoughts and tried to sound nonchalant. "Oh, really? What?"

"This." And then he leaned down and kissed me.

Twenty-one
❤ ❤ ❤

It was the hottest, wildest, most passionate kiss of my afterlife.

And the shortest.

One minute Ty's strong, purposeful mouth devoured mine, his tongue stroking and delving and leaving no secrets between us. And the next, I found myself staring at a dark, empty hallway. A door opened and closed at the far end. Footsteps sounded. The flutter of wings echoed the frantic beat of my own heart and then he was gone.

I blinked.

Huh?

I blinked again as my brain tried to process what he'd done and what I'd done and what it had meant and . . .

I shook my head, walked inside, and locked the

door behind me. Marvin had faded into a slow rock ballad from Nickelback. I headed for the bedroom to take a quick peek.

The walls seemed to vibrate and as soon as I opened the door, I discovered why. My loyal assistant hovered a good ten feet in the air, her face plastered on the ceiling. She slammed her head into the Sheetrock in time to the drumbeat and bits of plaster rained down on my Egyptian cotton sheets.

I snatched the iPod from its docking station and the room went silent. The headbanging stopped and Evie fell back to the mattress. Her forehead was cut and bleeding, her face puffy and swollen, and my chest tightened.

Reality hit me and I forgot all about Ty and my crazy, mixed-up feelings for him. I gave the room another spritz of holy water and then went back to the living room.

I bypassed the Yellow Pages (can you say *grasping?*) and snatched up my cellphone. As much as I hated to admit it, I knew I wasn't going to find an exorcist and get Evie out of this mess on my own. I needed reinforcements.

I scrolled through the numbers in my directory until I found what I was looking for, and then I hit TALK.

"You need a what?" Max's incredulous voice thundered in my ear.

"An exorcist."

"That's what I thought you said. Shit," he muttered. "I knew you were a fruitcake, but I never realized—"

"Not for me, dumbass. A close friend of mine is in trouble and I have to help her. Since I don't actually know any exorcists, I called you."

"What makes you think I know any exorcists?"

"You dated that nun one time. Surely she knows someone."

"Terry wasn't a nun. She was a secretary at St. Peter's Catholic Girls' School."

"Nun . . . secretary . . . What's the difference?"

"Let's see . . . one has years of training and is ordained by God, and the other writes out detention slips for chewing gum and has wild sex with vampires."

"Well, if you want to get picky about it."

"It's called being practical. You should try it sometime."

"Are you going to help me or not?"

"Why should I?"

"Because I'm your one and only sister."

"You're my one and only sister who narcs on me every time I turn around. You told Mom and Dad about that milkmaid. And the serving wench."

"Because I'm a fine, upstanding member of society?"

"You're a pain in the ass."

"Because if you don't help me, I'll tell Mom and Dad about your ongoing bump and grind with a certain werewolf neighbor."

"How do you know about Viola?" he asked, his voice suddenly sharp.

I smiled. "Lucky guess."

"Shit."

"Come on, it's not like it took a genius. I've seen the way you look at her and I've seen the way she looks at you and, well, to be honest, I would be more surprised if something wasn't going on. She's a beautiful woman."

"And smart," he added. "I can actually talk to her."

Since when did talking figure in with my brother? With any born male *vampere* for that matter?

"So that's what you and Internet bimbo were doing during the last hunt. And here I figured her for more of a moaner than a talker."

"Very funny." His voice grew quiet. "She was just a diversion."

"To keep your mind off Viola?"

"To keep Mom and Dad's minds off Viola. We don't want them to know what's going on yet."

"Yet? Are you trying to tell me that you two are—"

"Drop it, okay?" he cut in. "It's just sex."

And talking. And sex plus talking equaled serious business. That's what I wanted to say, but Max's sudden silence—as if he was still trying to wrap his head around the notion of actually falling for a woman—kept me from pushing.

What can I say? I'm a sucker for love.

"So what about it?" I prodded, shifting the subject back to yours truly. "Can you hook me up with an exorcist? Preferably one who offers cleanup services afterward. My apartment is such a mess."

"You really are a fruitcake."

What? You can't blame a girl for trying.

"So forget the cleanup service. Just find me someone. Anyone."

"I guess I could give Terry a call and see if she has any connections at the church. Maybe a friend of a friend of a friend. It might take a while, though. A few days maybe."

"I really need someone sooner than that."

"How soon?"

"A few hours." He let loose a few cuss words illustrating how impossible that was going to be and what a major nut job I really was and how I'd obviously been switched with his real sister at birth.

"Of course, if you can't," I interrupted when he launched into a very vivid description of how I'd most certainly been conceived via some weird science experiment that had gone crazily wrong, "I'll totally understand. I know I'm asking a lot. Imagine me expecting you to lie to our parents for pretty much the rest of your existence and conceal the fact that I'm having an illicit affair with Dad's arch enemy . . . No, wait. *You're* the one who's asking *me* to lie for the rest of *my* existence. I'm just asking for a measly exorcist."

"If you weren't my sister, I'd rip you into so many pieces your own mother wouldn't recognize you."

Promises, promises.

"Two hours." A pleading note crept into my voice. "Please, Max. I really need your help."

"Give me three," he finally muttered, and then he hung up.

My curiosity (and my survival instincts) got the best of me, and I punched in Vinnie's number.

"Yo. It's Vinnie. Leave a message." *Beeeep.*

"Hi Vinnie! It's Lil. Lil Marchette. The vampire who's doing everything in her power to make your dating experience as fruitful and as satisfying as possible. The vampire who's also doing everything in her power to please your mother. Speaking of mothers, did you show Carmen any pics of Mama Balducci? Did you mention the birthday party? The upcoming wedding and the eight possible kids? Call me."

I killed the phone and spent the next thirty seconds wondering if my fangs were going to end up on eBay.

Maybe.

Probably.

My stomach churned and my chest tightened and I gave myself a great big mental bitch-slap.

Sure, Vinnie wasn't perfect. But he had made *some* progress. He'd actually cleaned any and all body parts out of the trunk of his car. No bones hanging from the rearview mirror. No femur gear shift. No kill sheet taped to the dash. That had to count for something.

And if it didn't, well, at least I wouldn't have to worry over a demon head-banging in my bedroom. If Vinnie staked me, I'd have my own soul to worry about.

So much for making myself feel better.

I forced aside the negativity and spent the next five minutes checking my cell messages.

Nina One called to let me know that Rob had given her complete carte blanche—and his Visa gold card—to redecorate his apartment in Jersey. He was officially the sweetest, kindest, most virile born vampire to ever terrorize the earth. To think Nina had known him most of her entire life and had never realized it.

Hey, I'd known him even longer and I still thought he was a putz.

My mother called not once, but three times.

"I did not raise my daughter to behave so rudely. How could you stand up Remy like that?" *Click*.

"Do you really want to spend the rest of your after-life alone?" *Click*.

"Maybe I'll just forget the grandchildren and buy a dog." *Click*.

I should be so lucky.

I deleted the messages and left a quick "Hey, how's the date going?" on Mia's voice mail.

After two glasses of blood and a Tums (between my thoughts of eBay, Evie, and *ma mère*, I was *this* close to tossing) I headed downstairs to pick up Killer.

He was thrilled to see me, as usual.

What are you trying to do? Starve me to death? I haven't eaten a thing since you dropped me off on account of I just spent the past ten hours with two schnauzers, a shih tzu and three snotty French poodles. With their big asses in the way, I couldn't even see the food bowl, much less get a bite to eat.

"Nice to see you, too," I told him as we headed back to my apartment. "I missed your jovial personality."

Bite me.

I flashed him some fang and his eyes widened. "Don't tempt me."

He sniffed. *Geez, you don't have to be so touchy. It was just a joke. Lighten up.*

I tried.

Really, I did.

I fed Killer and tidied up what was left of my wardrobe, and I even called Nina One to tell her how happy I was that she and Rob had finally found each other. But no matter how I tried to distract myself and relax, I couldn't stop thinking about Evie and the exorcism and the fact that Max still hadn't called me back.

Or the possibility that maybe, just maybe, he wouldn't call at all.

Twenty-two
♥ ♥ ♥

I was just about to lick salt off Ty's nipples when the Pussycat Dolls started singing.

Whoa. Wait a second.

There were no Pussycat Dolls on this particular stretch of secluded beach. Just palm trees and lots of sand and a bare-chested bartender named Raoul who'd appeared to replenish my margarita and offer to rub coconut oil on my back. Since Ty had appeared at the same time, I'd given him the job and Raoul had faded into the shimmering white sand.

I paused, salt on my tongue and Ty's strong body slick and solid beneath me, and glanced around. The sand stretched for miles. The palm trees swayed. The water lapped at the shore. No, definitely no Pussycat Dolls.

I dipped my head and lapped at one male nipple.

The nub tightened against the rasp of my tongue. Ty groaned and my own nipples throbbed and—

"... *loosen up my buttons, baybeee* ..."

The song blared, shattering the sun-drenched fantasy. Ty faded, along with the beach and my margarita. Everything went pitch-black except for a tiny sliver of light just to my right.

Like a mad woman, I picked my way toward it. A few seconds later, I scrambled and shoved about a dozen throw pillows off my head. I rolled over to find myself flat on my back on the floor. I was wedged between the coffee table and couch, one hip numb from the shoe that was trapped beneath it.

Killer peered over the edge of the leather sofa and stared down at me. He blinked.

What? It's not my fault that you toss and turn when you sleep. It's not like I pushed you off.

I glanced at the tiny red claw marks that were rapidly healing on my upper right arm.

He blinked again. *Purely circumstantial.*

The song blared again and stopped me from reaching out to strangle my sorry excuse for a pet. I freed the trapped shoe, hauled myself to a sitting position, and groped for my cell, which had rolled a few feet away.

"What took you so long?" I blurted the minute I hit TALK. "It's five o'clock in the afternoon. What happened to a few hours? You didn't find an exorcist, did you?"

"Lil," Max's voice floated over the line, but I was on a roll.

Panic welled inside me and I was stuck riding the Freak-Out Express all the way to the first stop. "Please tell me you found one, otherwise with the way my life sucks, I'm just going to stake myself now and get it over with—"

"*Lil,*" he cut in again.

"What?"

"Chill, would you?"

"Easy for you to say. It's not your afterlife on the line here."

"It's not yours either."

Oh, yeah.

I held tight to the knowledge and tried to calm my pounding heart. It didn't work. Sure, it wasn't me. But we're talking the next best thing to me. Evie was my right hand. My peep. Part of my posse. My friend.

"I'm so screwed," I choked out, my throat suddenly tight.

"No, you're not. The secretary knows the secretary of one of the bishops who knows the personal assistant for one of the parish priests who happens to do black-market exorcisms." Hope fired to life even before he added, "You're meeting him tonight at ten p.m., at St. Anthony's in Newark."

"Are you nuts? I can't go to church." Unless I wanted to end up looking like a walking strawberry.

"Not the church. There's a coffee shop across the street. He'll meet you there and you can tell him what you need. And he isn't cheap. He does the exorcisms because he wants to rid the world of demons, but ridding the world costs money. He funds a lot of charities and so he'll expect you to ante up."

"No problem. Money is no object."

"You don't have any, do you?"

"Technically, yes. Theoretically, no."

"Meaning?"

"My closet had a knock-down, drag-out with Evie, and guess who won?"

"Here it comes. First you blackmail me into finding an exorcist and now you're going to extort money."

"I prefer to think of it as a loan."

"Are you going to pay it back?"

"No."

"Then it's extortion." He sighed. "Tell him to call Moe's and I'll write him a check."

"Have I told you that you're my favorite brother?"

"Just make sure you keep your mouth shut about Viola."

"Viola who?"

I hung up the phone, dragged myself to my feet, and headed for the bedroom. I took a quick peek in at Evie, who lay on the bed in the now frigid room. A layer of cold surrounded her. Wheezing and gasping echoed off the walls and sent a ripple of fear down my spine.

Tonight. Ten p.m.

I held tight to the hope and headed for the bathroom. My head throbbed and I felt as if someone had driven a stake right between my eyes. I stepped under the scalding spray of the shower and let the water drip-drop over me and wash away my troubles. My headache eased and my panic subsided. Unfortunately, said troubles waited on the other side of the shower curtain.

Other than what I'd slept in and a few trashed pieces, I was wardrobe-less.

The thought renewed the ache between my eyes as I put on my makeup and flat-ironed my hair. I added an extra coat of mascara to make myself feel better and glossed my lips with my favorite MAC juicy cherry. There. I felt a little better. At least I had *something*, I reminded myself as I pulled on the clothes I'd slept in last night. I could be going shopping au naturel.

Shopping.

The word was like a bright light waiting for me at the end of an otherwise dark smelly alley, and I hauled ass toward it. A half hour later, I was cruising one of my favorite boutiques.

Fifteen minutes after that, I'd found two perfect outfits, complete with shoes and accessories, and I was starting to think that things would actually work out.

I left the store in my fave of the two, a white off-the-shoulder peasant dress complete with some rocking silver Jimmy Choo stiletto slingbacks, and headed to work.

There were ninety-eight messages waiting, complete with a stack of mail and one irritated client who'd had an appointment that morning.

Geez, I missed Evie.

I spent fifteen minutes calming the client and promising a free prospect for the mix-up. I glanced at the mail and made it through four messages (all from my mother) before I finally gave up. I was too stressed and worried and this whole receptionist thing was *hard*.

I set everything aside and punched in Vinnie's phone number.

"So?" I asked the second he picked up. "How was it?"

"Not so good."

"She still didn't like you."

"Oh, she liked me, all right. She loved me. Even asked to see my chest when I told her I'd waxed. I had to turn her down 'cause it's still pretty irritated and I don't want to get an infection. I held the door open just like you said and smiled at the waiter even though he spilled my water and nearly decapitated me with a freakin' drink tray."

"I'm sure it was an accident."

"That's what Carmen said."

"And what did you say?"

"I said she was probably right and I tipped the guy anyway."

"Atta boy. It takes a real man to turn the other cheek."

"Are you kidding me? I felt like a pussy. It was the worst date of my life. Even worse than that time I hooked up with these redheaded twins—Heather and Leather. At least I thought they were twins. Turns out they were husband and wife and looking for a third in their little dress-up party. While I got nothing against a nice thong, I draw the line at a latex scrotum sac."

"Little too much info there, Vinnie. If you tell me Carm asked you to wear a latex scrotum sack, I think I'll stab myself with my letter opener."

"The only thing she asked me was to go out with her again."

"Cool."

"Yeah.

"She must really like you."

"My mama, too. Turns out her mother actually knows my mother. They volunteer at St. Anthony's every Saturday morning for the weekly bake sale. Carmen's even met my mother twice already and thinks she's great. Who would've known Jersey was such a small world?"

I did a mental hand-slide into the air.

"So my fangs are safe, then?"

"Maybe."

Okay, so where was the *"Gee, Lil, of course your fangs are safe, in fact I'm naming my firstborn after you"*?

"Vinnie, is something wrong?" Something other than the fact that he was going to have to wax, pluck, and coif for the rest of his life.

"This whole thing isn't going exactly like I planned."

"How's that? You wanted the perfect woman. You met Carmen. You wanted her to like you and now she does. You wanted your mother to like her, and she does. I'd say it's going exactly as planned."

"Yeah, but my back hurts like hell."

"The soreness will go away in a few days."

"And the skin? How long will that take to actually grow back?"

"Maybe a week." Or two. "The point is, it'll grow and the waxing will get easier. Sort of. And you'll forget you ever had unsightly body hair." When he didn't say anything, I prodded, "What?"

"Some kid stepped on my foot when I was picking up sausage at Machiavelli's Deli this morning and I didn't whack the little bastard. I told him not to sweat it. I even bought him a Yoo-hoo. Christ, I was *nice*."

"You say that like it's a bad thing."

"It is. I'm an SOB, dammit. We piss fire and shit pain."

And I thought *"where love is only a credit card away"* was lame. "You guys don't actually print that on hats, do you?"

"Koozies. We got this guy in Newark that does it for less than five cents each if you order bulk."

"You wouldn't happen to have his number?"

"I had it in the glove box, but you made me clean that out. The only thing in there now is a pack of wipes and a CD of Michael Bolton's greatest hits. What the fuck is happening to me?"

"You want the perfect woman and in order to get her, you have to become the perfect man. It's a small trade-off."

"That's what I thought. But we're talking *greatest hits*, as in two friggin' CDs. I swear if I hear another love song I'm gonna puke. This ain't me. I don't like all that soft, fluffy shit. I'm the kind of guy who likes Metallica."

"No, you're not. We peeled that layer away, along with everything crude, lewd, and obnoxious. You're now a guy who likes Michael Bolton."

"A pansy, right?" I could practically hear him shaking his head. "I don't want to spend the rest of my life being a friggin' wuss. I want to be able to burp and fart and rough up the newspaper guy if he throws my *Times* into the azalea bushes. Is that too much to ask?"

Uh, yeah. "Listen to me, Vinnie. You have to stop focusing on the past and think about the future. Your *wedded* future. Does your mother like Carmen?"

"I mentioned her when I dropped off the sausage and she went nuts. Said she couldn't wait to see her tonight and then she rushed to get ready for church. Said she was going to light a candle and pray to St. Benedict himself for us to name our first child after my father. Said I'd better snatch Carmen up right now if I know what's good for me."

"Then propose to the girl and make your mother happy." And give me my Get-Out-of-Death-Free card.

"I should."

"You would be a fool not to."

"That's true."

"It isn't every day that the perfect woman comes along. Stop worrying and embrace the new you. A little change never hurt anyone."

"Tell that to my back."

My next phone call was to Mia.

"How did it go?"

"Not so good."

"No sex?"

"We only did it twice."

"The impotent bastard." Twice? In three hours? That was more action than I'd seen during the entire Clinton administration. By my own choice, I reminded myself. I'd already decided to give up meaningless sex and find my one and only.

An image of Ty appeared, and my brain went *cha-ching!*

I *really* needed to get more sleep.

"I was going to play the sex down a little," Mia went on. "And just act like twice was okay. But I shouldn't have to put up a front just to please some guy. I want a man who likes me for who I am. I shouldn't have to pretend I'm something I'm not, should I?"

"No, no, pretending isn't good. At the same time, a little change never hurt anyone," I heard myself say for the second time that night.

"So who's next?" she demanded.

I pulled up my list of prospects, which consisted of last night's dud and Evie's cousin, Word.

"I do have this one guy. I wouldn't call him the most experienced lover on the block. He's a little quick on the draw, but he definitely gets an A for effort."

"Bring him on."

"There's just one thing." I thought of Word and his

rabbit fetish. "How do you feel about small, furry animals?"

"I love 'em. So does Pooky my python. He's always up for a good snack."

"I'll set it up."

Twenty-three
♥ ♥ ♥

I was at the coffee shop at a quarter to ten. I sat in a booth and stared at the church that towered across the street. It was an old stone building with lots of stained glass and a bell tower. Lights gleamed from inside, casting colorful patterns on the concrete steps. The place radiated an old-world charm that reminded me of rolling French countryside and a certain stable boy named Andre.

He'd been my first crush—a young, strapping human—at a time when I'd been intent on rejecting my inner *vampere* and pissing off my folks.

Oh, wait . . . I was still rejecting my inner *vampere* and pissing off my folks. Only now it wasn't intentional. Really. I *wanted* to embrace my born-vamp heritage. To do my duty and populate the species and give my mother a wallet full of grandkid photographs to pass around at her monthly huntress club meetings.

I just wanted to do it with someone I actually loved.

Like Ty.

I nixed the thought as soon as it struck.

I *so* didn't love him. For all the obvious reasons, of course. And even more because he was a selfish jerk. That was the only explanation for The Kiss. If he'd had even an ounce of feeling for me, he would have wished me luck with my life and said *adios*. But nooooooo. He'd had to kiss me and remind me exactly how fiercely the chemistry burned between us.

We're talking a full-blown nuclear reaction, as opposed to the tiny flicker I felt whenever I was around Remy.

Which had been his intention.

The rat bastard.

Fergie started singing, indicating my new ring tone, and I whipped out my cellphone. For a split second, I thought maybe Ty had smartened up and decided to apologize. I glanced at the caller ID.

Make that a stubborn rat bastard.

"Why are you calling me when you should be proposing to the perfect woman?" I asked Vinnie.

"I'm getting to it. I'm just waiting until everyone finishes eating. Then right before they bring out the cake, I'm going to pull Carmen off to the side and ask her."

"Does your mother like her?"

"She let her stir the spaghetti sauce."

"She likes her." I smiled. "Sounds like you're all set."

"Yeah. Shouldn't I be more excited about this? I mean, if she really is the perfect woman, this ought to be easy?"

"Think of it like a Band-Aid. You're dreading it, but once you work up the courage and just rip, it'll be over and done with."

"A Band-Aid," he said. "I can do that."

I hung up, slid the phone back into my purse, and went back to staring out the window. And trying not to think about Ty.

I pictured tomorrow's outfit and I went over my list of questions for the black market exorcist Father Duke. But then ten o'clock rolled around, and then ten fifteen, and then ten thirty, and, hey, a girl could only think so much about one measly outfit and an exorcism. My only saving grace was another phone call from Vinnie.

"I think I should wait until after the cake," he told me. "I wouldn't want to upstage Italian Crème."

"You're stalling."

"I'm just waiting for the right time. And for the Rolaids to kick in. And the wine. Then I'm gonna do it."

"Swear?"

"Fuckin' A."

I hung up and my thoughts shifted to the scarred tabletop, then the checkerboard curtains. I stared at the menu and glanced at the ancient Coke sign that hung above the cash register.

The Coke bottle made me think of how thirsty I was, which made me think of the great big bottle of O positive sitting in my fridge, which made me think about warming said blood in my microwave. Warm blood reminded me of Ty and just like that, I was thinking about him and his kiss and—whew, was it hot in here, or was it just me?

I tugged at the neckline of my glitter tee and reached for the ice water sitting in front of me. A huge gulp, and the glass was empty. I signaled the waitress for a refill.

"You sure I can't get you anything else?" She paused when she finished topping me off.

Melba Donelli. Mid-forties. Married. No kids. She wore a bright pink uniform and white Keds. Her bright red hair was teased and sprayed within an inch of its life and she wore an even brighter red lipstick. A Jersey native, she'd been born and raised just a few blocks over. She knew everybody in the neighborhood. She also knew every piece of gossip.

"A piece of pie?" she went on. "A burger? Tonight's special is meatloaf." She wiggled her carefully painted-on brows. "How's about I cut you a nice big slice?"

"No, thanks. Could you tell me what time it is?"

"Five minutes since you asked the last time." She shook her head. "Can I give you a piece of advice, sugar?" I nodded and she added, "If he ain't here by now, he ain't coming. You ought to just cut your losses, have some pie, and start fresh again tomorrow.

Life is one great big cookie and you can bet there are plenty of chocolate chips where that one came from."

Her meaning hit and I shook my head. "It's nothing like that. I'm not waiting on a date—"

"A date," she cut in, "a friend, an acquaintance, a sex buddy—whatever you kids call it these days—you're much too pretty to let some guy string you along. You ought to be out living it up instead of warming the vinyl in a place like this. Bowling. Now there's a fun pastime for you, and a surefire way to meet a man."

"Bowling, you say?" Hey, I'm always looking for new hook-up venues.

She nodded. "Met my husband Don when I joined the Rock 'n Bowlers over at Fairbridge Alleys. Watched him bowl that first strike and bam, I fell hard and fast. I showed him my curve technique and we've been together ever since. Just celebrated our fifteenth anniversary. He got us matching balls."

I smiled. "He sounds like a keeper."

"You're telling me." A wicked gleam lit her eyes. "And lemme tell ya, the man knows how to bowl a strike, if you know what I mean. Say, my Don has a younger brother. Been divorced a couple of times, but only because he has a bad habit of mistaking sex for love. I swear the boy's a nympho—but then what man isn't, right? Forget the tramps, I tell him. Find yourself a nice girl." She eyed me. "You look like a nice girl."

"Thanks, but I'm already seeing someone."

Or I would be just as soon as I saved Evie from the bowels of Hell and called Remy.

Lil Tremaine. Lilliana Tremaine. Princess Lilliana Tremaine.

It had a ring to it.

Sort of.

"It figures," Melba went on. "The good ones are always taken."

"Not necessarily." I thought about Mia and the crappy time she was undoubtedly having with Word at that very moment. "I just might be able to help him out." I pulled a DED card from my wallet. "Tell him to give me a call and I'll find him the perfect woman."

She eyed me again. "You sure you're spoken for?"

"Yes." The word came out as more of a croak than the confident reply of a born vampire eager and excited to take the next step in her life.

Princess Lilliana Marchette-Tremaine.

I swallowed the sudden lump in my throat. "You wouldn't happen to have a chocolate martini, would you?"

"I've got chocolate meringue pie?"

"That'll work." Hey, if I couldn't drink it, I could at least smell it.

Just as Melba walked away, the bell on the front door jingled and the youngest priest I'd ever seen walked in. His hair was mussed and he had a zit on his chin.

No, seriously. A *zit*.

"Father Duke?"

He shook his head. "I'm Father Bryce."

No, seriously. *Bryce.*

"Father Duke's assistant," he added. His gaze collided with mine and his stats ticked off one by one.

Father Bryce McGhee. Twenty-one. His two best friends had gone into the police academy and he'd joined the church. While most boys had spent their childhoods fantasizing about becoming a firefighter or a Power Ranger or Brett Favre, Bryce had envisioned himself as the Pope or Gandhi or Mr. Rogers.

No, seriously—never mind.

"So how long have you been a priest?"

"About six months. How about you?" He arched an eyebrow. "How long have you been a vampire?"

"My entire—wait a second." I stared into his eyes, which glimmered with a knowing light. "I'm, uh, there's no such thing," I blurted. *Vampires DO NOT exist.* I sent the silent thought and he smiled.

"Forget it. It doesn't work."

I'd never heard of priests being immune to born-vamp charisma, but hey, what do I know? I wasn't exactly the worldliest born vamp in existence. "Religious immunity?"

He shook his head. "Drugs. One tiny pill and bam, we're vampire-proof."

"Really?"

"No." He started laughing. "Just a little secular humor. Actually, we're vamp-proof because we're celibate. Vampires are, in their most basic form, extremely sexual creatures. They draw power from their sexuality and influence others with the unspoken promise of pleasure of the flesh. Since I'm not interested in fleshly pleasures, I'm not susceptible. Of course, I'm not made of stone either, so I can still hear you. So how long?" he persisted.

"I . . ." I caught my bottom lip and debated my options. I could stay incognito, forget the exorcism, and head for the door, or I could shove him up against the nearest wall and pat him down for concealed weapons.

"Don't worry," he assured me. "I'm in the demon department. The church, for the most part, leaves the vamps to the SOBs. We deal strictly with evil spirits."

I stared deep into his eyes for a little confirmation. No, no stakes. But he did have a handheld cassette recorder in his coat pocket, a cellphone and a travel-sized toothbrush and floss because, while his mother had been a religious zealot, his father had been a dentist.

"I've been fanged and fabulous my entire life," I finally said. "Five hundred years old." And holding. "You couldn't tell?"

"We've been trained to sniff out a vamp, but it's impossible to know if they're born or made. I've met my share of made ones, but you're my first born vampire." He whipped out the cellphone. "Do you mind if I get a picture?" He slid into the booth beside me, held out the phone to arm's length, and snapped. The camera flashed and I blinked.

"Is that standard procedure? To take a picture of any vampire you meet?"

"Just the ones on TV. So far I've got you and Angelina Jolie."

"Angelina?" I wasn't an expert when it came to Others, but I knew my own kind. "She's not a born vampire."

"Made." When I looked surprised, he added, "You didn't think an actual human could be that hot, did you?"

The man had a point.

He slid off the vinyl and folded himself back in the seat opposite me. Excitement lit his gaze as he proofed the pic. "I can't wait to show the monks over at Lady of the Blessed Virgin. They're going to *die*—"

My ringtone cut off the rest of his sentence and I reached for my phone. "Could you excuse me one sec? I just need to get this. Don't tell me you're waiting until after the presents?" I asked Vinnie once I'd hit TALK.

"Communion."

"At your mother's birthday party?"

"I told you she's very religious. Goes to Mass as often as I go to the crapper. Father Paul is even here— he's the head priest from St. Anthony's and he doesn't come out for just anyone. The last time he attended a social event, he was at Madison Square Garden with Tyson. Anyhow, he's going to say a few words and give my mother a special blessing before she starts opening her gifts."

"And then you're going to pop the question?"

"Damn straight. Just as soon as I do communion. And maybe pop a few more Rolaids. And definitely have a couple more drinks." His voice took on a desperate note and my heart clinched. "Maybe I ought to forget the whole thing and just dedicate myself to killing vampires and Others."

"Nonsense. You need someone to have fun with and make babies with and grow old with." And, more important, someone to distract him from killing vampires and Others.

In particular, a certain fabulously dressed blond matchmaker in desperate need of an exorcism.

"Getting married is the right thing to do," I went on. "You owe it to yourself. You owe it to your mother."

"She did go through seventeen hours of labor."

"Band-Aid," I reminded him. "Don't think about it," I told him. "Just rip the sucker."

"Right. Bye."

"So what about the exorcism?" I asked after I slid the phone into my purse. "Can you do it?"

"That depends. While we take on cases that don't meet the specific documentation requirements of the church, we still require proof of the possession. Father Duke will have to meet with the person to determine authentic possession."

"And then?"

"If the person is truly possessed, he'll do the exorcism immediately. So"—he pulled out a small black day planner—"let's just take a look and see when he can meet with you. How about next Friday?"

"How about tomorrow?" When he shook his head, I added, "This is urgent. This isn't just some nasty demon."

"He's wanted by the Prince brothers?"

"You know about Ash?"

"Of course we've heard of Ash Prince. He's completely at odds with everything we stand for. We're into preserving human life and salvaging souls, while his main goal is to maintain law and order. Satan's law. If he wants this demon, your friend is as good as dead."

"Which is why you have to schedule something sooner. My friend," I started, and he flashed me a strange look. "That is, my assistant doesn't have much time."

"Let's see." He eyed the planner. "We've got a eulogy tomorrow evening, but I suppose I could set it up after that."

"I'll take it."

He scribbled frantically. "There. It's all set. We'll meet here at the diner and you can follow me to Father Duke's home. He'll do the exorcism there if warranted." He reached into his pocket and pulled out a piece of paper. "Here's a list of instructions to follow prior to the ritual and a consent-and-release form."

"I thought this was unofficial."

"Officially unofficial," he corrected. "Father Duke has to protect his interests."

I scribbled my name and was just handing the form back to Father Bryce when Fergie started singing again. I pulled out my phone while Father Bryce added his signature to the form as a witness.

"I don't think I can do it," Vinnie said. "I've got the ring and I tried to pull it out of my pocket, but then I got sidetracked with a meatball sub and now everyone's busy talking and, well, I'd hate to butt in."

"I'll be there in five." When Father Bryce arched an eyebrow, I covered the phone and whispered, "My blood slave."

"Really?"

I grinned. "No. Just a little vamp humor."

I know, I know, but I couldn't resist.

"A friend of mine is having a birthday party for his mother and I promised to stop by," I told the young priest after I hung up with Vinnie and stuffed the instructions into my purse.

"Teresa Balducci?" Father Bryce asked.

"You know her?"

"She's one of our most devout members at St. Anthony's. She helps out with the weekly bake sale and heads a clothing donation for a nearby women's shelter, and she even organizes the monthly spaghetti dinner for the clergy. The woman's a saint. Please give her my best and tell her Father Duke was planning on attending tonight with Father Paul. Until the throw-up incident."

"I'll relay the message." I gathered up my purse and pushed to my feet. "So we're on for tomorrow night?"

He gave me a solemn nod. "We're on."

Twenty-four
♥ ♥ ♥

Since I didn't make it a habit of partying with the local clergy (forget popping a few Xanax—my mother would down the whole freakin' bottle), I bypassed the front walkway of the two-story colonial and headed around the side of the house.

It was a nice house in one of the better Newark neighborhoods, with several feet of carefully manicured lawn and a six-foot-plus fence separating one lot from the next. The moon hid behind the clouds and so the shadows were thick alongside the house. Definitely a prime opportunity to do my best Peeping Vamp impersonation.

I thought so until I felt a prickle of awareness ripple down my spine. I turned and caught a flash of red light peeking through the slats between the fence.

The light disappeared in a blur of blue polyester.

"Who are you?" demanded an old, crackly voice.

"A friend of Vinnie's," I blurted. "And Mama Balducci. I thought I'd slip around the back and surprise everyone," I rushed on, explaining why I was skulking in the dark instead of waltzing up the front walkway. "It's her birthday."

"Birthday my ass," the voice muttered. I heard the squeak of rubber soles and the creak of wood and a silver white updo peeked over the top of the fence.

The hair was teased and coiffed and a good twelve inches tall.

I watched as the hair grew higher and higher.

Okay, make that a good fourteen.

Finally a creased forehead appeared, followed by a pair of night-vision goggles sitting on brightly rouged cheeks.

No, really.

A red light beamed in the center between two mirrored round lenses, which made her look like an ancient fly and blocked my BV view into her thoughts.

"That party is just an excuse," the woman went on, "to get the whole neighborhood together to make a bunch of racket and disturb my sleep. Why, the whole thing's been keeping me up all evening. I couldn't even watch *Wheel of Fortune*."

I could barely catch the occasional sound of laughter and a very faint "Moon River" playing softly in the background, and I've got preternatural hearing.

No way was this geriatric fly—whose wrinkled face looked even more ancient than her hair—hearing a thing.

"You would think the police would have shut it down when they came out the first time," she went on. "Or even the second. But nooooo. They stayed for pasta first, the bastards, and then came back around for dessert." The silver updo bopped in confirmation. "You can bet your hind end I'm filing a complaint with Internal Affairs just as soon as they open tomorrow morning. In the meantime, it's up to me to keep things on the straight and narrow. Fifty years," she muttered. "I've been putting up with this crap for *fifty* years."

"The Balduccis have a lot of parties, do they?"

The forehead wrinkled even more. "What'd you say your name was again?"

"Actually, I didn't say. But it's Lil. Lil Marchette. I own a dating service in Manhattan. You might have heard of it. Dead End Dating?"

"I don't get to the city much."

Ya don't say?

"Well, if you ever do." I slipped her a DED card along with my standard bribe when I needed to get out of a sticky situation and my vamp charm wasn't enough. "Call me. I'll give you a free profile and set you up with three prospective matches."

"For free? Why on earth would you do that?"

Because you're annoying the hell out of me and sucking up my time when I'm in a hurry and I'd do anything—anything—to shut you up. I smiled. "Our senior citizen special."

"Are you trying to say I'm old?"

And sort of scary.

Not that I was scared, mind you. Vampire equaled superior shitkicker. But if I hadn't been a BV . . . We're talking *night-vision* goggles. I could only imagine what she used those for when she wasn't spying. Maybe burying bodies in the backyard or something.

I swallowed and gave her my most charming smile. "Did I say senior?" I tried for a convincing laugh. "I mean *single* discount. You are single, right?"

"For the past twenty years since Merv kicked the bucket, the bastard."

"Perfect. Then you're totally available for the special. As personable as you are, I'm sure I'll have no trouble finding you the perfect man. And speaking of personable, why aren't you partying it up with the rest of the neighbors?"

"I've got better things to do with my time."

I arched an eyebrow. "Like lurking around the bushes?"

"You want me to climb this fence and kick your ass fifty ways til Sunday? I can do it. These new orthopedic shoes have aluminum toe reinforcements on account of my grip ain't what it used to be and I drop things a lot. One kick in the shin and you're old news, just like that dress you're wearing."

Wait a second. Did she just . . . Did I hear . . . Oh, no, she *didn't*.

"Where'd you get that?" she went on, the goggles bobbing. "A garage sale?"

I . . . She . . . It . . . My mind raced for something to say that didn't involve a four-letter word or several big fat tears.

Easy. She's old and severely fashion-challenged (we're talking powder blue *and* polyester). It couldn't be easy.

I bit back several choice replies and considered sending her a nice, persuasive *You're not a mean, cranky, nosy bee-yotch. You're nice and sweet and you think I'm the hottest, most well-dressed hottie you've ever seen.* But she was wearing the goggles. On top of that, she was female and could probably barely remember sex, much less lust after it. "I didn't mean to disturb you. I'm just here to have a little fun."

"Make sure you tell Teresa she'd better keep all that *fun* to a respectable level or I'll head over there and stick my foot up her—"

"It'll be the first thing out of my mouth," I cut in. "Seriously," I added when she stared me in the eye with that stupid red beam. "Cross my heart and hope to die."

Okay, like I was already dead so it didn't really count. But it's the principle of the thing, right?

"Are you one of them floozies Vinnie's always bringing home?" She swept the beam from my pink-tipped toes peeking through the tips of my Jimmy Choos, clear up to the fab highlights I'd had done just last week. "You look like a floozy to me."

First off, *nobody* said floozy anymore.

Second, *floozies* didn't drop a small fortune for sea-salt facials and Swedish massages at Christine Chin once a month. Unless they were filthy rich floozies, which would make them escorts. We're talking an entirely different tax bracket.

And third . . . why the hell was I kissing the fly's ass when I should be doing a search and rescue for Vinnie?

Oh, yeah. Skulking in the dark. Low profile. Preservation of the entire BV race.

"I love your hair," I blurted. "Is it natural?"

"Smartass." She snorted. The red beam shifted. Wood groaned. The hair disappeared.

I listened to the *clop-clop* of her shoes and waited for the screech of the screen door. Turning, I picked my way through the thick bushes a few feet until I reached the nearest window.

A basement ran along the bottom of the house and pushed the first floor several feet above ground level. Even with five-inch stilettos, I wasn't tall enough. I pulled good old levitation out of my bag of vamp tricks, floated up a few inches, and peered inside.

The living room was packed with people.

Some sat on the overstuffed sofa and chairs, others milled around a massive dining room table decked out with every sort of pasta known to mankind—ravioli, manicotti, lasagna, angel hair. A huge platter of meatballs—make that *seven* platters—dominated the center of the table, while the bowls of pasta edged the perimeter. The coffee table overflowed with gifts. A banner that read HAPPY BIRTHDAY MA! hung from one corner of the room to the next.

My gaze swept the sea of faces until I spied Carmen. She sat on the sofa next to a short, gray-haired woman with plump cheeks, a wide smile, and a flower-print dress.

Teresa Balducci.

I knew it even before I noticed the miniature black Yorkie that sat on her lap. Or the large crucifix that dangled around her neck, along with a St. Benedict medal and a few others I didn't recognize.

The doorbell rang. The old woman handed the dog to Carmen and pushed to her feet. She waddled to the front door, much to the objection of everyone else, including Father Paul. The old priest urged her to sit down and save her energy for emptying bedpans at the senior center the following morning.

"Nonsense. I don't even think of that as work. It's a pleasure just to help out those less fortunate."

Yikes, the woman *was* a saint.

Mama Balducci pulled open the door to an elderly couple. The man carried a large gift-wrapped box that contained an in-home spa treatment for bunions and a doggie toy for the Yorkie.

FYI—I'm not Superman, folks (blue and red and yellow? So *not* my best color combo). It's just that the old man had wanted to keep the spa treatment and the truth flashed in his eyes when he handed over the gift.

As soon as he got home, he was ordering his own off the QVC—regardless of what that podiatrist had said. Why, that old doc didn't know his bunions from his plantar's warts.

Uh, *ewwwwwww*.

I shifted my attention to Mrs. Bunions. She carried

a suitcase-size white patent leather purse and a platter of—wouldn't you know it?—meatballs.

"They're my special recipe," the old woman said. "I know how much you and Marlon like them." Marlon being the Yorkie. She hugged and kissed Teresa on both cheeks before grabbing her husband and dragging him toward the food table. "Oh, look, Walter! Eileen Stanover brought her cannolis!"

I took a quick peek in the rest of the windows but I couldn't find Vinnie. Either he'd left, or gone into hiding. Since Vinnie was a devout man (in the sense that his mother had him scared shitless and convinced he was going to hell should he defy her wishes), I knew he wouldn't just leave.

Okay. Think. Let's see . . .

Nervous.

Anxious.

Semi-drunk on wine and antacids.

Where do you go?

I headed into the backyard and searched for the nearest pool house.

But there was no pool, much less a house. Just a flower garden, a small barbecue pit, three plastic lawn chairs, and a toolshed—*bingo!*

A few steps and I found Vinnie crouched inside on a red Husky toolbox. He sat crammed between a weed whacker and several bags of fertilizer.

"Nice party." I swept a glance around. "I'm sure you and the lawn mower will be very happy."

"Very funny." His glasses reflected the light off the

back patio as he shook his head. "I don't feel so good."

"It's the waxing. It'll sting for a few days."

"It's not the stinging. It's . . ." He shook his head again. "I don't really know her."

"Sure you do. Catholic. Good-looking. Wants a big family. You know all the important stuff."

"But what if she's putting up a front like me? What if she isn't all of those things?"

"She is."

"How do you know?" I gave him a get-outta-here look and he shrugged. "Okay, so you're a bloodsucking fiend and you know."

Talk about harsh. "I prefer fantabulously dressed creature of darkness."

"Like I care."

If my afterlife hadn't been on the line, I would *so* have taken my chances and punched this guy in the teeth. "Sensitivity, remember?"

"But that's the point. I ain't sensitive. I don't want to be sensitive."

"What about your mother? I'm sure she would love to see the sensitive side of you. I bet she would cry tears of joy if you were to drop to one knee, pour out your black heart to Carmen, and ask her to marry you."

"And then when she realizes I'm an SOB?"

I shrugged. "By that time she'll have seen the kinder side of you"—sort of—"and she'll be more forgiving. She might even like the macho streak once she gets used to it."

"Ya think?"

"Anything's possible. But you'll never know if you stay out here. Give her the ring and get it over with already."

"We could make it a long engagement. My ma never said anything about praying for me to get married. She wanted me engaged."

"*Voilà*. Prayer answered."

"That's right." He pushed to his feet. "We don't even have to set a date yet. We'll just get to know each other. I'll get a chance to make sure her tits are real and she'll get to know who I am, and she'll come around. Provided, of course, that the tits *are* real."

"Sounds like a plan."

"Course I won't be able to just lay it all out right away. I'll have to keep the trunk free and clear at first. And the glove compartment. I'll take things slow and ease her into it gradually. Before you know it, she'll be holding the flashlight while I pull out the fangs."

"That's the spirit." What was I saying?

What you have to say. No engagement, no deal. No deal, no more afterlife.

"I'll do it." He pushed to his feet and reached for my hand. "Come on."

"Oh, no. This is a moment strictly for friends and family. I wouldn't want to impose—"

"You'll impose, all right." He nailed me with his Ray-Bans. "Just in case she says no. If that happens, I've got a stake with your name written all over it."

A few seconds later, I stood off to the side and watched Vinnie approach Carmen. He did the ring bit, much to Carmen's surprise, and she burst into tears. Happy tears, thankfully. Vinnie slid the ring onto her finger and an arm around her waist, and a few seconds later they were being toasted by a tearful Mama Balducci.

"I don't think I know you," Mama said when I stepped forward to offer my congratulations once things had settled down. Her gaze collided with mine and recognition sparked in the dark brown depths of her eyes.

"A friend of a friend of a friend," Vinnie jumped in before I could open my mouth. "She's Martin Morelli's sister's husband's cousin. We go way back. I saw her down at the deli and invited her over for cake. Really, Ma," he added when she stared at him as if he'd just told her the dog had eaten his report card.

"Italian Crème," I murmured. "My all-time favorite."

But Teresa wasn't convinced. Something wasn't sitting well with her about me. She had the distinct feeling that I was someone very different from what Vinnie had told her.

"Where's that cake?" I whirled, breaking the connection into her thoughts, and glanced frantically around. "I'm diabetic, and if my blood sugar goes too low I'm dead meat."

She couldn't . . .

No way did she realize I was a . . .

"I don't mind vampires around here," I heard her

whisper to Vinnie. "Just so long as she keeps her fangs to herself."

I did a double take, but Teresa had already shifted her attention to another well-wisher.

"Did you tell her?" I asked Vinnie as he shoved a cake plate in my hand and propelled me toward an empty seat on the far side of the room.

"Not me. The woman's got a direct link to the Big Guy Upstairs. She knows *everything*."

I was starting to believe it.

I spent the next forty-five minutes nursing a glass of champagne, pretending to eat cake, and trying not to feel so crappy.

Moment of triumph, I reminded myself. I'd done it. I'd saved my fangs and written myself onto the top of the SOB's Hands-Off list. I should be over the moon right now.

But as I watched Vinnie and Carmen—or at least Carmen, because the big V looked as if he might throw up at any moment—my thoughts shifted to Ty and the kiss.

What was *that* about?

Obviously it meant goodbye.

But *goodbye* as in: I never want to see you again you two-timing born-vamp bitch?

Or *goodbye* as in: I don't care if I ever see you again but I'm so narcissistic that I want you to think about what you're missing every day of your afterlife?

Or *goodbye* as in: I'm kissing you right now because I don't know what else to do to convince you to please, please, *please* give me a second chance?

Yeah. Like that last one was even in the realm of possibility. He couldn't and I couldn't and, well, *never*.

But when his lips had touched mine, I'd actually started to think that if I wanted it bad enough and he wanted it bad enough, then maybe it could happen. *If*.

"Vinnie told me about you." The deep voice echoed in my ear and yanked me back from neverland a split second before the couch dipped next to me and I found myself sitting next to three hundred and fifty pounds of Italian attitude.

His name was Crusher, and he was Vinnie's younger bro. He wore the same black suit and Ray-Bans. His hair was greased back à la Vinnie and he wore the same collection of bling around his neck. But instead of looking at me as if he wanted to stake first and talk later, he eyed me as if I were the last pepperoni sub in the deli case.

Panic bubbled inside me and my heart started to pound. "Vinnie's engaged," I blurted. "I'm off the hook. That means DO NOT TOUCH in SOB language."

"I don't want to touch." He smiled for a split second before his expression grew serious. "I want to see if you can hook me up. I don't need a fiancée or anything like that—Vinnie's the oldest so Ma's riding him, not me, when it comes to settling down—but I do need a date for the yearly SOB Christmas party. It's in Atlantic City this year."

"Christmas is over six months away."

He shrugged. "I like to plan ahead." One black brow inched up over the Ray-Bans. "So you think you can hook me up?"

"Or else?"

"Or else what?"

"Or else you're going to rip out my fangs and turn me into a popsicle, right?"

"Nah. You're in Vinnie's territory. Besides, your brother Rob keeps the office fully stocked with everything from copy paper to binder clips, and I got a business to run. That shit don't come cheap."

"Neither do I." I summoned my courage. Even though I couldn't read his thoughts through the glasses, I didn't get the same threatening feel from him. "I don't work for free."

He reached for his wallet. "You take Visa?"

I smiled. "Do born vampires fudge on their tax returns?"

Twenty-five
❤ ❤ ❤

Instead of heading back to the office to get some work done after I left Mama Balducci's, I mapped a flight plan for my apartment to check on Evie.

She was exactly the way I'd left her—hovering on the ceiling, her eyes rolled back into her head, her hair tangled and matted, her skin pasty white. The walls looked as if someone had paintballed the room in slime green, and there was a nice big pile of gunk in the middle of my bed.

My chest hitched and my eyes started to sting. Seeing Evie like that . . . Seeing my sheets like that . . .

I blinked frantically and sniffled.

Easy. You can handle this. You've got guts. You've got optimism. You've got renter's insurance.

"Good news," I announced on the off chance that maybe, just maybe Evie—the real Evie beneath the layers of vomit and really bad skin (can you say sea-salt facial?)—could hear me. "I found someone to do an exorcism."

"So?" The deep guttural voice slid into my ears and I glanced up to see a pair of blazing yellow eyes staring back at me. "You won't save her."

I ignored the tiny voice that whispered *"He's right. Ugly, but right."* I straightened my shoulders and nailed the demon with my most confident stare. "I *will* save her."

Cold, chilling laughter bounced off the walls. "You can't do anything. You're weak. Just like your friend here. She's a whiny, pathetic, insecure bitch. No wonder she can't keep a boyfriend."

Okay. I could put up with a lot of things—the sliming and the smell and the ruined wardrobe and even the soiled sheets. But I wasn't about to stand here and let some serial-killing demon talk smack about one of my BFFs. "I am so going to kick your ass."

"You and what army?"

"No army." I held up my bottle of holy water. "Just me and my spritzer."

That was enough to cause a loud *hissssss* and send the eyes rolling back into the head again.

"I thought so," I said.

The mouth opened and a wave of projectile vomit shot straight at me.

I summoned my BV speed and in a split second I stood outside in the living room, my new outfit still immaculate, while slime glazed the walls of the bedroom. There were definitely some perks to being a bloodsucker.

Unfortunately, lying wasn't one of them.

"For the last time, I don't know anything about your demon," I told Ash when he called just after I picked up Killer from my neighbor's apartment.

"That's odd, because we happen to know that he's possessing your assistant."

"Oh, really?" I feigned ignorance as I opened a can of cat food. "Who would that be?"

"You only have one."

"Oh, you mean Evie. I thought you meant her cousin Word. He works for me every once in a while. I should have known something was up. He's got really bad skin and a fetish for small animals, and he's addicted to heavy metal goth."

"That doesn't say demon. It says horny adolescent. Besides, I already checked him out. Caught him doing it with some woman with a bunch of tattoos earlier tonight."

"Her name's Mia." I tossed the empty can into the trash and reached for some imported sardines to top off the cat food. "Was she smiling?"

"She was beating the shit out of him for being too quick."

"Poor thing."

"He seemed to like it."

"I was talking about Mia." I made a mental note to send her something to keep her spirits up, maybe some flowers or a spa basket or a new high-powered vibrator.

"Where is Evie?" Ash demanded. When I didn't say anything, he added, "Come on, Lil. There are a lot of lives at stake. You don't want their blood on your hands."

"I love blood on my hands. I'm a vampire."

"Yeah, right."

"What's that supposed to mean?"

"That you're soft."

"I may not be as hardcore as most, but I am most definitely *not* soft." I forked the sardines into Killer's bowl and set it on the floor for him.

"You're a marshmallow," Ash said. "You're too nice."

"I am not." Killer sniffed and blinked at me and I realized I'd forgotten a few sprinkles of Tuna Sparkle. I grabbed the seasoning, topped off his dinner, and he started to eat. "I'm as mean as Brad Pitt is sexy."

I could picture his smile as he said, "Just calling 'em like I see 'em."

"You can't see me right now." I glanced around my kitchen, my senses instantly alert. "Can you?" While I'd learned a little about the various Others out there (particularly werewolves, who had great taste and liked to hump during the full moon), I was still learning as far as demons went. "What am I wearing?"

"Let's see . . . outfit, shoes, thong."

"What color is the thong?"

"Pink."

Panic bolted through me followed by a rush of *nahhhhh*. "How do you know that?"

"Lucky guess."

A girl could only hope.

Even so, I pulled my shoulders back and did my sexiest walk as I headed for the living room and my overstuffed sofa. "Maybe the demon body hopped after Evie, which would mean she's no longer possessed and you're looking for the wrong person."

"Then where is she?"

"Good question." One I wasn't about to answer.

"If you know something, you have to tell me," Ash said as if reading my thoughts.

I tamped down my nerves and chose my words carefully. "Well, I know she hasn't shown up to work in the past few days." It wasn't a lie. She hadn't shown up for work. My overflowing answering machine could testify to that. "I've called her at home, but she's not there." Because she was here. "Maybe she skipped town. That's what I would do if I were possessed by a demon." Unless I was confined by holy water in my fantabulously dressed employer's bedroom. "I'd take the first plane and head for Cancún."

"Demons don't do warm climates too well. Reminds them too much of what they're trying to escape."

"Then maybe she hopped a plane for the Poconos. Or Antarctica. How do I know? I'm a matchmaker, not a bounty hunter." And speaking of bounty hunters— "Say, have you talked to Ty by any chance?"

"About what?"

Me. The kiss. Us. Me. "Um, nothing." It was crazy to even think that Ty would talk to Ash about his personal life. What were we? In high school? Then again, I was all but bursting at my designer seams to talk to someone, so there was always the chance that he might be just as anxious. "It's just that I ran into him, and he mentioned that he was helping you guys on this and I just thought you might have talked to him recently and he might have mentioned that he talked to me." And that maybe, just maybe he's desperately in love with me and doesn't know what to do.

"He said you were a stubborn pain-in-the-ass and that you were driving him crazy."

"Crazy in a good way, or crazy in a bad way?"

"The why-don't-I-just-get-it-over-with-and-shove-a-stake-into-myself way."

"Oh." Well. Whatever.

"He's helping us follow up leads from the sighting at Times Square," he went on, as if I'd just reminded him about something. "Look, I've gotta go. I'm meeting with the employees at that dyke club in a few minutes."

I had a quick vision of the bartender and remembered that I hadn't glammed her with a quick *I wasn't here and I wasn't asking questions about Evie and I surely didn't hunt her down* or *drag her back to my place and please, please, please don't mention me to anyone, especially a hunky trio of demon brothers.*

Uh-oh.

At the same time, according to Ty, they already knew I'd been to the club with Evie. They just hadn't figured out that Evie wasn't exactly Evie at the time.

Yet.

My heart catapulted as Ash's voice rumbled through my head.

"If you see her, call me immediately. I'm going to talk to a few of her relatives tomorrow to see if they've heard from her and then I'm headed over to talk to her neighbors."

And then he would most likely put two and two together and come knocking on my door.

But not until tomorrow. And by then, all of this would be over. I would meet with Father Duke, we would do a little demon-busting, and bam—problem solved.

I held tight to the hope and spent the next fifteen minutes going over the prep list Father Bryce had given me. I packed a bag of needed items, made a note of what I still had to pick up at the store, checked on Evie again and dodged a loogie, and gave Killer, the glutton, a few more sardines sprinkled with Tuna Sparkle.

By the time I collapsed on the couch, I was more than ready to close my eyes and get some much-needed sleep. My body felt tired, drained. Unfortunately, my mind wasn't as wiped out.

Between the possibility that Ash would catch on sooner rather than later, my worry over the upcoming exorcism, and my *what-the-fuck-is-up-with-that?* thoughts about Ty and his kiss, I spent the majority of the day tossing and turning and growing more anxious by the minute.

By the time I finally pushed to my feet and downed my breakfast (warm O positive with a chaser shot of

AB negative), I was a bundle of nerves. I'd come to the conclusion that my afterlife really and truly sucked (and I don't mean in a good way).

I know, right? The vein-is-always-half-full *me*.

Anyhow, I tried to counter the negative thoughts with a distraction—I fed Killer and looked over the exorcism prep list and even watched *The Tyra Banks Show.*

But when I found myself watching Tyra interview some actor from one of the daytime soaps who happened to have long dark hair and very blue eyes, I started thinking about Ty and the kiss and . . . well, so much for distracting myself.

Enter denial.

Crappy life? I most certainly did NOT have a crappy life. I was a hot, happening vampire with a successful dating service and really great hair.

And a demon trapped in the next room, a voice reminded me. And feelings for a made vampire who obviously didn't feel the same. And a nagging mother. And a date with a made vampire who obviously liked me more than I liked him. And a minuscule wardrobe that consisted of—count 'em—two outfits and a shopping bag full of perfume samples.

Okay, so I had a crappy afterlife. But things were going to get better.

At least that's what I was telling myself. I just wasn't so sure I believed it anymore.

"What do you mean he's not coming?" I asked Father Bryce at exactly 7:00 p.m. when I slid into a booth across from him at the coffee shop that night.

Melba was off duty. Thankfully. I was being stood up for real this time, and if she'd been there with her knowing looks and her *poor thing* expression, I would have burst into tears. Guaranteed.

I blinked frantically and tried to calm my frantic heart. "But he has to come," I rushed on. "I've got everything ready."

Vinnie and Carmen were having dinner with her folks tonight—her idea, not his—and so I'd offered Crusher a discount if he would pick me and Evie up at my apartment, no questions asked. He'd agreed (we're talking twenty percent and a Starbucks gift card) to drive us to Jersey, wait outside during the exorcism, and get us back to the city (*sans* demon) before daybreak. He now sat behind the wheel of an old dark blue sedan that idled at the curb.

Across the street at the church, the choir had just finished up practice. The sound of an organ and the closing notes of "All Hail the King" filtered through the voices in the diner and slid into my super vamp ears.

"I followed the pre-exorcism instructions to a T," I went on. "Evie is hog-tied in the trunk of the car and I'm wearing the mandatory crucifix." I held up the tiny gold symbol (do NOT tell my mother). I'd even worn all purple—a plain jogging suit I'd picked up on my way out of the city because I *so* wasn't screwing up the only two outfits I had by letting them get slimed. The color was symbolic of the stole Father

Duke would use to calm the demon during the exorcism.

I was stoked.

And now it was off.

"The kid who threw up on him last night has the flu and passed it on to Father Duke," Father Bryce explained. "He's really sick. He usually joins in on the choir." He indicated the church across the street. The organ had stopped and people were now filtering out of the massive double doors. "But he couldn't even get out of bed."

"What about antibiotics? Surely there's something he can take to get back on his feet."

"Flu is viral. There are no antibiotics."

"Vitamins?"

"They won't work in time."

"Energy drink?"

He shook his head. "It's not going to happen tonight. I'm sorry, but that's just the way it is. He's got a very high temperature."

"Yeah, but he's still alive, right?" I know I sounded cold and unfeeling, but I had my best friend trussed up in the trunk and a crew of demons dogging me. I was D-E-S-P-E-R-A-T-E.

"He'll be happy to help you next week." Father Bryce pulled out his black scheduling book. "Maybe next Friday?"

"I can't wait until next Friday. I need him tonight." I remembered Ash's phone call and my chest hitched. He could very well be on his way to my place right now. And if he saw the shambles that had once been my bedroom . . . *"Now."*

Father Bryce shook his head. "I'm sorry. An exorcist must be strong and healthy during the ritual. Otherwise, it's a sure disaster."

"Can't you do it?" I swept a gaze from his black loafers to the top of his gelled hair. "You're young, but you're still a priest, right?"

"I don't know the Latin."

"So do it in English."

"It might not be as effective. Besides, I work for Father Duke." He shook his head. "I can't defy his wishes. The last time I went against his orders, he got very upset."

"Did he take away your PlayStation?"

He shook his head. "My Xbox."

"That was a joke."

"Oh." He scribbled something in his notebook. "I'm penciling you in for the following Friday. Just keep your friend contained with the holy water and we'll see you here next week."

But I didn't have that much time. I knew that as surely as I knew the sun would set and my mother would nag me about Remy and Britney Spears would wind up on the cover of yet another tabloid.

I watched Father Bryce push to his feet and leave the diner. He crossed the street and headed for the church rectory. From the corner of my eye, I caught movement and shifted my gaze to the actual sanctuary. The doors had opened again and a group of choir members herded outside. I recognized one of them and Vinnie's voice echoed in my head.

"The woman's a saint, I tell you. A bona fide saint."

An idea struck—a crazy, out-there idea that probably wouldn't work—but I grasped at it anyway for lack of anything better. I summoned a smile.

If I couldn't find a priest, I'd just have to settle for the next best thing.

"Mama Balducci?" I caught the woman just before she turned the side of the building to head for the fellowship area.

"Yes, dear?" Her gaze met mine and recognition lit. "Oh. It's you."

The vampire.

The truth blazed in her eyes and I felt a moment's hesitation. I wasn't used to having humans aware of my identity, and it sort of freaked me out (and made me feel massive amounts of guilt because I was breaking the number one BV commandment—Thou Shalt Keep a Low Profile).

Then again, it wasn't my fault that she knew. She had a direct link Upstairs, and so any information leaks belonged to someone a lot more powerful than *moi.*

I summoned my courage. "A friend of mine is in trouble and I really need your help. Can I please talk to you?" I shifted my gaze to the three old women who'd stopped to wait for her. "In private?" I was out of the closet with Teresa Balducci, but that didn't mean I was flaunting it for the whole geriatric gang.

She stared at me a long moment before directing her attention to the women. "You ladies go on and have some coffee cake. I'll be there shortly."

"Is she pregnant?" Mama asked after the women had disappeared through a nearby door. "I volunteer at the local shelter for unwed mothers and I would be happy to counsel her."

I shook my head. "She's not PG."

Her face took on a worried light. "Drugs?"

Another shake.

Her frown deepened. "Prostitution?"

"Possession." There. I'd said it.

Before I had a chance to wonder whether or not she even bought into the big P concept, Mama B arched an eyebrow. "How possessed?"

I motioned her across the street to the blue sedan.

She adjusted her glasses as we started across the pavement. "Is that my son behind the wheel?"

"He's helping me out in exchange for a discount. I'm finding him a date for the Christmas party."

"Hey, Ma. How's it hanging?" Crusher gave her a little wave before going back to polishing a large, menacing handgun.

"Don't worry," I told her when she frowned. "I'll make sure he gets the body parts out of the glove box before the actual date."

She flashed a relieved smile and followed me around to the trunk.

I slapped the end of the car. "Pop it," I told

Crusher. The lid gave a click and a gasp and then lifted. I motioned to Evie, who looked like a cross between Linda Blair and a trussed-up turkey.

"I need an exorcism," I went on as Mama adjusted her bifocals and peered at Evie, who had green foam oozing out from beneath the scarf tied around her mouth. "I was going to get one tonight, but the priest who was supposed to perform it got sick."

"Father Duke." She nodded. "He does all the black-market exorcisms in Newark."

"Since vamps aren't the most popular among the clergy, I can't go through the church and my time is running out. You're such a devout woman, I thought you might know someone who could help me."

She eyed Evie a moment longer before turning to me. "You're looking at her. Not that I've done an exorcism all by myself, but I've assisted Father Duke many times doing backup prayer whenever he gets tired and needs a break."

Hope blossomed and ballooned in my chest. "Really?"

Mama nodded and glanced down at her flower-print dress. "I'll need to stop off at home for my exorcism clothes first. Crusher can drive me. You stay here with your friend. Take her to the old building behind the church." She motioned to a slim edge of maroon brick barely visible behind the main structure. "It's the children's recreation center now, but it was once the actual sanctuary before the church expanded. The place has been remodeled, but the altar is still there." She pulled out a key ring. "I head up the monthly toy drive and I'm always dropping off donations, so I have my own key."

"Thank you." I took the key.

"Don't thank me yet." She cast one more glance at Evie, a serious expression on her face. "We still have to kick some demon butt first."

Twenty-six
♥ ♥ ♥

Crusher dropped Evie and me off behind the brick building before heading home with his mother. I took a long swig of the Benadryl I'd picked up (my own little addition to the prep list), summoned my courage, and opened the door to the building.

With the exception of the red-carpeted altar and vestibule at the far end, there were no telltale signs that the place had ever housed the main sanctuary. The walls were bright yellow with tiny rainbow-colored handprints here and there. Glossy navy blue linoleum covered the floors. There were miniature tables and chairs situated here and there, along with bins of toys and shelves holding everything from coloring books to tempera paints.

I bypassed the Kid Zone and headed for the large altar that sat at the top of a small set of carpeted steps. Setting Evie down, I checked the ropes on her hands and feet (still snug). Her eyes were still rolled back into her head. A steady stream of hissing and wailing drifted from the corners of her mouth and my throat tightened.

I touched a hand to her forehead, which was ice cold. "You'll be back sipping lattes and matching up singles in no time."

She didn't respond, but neither did the demon, and I took it as a sign that maybe he was feeling the holiness of the place closing in on him.

I know I was.

My shoulder gave a twinge and I barely resisted the urge to scratch. I walked back down the steps and sat at a nearby table. I spent the next few minutes listening to my voice mail and trying to kill some time.

My mom. My mom. My mom. Nina One. My mom. Remy. My mom. Ash.

"I'm at your apartment," he said, his voice deep and sexy and oh-so-pissed. "Call me *now*."

Shit.

No sooner did the thought strike than I sent up a silent *Please forgive me for being a dumbass—er, that is, an ignorant idiot. Amen.*

Hey, I'm a vampire, not an atheist. Besides, it was a once-upon-a-time church, for Damien's sake.

Oops.

I did another *excusez moi* and my right shoulder gave another twinge. I balled my fingers and prayed (that's *meditated* if my mother should ask) that the Benadryl would kick in.

I perked my ears, trying to pick up any nearby voices as I tapped my shoulder to relieve the itchy sensation. Apparently the choir crowd had already finished up their coffee cake. Not a peep drifted from the surrounding buildings. A quick peek outside confirmed my thoughts. The buildings surrounding us were dark. I slapped at my shoulder again. Once. Twice. Ugh.

The itch, along with several red welts, had spread to my chest by the time Mama finally showed up at close to ten o'clock.

She wore an old purple smock covered with a clear plastic apron and a pair of goggles.

I arched an eyebrow at the rubber galoshes covering her feet.

She shrugged. "Once they start vomiting, it can get pretty deep."

I glanced down at my own flip-flops. Now she tells me.

"Where do you want her?" Crusher asked as he pushed through the doors, Margaret Weisenbaum bundled in his arms. Her hands and feet were tied, her mouth taped. He hefted the old woman, a gleeful look in his eyes as if he'd finally gotten to have a little fun instead of just playing chauffeur.

Uh-oh. Here we go again with the layers.

"Next to the altar," Mama told her son as she led him toward the front of the building and Evie.

I was right behind them.

I tapped Mama on the shoulder. "What's she doing here?"

"The demon has to go somewhere, dear. I can barely fit my triple D's into this girdle. There's no room for a tic tac, much less a demon. And you"—she spared a glance at me—"you don't strike me as the usual deserving vampire."

"Not snotty enough?"

"Not bloodthirsty enough. When was the last time you've actually bitten someone?"

Okay, so like my last "official" chomp had been Ty. But I'd been wounded and delirious with pain and he'd instigated it.

No, the last time I'd actually stalked someone and sunk my fangs into his neck had been back during Prohibition. The Ninas and I had been at a flapper party and we'd had a little too much to drink (isn't that always how it starts?). Anyhow, I'd been out of it and he'd been right there and one thing had led to another, and bam, I'd drunk. But I hadn't enjoyed it. At least, I don't think I did. The next morning, I'd had a whopper of a headache and a mountain of regret. The entire experience had furthered the point that I was sick of one-night stands. I'd hitched a ride on the No-Biting Express and had been bouncing along ever since.

Until Ty.

"I sort of scarfed on someone a few months back."

"Sort of?"

"I didn't want to," I admitted.

"My point exactly. What vampire doesn't want to bite people?" She shook her head. "You'd be easy pickings for this demon."

"I've faced him before and he didn't jump ship."

"Was he possessing a human?" I nodded and she added, "Then that's why. No demon would willingly jump ship into a vampire unless he had no other choice. If his current vessel were dying or he were being forced out by the Almighty Himself and had no place else to go." She motioned to Margaret, who now lay a few feet away from Evie. "That woman's so hateful she wouldn't notice if Satan himself jumped in. Spies on everyone in the neighborhood and is always making trouble. She even tried to kill my precious little Marlon Brando."

"Poison?"

She nodded. "Served him up a great big chocolate fudge cake. She swears she didn't do it, but I smelled the chocolate in her house when I went over to confront her. I even saw the cake pans sitting in the sink, too."

Margaret murmured "circumstantial" which, because of the tape, came out more like *"shhirrm-melcha."*

"She did it," Mama declared, sparing a glare for the woman before motioning Crusher to leave us alone and wait in the car. "I know she did it."

I knew, too.

I took one look into Margaret Weisenbaum's eyes (minus the night-vision goggles this time) and I saw a rap sheet a mile long.

She'd served up her infamous three-tiered choco-late cake with fudge filling and dark chocolate sprinkles to twelve of the neighborhood dogs, including

Marlon. He'd been the only survivor because Mama had taken him to the vet right away. The other animals had died a slow, painful death. She'd also "accidentally" spilled antifreeze in the neighborhood bird baths. She'd taken out eight cats, sixteen birds, and all of Mr. Schwartz's goldfish. She'd paintballed Mr. Jackowski's fence and ripped up Mrs. Wallingford's rose bushes, and she'd even stolen a case of Thin Mints from Mr. Berryman's granddaughter's wagon when the little girl had been going door-to-door.

I patted her hand. "Good to have you, Mrs. Weisenbaum." Stealing Girl Scout cookies? Talk about a one-way ticket straight to Hell.

I excused myself to make a quick call to Ash. I got his voice mail and left a message for him to meet me at the church as soon as he got the message. I gave a quick confession that Evie was the one possessed, but told him not to worry because I had things under control and was going to save her.

My plan? A super-quick exorcism while Ash was en route. Then by the time he arrived, I could hand over Mrs. Weisenbaum, aka The Demon, and let him handle things from there.

I made a mental note to remember the antifreeze the next time Killer annihilated a pair of my shoes and reached into my pocket for the bottle of Benadryl. I downed another long swig, slapped at the itchies spreading across my chest, and turned to Mama. "Let's do it."

I watched as Mama retrieved her giant patent leather purse and started pulling out various items—

her bible, a book of prayers, a beaded rosary, a long
purple stole, a medal of St. Benedict that matched the
one worn around her neck, a large crucifix, several
handkerchiefs, a vial containing holy water, and a ton
of votive candles.

She spent the next few minutes lighting one after
the other until the altar blazed with soft, flickering
light.

"I didn't realize candles were such an important
part of an exorcism."

"They're not. They set the mood and help mask the
smell." She eyeballed Evie and waved a hand in front
of her face. "I swear this is worse than Vinnie and
Crusher after a pot of my corned beef and cabbage."

She put her matches away and reached for the
extra St. Benedict medal. "Put this on. It's not fool-
proof, but it'll help protect you during the exorcism."
She placed the stole around her own neck, doused her
handkerchiefs with holy water, crossed herself, and
reached for her bible. "Let's get this party started."

She took the end of the stole and slid it around
Evie's neck.

At first Evie hissed and bucked against her re-
straints, but after a few seconds, she collapsed back
atop the altar. Mama pulled the tape from Evie's
mouth and an agonized wail pierced the air.

Ouch.

"Our Father who art in heaven," Mama started,
launching into the opening prayer. The candles flared,
the flames popping and crackling before dying a
quick death. Smoke curled into the air and a rush of

cold wind whispered over my skin. A loud drumming echoed through the room and thundered in my ears.

I chanced a glance at Mrs. Weisenbaum. Her eyes went wide, but not from fear. Expectancy gleamed hot and bright as she watched the exorcism unfold.

Mama kept reciting prayers, pausing every now and then to touch the crucifix to Evie's forehead. Skin sizzled and the smell of burned flesh made even a bloodthirsty *vampere* like me want to toss her cookies.

But Evie was doing enough of that for the both of us. And levitating. And snarling. And cursing.

I held tight to the St. Benedict medal, which was making my palms itch even more than my shoulders and chest.

Meanwhile, Mama kept going. After several more prayers, she made the sign of the cross over Evie and demanded, "Who are you demon? Reveal yourself."

After a lot of snarling and spitting, the demon finally admitted the truth—he was the spirit of the deceased serial killer from the sixties. Score one for Ash.

"A newbie in demon years," Mama told me. "This shouldn't take long." She wiped Evie's barf-stained cheeks with the handkerchiefs drenched in holy water and ordered the demon out.

"Leave this woman," she bellowed. Over and over. Until Evie opened her mouth and screamed.

It was a man's voice at first, but the louder the screams grew, the higher the pitch became, until a burst of flames erupted behind the altar. Evie bucked and gasped one last time and a putrid green mist spiraled from her mouth.

The mist took on its own form until the shadow of a vicious-looking creature hovered above us. He looked like a cross between a dragon and a lizard. Fangs gleamed in the dim light and a forked tail whipped at the air.

Mama kept praying, pushing the demon father away from Evie until he hovered over Mrs. Weisenbaum. Mama leaned forward and snatched the tape from her neighbor's mouth.

Mrs. Weisenbaum let loose a string of cuss words before she opened wide, as if to say *"mi casa es su casa"* to the forked demon.

But instead of taking her up on her offer and diving inside, the demon pulled back. A split second later, I realized why.

A nearly identical green mist poured from the old woman's mouth and hovered just above her face. I heard a hiss and a "Find your own fucking body," before Mrs. Weisenbaum sucked the mist back into her mouth and clamped her lips shut. Her eyes flashed a bright yellow before dimming to their usual color.

Well. That explained it.

"It figures," Mama murmured. She grasped her crucifix and held it up. "The demon's got nowhere to go now."

Who knew demons had a no-double-occupancy policy?

A wave of panic shot through me and my mind raced. "What do we do now?"

Her gaze shifted from the demon to Mrs. Weisen-baum to me. "We run."

I made it halfway across the room (bless my preter-natural feet) before I heard the tormented wail. It pierced my ears and sent another bolt of panic through me. I picked up my steps and was *this close* to the door when I felt the icy grip snake around my neck. Something jerked my head backwards and sud-denly I was flat on my back on the hard floor. I stared up in time to see the demon hovering over me, his mouth open, his fangs glittering.

"You're so screwed," he spat.

"Ya think?" I'd barely gotten the words out when a white hot sensation hit me in the solar plexus. I gasped and my mouth opened. The demon went *poof* and suddenly he was in mist form, spiraling straight for me.

Heat rolled through me, over my tongue, down my throat, into my chest, my abdomen, clear to my toes.

I had a moment of startling realization—me, the demon, the demon, me—*no!*

I was a vampire. I was wearing the crucifix *and* the medal. I reached up, but I felt only itchy, inflamed skin. In the corner of my eye, I caught a gleam of gold on the floor. I'd either dropped them or they'd been ripped away. Either way, they were gone. *Gone.*

I couldn't . . .

I wouldn't . . .

Nooooooo!

I hauled myself to my feet and tried to take a step, but the fire blazing through me grew hotter, more

consuming. My legs trembled and the floor shook. I
heard Mama's voice somewhere to my right, but I
couldn't see her. In the far-off distance, the sound of
footsteps and voices echoed. Familiar voices.

"Where are you?"

Ty whispered through my head and hope blossomed. I tried to form a thought, to send it back to
him, but the only thing I could think about was how
much my body hurt and how scared I was and how
friggin' *hot*—

"I'm coming, baby. I'm coming." It was his voice
again. Loud. Clear. Close.

He called me *baby*.

The thought registered along with a tiny burst of
happiness before I felt a stab of searing pain, like a
hot knife slicing into my chest. I groaned and gasped,
fighting the sensation that threatened to drive me to
the floor. I forced my eyes open. I had to hold on, to
focus, to *see*, but a green fog clouded my vision. I
stumbled forward, Ty's thoughts rumbling in my
head, leading me on.

"I'm here."

"I'm coming."

"It'll be okay."

A door crashed open and footsteps scrambled.

"Holy shit." It was Ash's voice this time.

"Fuck," Ty growled.

Double fuck declared a voice inside of me.

I knew then, just as surely as I knew my mother
would never give up her quest for multiple grandchil-

dren, that my forked buddy and I were headed straight to Hell.

Chaos erupted. Hands reached for me.

"No!" It was Ty's voice that blared in my ears. "Not her, you asshole," he growled. "Me." And then his arms closed around me. *"Me."* And his fangs sank deep into my neck.

The fire grew unbearable. Screams echoed in my ears. My afterlife seeped away. And then everything went pitch-black.

Twenty-seven
❤ ❤ ❤

When I finally opened my eyes, I was lying on my stomach in the middle of a king-sized bed with a goose-down comforter and a pile of soft, fluffy pillows. Ty's familiar musky scent—fresh air, freedom, and a hint of danger—teased my nostrils. I buried my head in the pillow and inhaled.

Heaven.

That's what this was. I was dead. Not in Hell, obviously, which meant I'd gone the opposite direction thanks to all of my hard work as a dedicated matchmaker. I'd helped the lost lonely souls of New York find true love, and *this* was my reward.

I took another whiff before lifting my head to see what else waited for me in the hereafter. Let's see . . . A heavenly beach. An endless supply of designer clothes. A hot-looking demon sitting on the sofa watching NASCAR—

Get. *Out.*

I blinked, but he was still there, sprawled several feet away, legs propped on the glass and chrome coffee table, remote control in hand. He pressed a button and Talledega morphed into the latest Nickelback video.

O-kay.

While I wasn't an expert on Heaven, I'd be willing to bet my next retainer fee that demons were not allowed. Not even good-looking ones.

I rolled over and winced. My body ached and my skin felt numb and tight. I wore an oversized man's T-shirt and my undies. My legs were bare beneath the soft sheets. I struggled into a sitting position and blinked. Once, twice and my vision focused beyond the sofa and the demon.

Nix the white sand beach, the palm trees, and the bamboo hut filled with Calvin Klein dresses and Ferragamo purses and yummy Christian Louboutin booties.

Instead, I saw the familiar wall of glass windows overlooking a quiet neighborhood in the Meatpacking District. Beyond, a full moon pushed past the edge of the building across the street, illuminating the massive room.

Ty's loft.

I'd crashed here a while back when I'd been wanted for murder and had gotten up-close-and-personal with the layout. We were on the top floor of a three-story warehouse filled with rich leather furniture, chrome tables, a gonzo entertainment center, and a state-of-the-art kitchen with lots of stainless steel and granite countertops (Ty, obviously, didn't need such an impressive kitchen, since the most he ever did was open the occasional bottle of blood or pop the tab on a beer, but it had come with the place).

I shifted my attention to the demon sitting on the black sofa.

Zee Prince.

My throat burned and I swallowed. "What . . ." I started, but my voice seemed to stick on the one word.

It was enough to draw Zee's attention. He pushed to his feet and walked over to me. He pulled up a chair near the bed. "You're finally awake."

I swallowed and licked my dry lips. "W-what am I doing here?" It was only one of about a zillion questions that raced through my fuzzy brain, but there were too many and I had a pounding headache that kept me from prioritizing.

"We brought you here after the exorcism. You were possessed," he told me in much the same way he might have said "You were sleeping." He folded his arms and eyed me. "Ty forced the demon out and saved you."

How?

Even as the next question bubbled to the surface, I already knew the answer. I touched my neck and felt the deep puncture marks. A tiny drop of blood oozed over my fingers and slid down my skin.

Zee grabbed a Kleenex off the nightstand and handed it to me. "Easy. It's still fresh."

I wiped at the blood and Zee relaxed back into his chair.

"It was the only way for Ty to force the demon out," he went on. "He had to drink from you until the demon jumped ship. He finally did, but only after Ty had drank so much that the demon feared you might die. If the vessel dies, it's an automatic trip back to Hell. The demon had no choice but to hop into the nearest body."

Images pushed and pulled and suddenly I was back in the old sanctuary, Ty's strong, purposeful mouth on my skin, his fangs pushing deep. I heard the tormented wail of the demon, felt the thrashing inside of me and the draw on my neck, and then . . .

"*No.*" I teetered as I struggled to throw my legs over the side of the bed.

"Calm down." He gave me an odd look, as if he couldn't quite believe I was so freaked.

"But it's Ty," I gasped. "He's possessed now." And all because he'd tried to save me.

The thought struck and the reality of what he'd done hit me. A lightbulb flipped on and suddenly I knew. I *knew*.

Made or not, Ty Bonner was The One.

Yeah, I know. I'd always sort of known this, but I'd never seen it so clearly. There'd always been too many obstacles in the way and so my view had been limited. But now I realized how all of that paled in comparison to the thought of losing him forever.

"He can't be possessed," I blurted. "Not now. Not when I'm finally sure—"

"He's okay." Zee got to his feet. Large hands forced me back to the pillows. "Ty's a vampire with a strong will. He was able to contain the demon. He and Ash headed for Riker's Island and a piece-of-shit child killer we've had our eye on who's been sitting on death row. Ty touched the guy, deposited the demon, and then Ash took control."

"And sliced and diced and sent the demon and the child killer straight to Hell," I finished, relief seeping through me as I realized that Ty was okay and he wasn't jetting for Hell at that very moment.

Zee nodded. "That part's happening right now."

"What about Evie?"

"She's got a few cuts and bruises and she doesn't smell all that great, but otherwise, she's fine. We dropped her at her apartment so she could recuperate. She doesn't have any memory of the demon— that goes with being possessed—and so she's a little confused. She thinks she tied it on at one helluva party and now she's paying the price. Some sleep and a hot shower, and she'll be as good as new."

"Mama Balducci?"

"She hauled ass out of there as soon as the demon jumped into you." He shook his head. "Never knew an old lady could move that fast in a pair of rubber boots."

"Mrs. Weisenbaum?"

"Crusher took her back home."

"But she's—"

"—possessed? We know. But Bucky—that's the demon who's got her—is small potatoes compared to some of the other bastards we have to deal with. Back in the early eighteen hundreds, he got messed up in the head in some war and became a hermit. Started torching animals for fun and stealing chickens for food, but he's pretty much harmless to humans. Besides, as old as that woman is, he'll be on his way back to Hell pretty soon anyway."

I closed my eyes and let everything sink in. I'd done it. I'd saved Evie and no one had gotten hurt in the process and it was now all officially over.

"So where's Ty?" I finally asked.

"Helping Ash and Mo. They needed a third and since he had to go make the deposit, he gets to help send the demon back. Mo and I flipped a coin to see who would stay here and babysit you."

"And you lost."

He shook his head and his eyes took on a bright gleam. "Actually, I won."

A few days before, I might have felt a tiny twinge of desire (I *am* a born vamp, so being a ho is practically genetic). But instead of thinking about sex, I found myself thinking about how soft the bed was and how I couldn't wait to see Ty and tell him the truth—that I didn't care if he was made or born and that I absolutely could not exist another day without him. "I'm really tired right now."

Yeah, right flashed in his gaze and he grinned. "You can't blame a guy for trying." He stood. "You thirsty?"

I nodded. A few minutes later, he reappeared with a glass of clear liquid. I sipped at the cold water as images from the church replayed in my throbbing head.

"They'll be back soon. You should rest. You'll never get rid of those splotches unless you sleep."

Demons and exorcisms faded in the face of real tragedy. "I have splotches?"

"It's more like a full-blown rash."

I glanced at the hand holding the glass. Sure enough, my skin looked red and angry. My gaze shot upward, over my forearm to my biceps that disappeared beneath the sleeve of the T-shirt. I yanked up the material on my right arm and studied my shoulder. Yikes. My stomach churned as I turned my inspection to the right arm and saw more of the same. I kicked the comforter away and surveyed my legs.

"I need a mirror," I blurted. It couldn't have spread everywhere, right? I'd taken the Benadryl. I'd even said a few Hail Marys (mum's the word). There had to be a part of my body—the most visible part—that had been spared. *Right?*

Zee shrugged and headed for the bathroom while I did my do-*not*-freak-out deep breathing. Needless to say, I was still freaked out (and a little lightheaded) by the time he returned. I took the small compact and drank in my reflection.

Rule number one—when suffering from a bad case of hives, DO NOT ask for a mirror.

A bright pink bloated face dotted with dark, angry splotches stared back at me. I was puffy. I was spotty. I was a freakin' strawberry.

Worse, I was a strawberry with fangs. Besides being dehydrated, my nerves were still buzzing from Ty's mouth on my neck. My primal instincts had obviously kicked in and I was still semi-aroused.

I was also mortified.

My chest tightened and my eyes blurred. "I can't believe I look this awful."

"You think that's bad, you should have seen yourself right after the demon hopped out. You've been sleeping a few hours, so it's actually gotten better."

Great.

Just friggin' *great*.

I'd waited my entire afterlife for the right vampire to come along, sweep me into his arms, and bite me. Finally it had happened and I'd spent the moment not only possessed, but looking like a bloated piece of fruit.

Was I cursed when it came to men or what?

Twenty-eight

♥ ♥ ♥

I spent the next half hour crying my eyes out while Zee went out for a pack of cigarettes. Not that he smoked, but what else was a guy to do when faced with an overly emotional female vampire?

Finally, the tears slowed down and I felt somewhat more calm. Miserable, but calm. I buried my head in the pillow, closed my eyes, and fell sound asleep.

When I finally opened my eyes, it was Ty who sat by my bedside instead of Zee.

Moonlight beamed down through the windows and illuminated his tall, muscular body sprawled in a nearby chair. He wore nothing but a pair of worn, faded jeans and a concerned expression. Broad shoulders framed his muscular chest and ripped abs. His dark, shoulder-length hair was mussed, as if he'd been running his hands through it. Shadow stubbled his jaw and gave him a dark, dangerous edge.

His electric blue gaze sparked as it met mine and I became extremely aware of how little I wore and how horrible I looked. "It's about time you woke up. You've been sleeping for two days." He looked worn and worried and my heart hitched.

I burst into another round of tears.

"Easy," his deep voice slid into my ears a split second before the mattress dipped. He sank down next to me and one strong hand touched my cheek. "You shouldn't get upset right now. It's not good for you."

I knew that. My skin was still itchy and tight and every bone in my body felt heavy. I needed to heal, not freak.

I needed . . .

The tears came harder, faster.

"You bit me," I finally managed, wiping frantically at the stream of wetness on my face.

"I'm sorry. I had to."

I slapped at my cheeks, which made them start to itch, which made me cry even more. "You . . . bit . . . me," I finally got the words out again, in between huge, racking sobs. "And"—*sniffle*—"I didn't"—*sniffle, sniffle*—"even get to"—*sniffle, sob*—"enjoy it."

His expression shifted and a fierce hunger fired in his neon blue eyes. A grin tugged at the corner of his sensuous mouth.

"Is that what's with the waterworks?"

I nodded. "That"—the word ended on a catch as I sniffled again and swiped at my face—"and the fact that I look really awful and I'd pictured things totally different when I finally found The One and you don't get a do-over when it comes to first bites and—"

"You think I'm The One?" he cut in. His gaze darkened and he suddenly looked as if he wanted to pound something.

Which wasn't exactly the vamp-stranded-in-a-blood-bank grin and euphoric "I feel exactly the same way about you" I'd been hoping for.

I stiffened and started to ramble. "Not that you are, you know. It's just that I was possessed and my brain obviously short-circuited and now that I think better of it, I can clearly see that you're not even close to my vamp in shining armor. Your hair is too long and—"

"Lil."

"—your eyes are too blue and you don't have near the taste in clothes—"

"*Lil.*"

His deep voice slid past the frantic pounding of my heart. I blinked. "What?"

"Give it a rest." His anger faded into something hot and intense.

He leaned forward, his face just inches from mine, and my nerves went on instant alert. Anticipation bolted through me. "Are you going to bite me again?"

"No." He grinned and leaned even closer, forcing me back down into the mattress. "Not yet." His lips barely brushed mine as he loomed over me. "Not until I do this." His tongue darted out to sweep my bottom lip and then he was kissing me. Slowly. Deeply.

Oh.

"And this," he murmured, dipping a hand beneath the hem of the T-shirt to stroke my bare breast. He played with my nipple, rolling and plucking until a moan worked its way up my throat. He hiked up my shirt and touched his mouth to my bare nipple. He sucked the ripe tip before moving on. His lips trailed from my breast, down the tender skin of my abdomen to the vee between my legs. He trailed his tongue over the thin material of my lace thong and traced the slit between my legs. "And this." He swept the lace aside and gave me a long, luscious lick.

Oh.

Ty had a mouth to die for, and he definitely knew how to use it.

He nibbled and sucked at my clit until I gasped and came up off the bed. Large, strong hands urged me back down, holding my legs apart as his lips and tongue worked their magic.

I dug my fingers into the sheets as he lapped at me and suckled and . . . *ahhhhhhhhhh.*

A delicious heat simmered between my legs and spread through my body until I burned from the inside out. He kept tasting me and I spread my legs wider, wanting him closer and deeper and—

Geez, this vampire was *good*.

So good I didn't think I could hold on for much longer. Sensation built and my body started to hum.

I was going to . . .

But I didn't want to . . .

Because I'd been waiting to . . .

"Bite me," I gasped as he thrust his tongue deep inside me. "Just . . . one . . . *bite*."

"*Soon*." His deep voice whispered through my head and stirred my senses even more. I plunged my fingers into his hair, holding him closer, urging him on.

"*Now*." I sent the silent message. "*Please*."

He suckled me for a few more mind-blowing seconds before replacing his lips with his fingers. He pushed all the way in and pleasure pierced my brain. He shifted his mouth an inch to the right, to the inside of my upper thigh. His muscles went tight and a growl tickled my skin.

The first convulsion hit me—so hot and delicious—just as he sank his fangs deep. Pleasure sliced through me as the most delicious orgasm of my afterlife gripped me.

He started to drink and the convulsions kept coming, over and over, fast and furious, until I spiraled so high on a cloud of satisfaction that I thought I would never come down.

I floated for several long moments, my heart pounding, before he finally drew back. He lapped softly at the blood that trickled from my thigh before pushing to his feet and shedding his jeans.

I caught a quick glimpse of his massive hard-on before he reached for me. He grasped the edges of the T-shirt and pulled it over my head. His gaze hooked on my breasts and my nipples pebbled in anticipation.

"*Beautiful.*" The word echoed through my head.

I smiled. "You're not so bad yourself."

The bed dipped and he settled himself between my legs. He braced his arms on either side of me and captured my mouth again. I tasted my own salty sweetness on his lips as he nudged my slick folds with the head of his penis and thrust deep.

Yowza.

He started to move, pushing deep and then withdrawing. Once. Twice. Again and again. His hard length rasped my insides and created a delicious friction that worked me up all over again.

I lifted my hips, meeting each thrust. In and out. Deeper and harder. Until he bucked one last and final time. His penis twitched and throbbed and I felt a warmth rush through me. The sensation sent a jolt of pure desperation through me. I grasped at his shoulders and pulled him closer.

I lapped at his salty skin and felt the pulse of his artery beneath my lips.

"*Do it,*" came the deep rumble in my head. "*Come on, baby.*"

My hunger stirred and raged and I felt the sharpness of my teeth against my tongue.

With a loud hiss I pulled my lips back, sank my

fangs into his neck, and started to drink. Without regret or remorse or the never-ending fear that my ma was going to kill me.

Because Ty Bonner was The One and I loved him. End of story.

Epilogue

❤ ❤ ❤

I absolutely, positively DID NOT love Ty Bonner.

I'd simply been caught up in the heat of the moment, freaked over the possession and thirsty.

Yes, I'd been *really* thirsty.

Stress and dry mouth definitely made for an altered state of reality. To think that I'd actually thought . . . that he and I . . . that we . . .

Temporary insanity, all right.

That's what I told myself over the next few days as I settled back into my normal routine. With a little help from Maids-R-Us (okay, so a lot of help), my apartment made the transformation from drooling demon den back to posh vamp digs. I borrowed Max's Visa Gold card (I'd kinda sorta maxed out mine and forgot to pay the bill because I'd been so worried about Evie) and replaced my wardrobe. I'd even thrown in a few extras—a Tiffany bracelet and a Swarovski crystal belt that was the *total* bomb—to cheer myself up and distract me from you-know-who.

Evie came back to work right away (yeah, baby), typing and filing and sucking down lattes as if she'd never been possessed by a vicious demon. The bruises were still there, but she'd explained them away as the result of a wild party, too much to drink, and rough sex with a guy she still couldn't remember.

"All I know is I'm never drinking appletinis again," she'd vowed on her first day back in the office. *"Ever."* She'd handed me a stack of messages and a pile of bills, and just like that my afterlife had morphed back into the same old, same old.

No more demons.

No more Vinnie (he'd called off the engagement with Carmen—much to his mother's dismay—but since I'd fulfilled my end of the bargain, he'd let me off the hook). I was still trying to match him up, but at least I didn't have to worry about getting staked and stuffed into his trunk. I also had Crusher on my side because I was the Great Vamp Hope when it came to finding a date for his yearly Christmas party. Not that I'd found him one yet. It was only April and I had oodles of time.

No more mom bugging the hell out of me (at least when it came to Remy). I'd agreed to a real date with him. No hunt, no parents. Just the two of us sipping drinks at the Waldorf, plenty close to Nina One, who'd promised to bring reinforcements (Rob, along with Jack and Mandy, who were now back from their honeymoon, much to my mother's delight) and save me after the first fifteen minutes.

No more Ty.

Really.

How could I possibly love a guy who'd dropped me off at my apartment after a night of fantabulous sex and mutual biting, and hadn't so much as called me since?

He'd had to go away for a few days and tie up some loose ends. That's what he'd told me and I'd been fool enough to believe him.

I'd believed a lot of things after that scrumptious night.

Like maybe, just maybe my mom wouldn't freak when she met him. And even if she did, she might actually grow to love him the way I did (or the way I'd thought I did during my moment of temporary cuckoo).

I'd also believed that Logan (the badass vamp who'd made Ty and held a world of guilt over his head) wouldn't get pissed and come after us. Who knew? Maybe Logan would see us together and think *awwww*. Maybe his black heart would soften and he would buy us a really great present to wish us well on our afterlife together.

Even more, I'd believed that Ty had actually returned my feelings.

Stupid, right?

It was now five days later and I'd come to my senses.

Ty was a jerk and I wasn't wasting another moment thinking about him or the fact that he hadn't called, e-mailed, or even texted since he'd gotten back into town yesterday. Ash had dropped that bomb when he'd stopped by to see how Evie was doing (and to flirt with me, of course).

I'd dodged the effort by slipping him a DED card and begging him to let me hook him up just once.

Things were back to normal, all right.

"I've got a live one for Mia," Evie said as she walked into my office with a stack of folders. She wore a green smock dress, matching patent leather knee-high boots, and a ton of bling-bling. "Twenty-one-year-old computer geek. Glasses. Awful taste in clothes. Hasn't had an official date *ever*. He's so horny he can hardly speak. I met him yesterday. He's my landlord's nephew." She handed me the folder. "Since we haven't had much luck with the really hot studs, I thought we might go the opposite direction. Maybe someone so sexually repressed will have more pent-up *oomph* and can keep up with her once it's unleashed."

It made sense. "Have I told you what a great assistant you are?"

She grinned. "Three times in the past hour."

What can I say? I'd missed her.

"I really am glad you're okay."

"So am I. I haven't had a hangover that bad since my senior prom."

I felt a pang of envy. Sometimes, just sometimes, I wondered what it would be like to actually be human.

Not half as great as being a born vamp, I knew. But still. A girl could fantasize.

I flipped through the folder. "Looks like a go. I'll give Mia a call and set it up."

"Could you help me in the outer office first? We had a delivery for you and it's kind of big."

"Office supplies from Max?" Amazing what a little blackmail (he *so* didn't want my parents finding out about his fling with Viola) could accomplish.

"Better."

My excitement bubbled. "The hobo bag I ordered off the QVC?"

"Bigger."

I couldn't help but smile. "The three pairs of Chanel boots I ordered off the Internet?"

"Smellier."

I followed her into the outer office and came to a dead stop a few steps from her desk.

At least I thought it was her desk, but I couldn't really tell because it was covered by a monstrous vase stuffed full of bright pink roses.

"Go on," Evie said, a smile spreading from ear to ear. "Read the card."

My heart stalled and my hands shook as I reached for the small white card. "You didn't have to do this."

"Are you kidding? You don't pay me nearly enough for roses. Maybe carnations." She wiggled her eyebrows. "Besides, these are clearly *after-sex* flowers and, while I think you're really hot with fabulous taste, you're not my type. I mean, you would be if I were into girls, but I'm totally not."

Well, maybe.

The window into her thoughts opened and I slammed it shut just as fast. While I liked being a vamp and knowing what was up when it came to humans, there was such a thing as too much info.

Especially if the info came from my assistant, whom I loved like a sister.

A sister. Got that? I sent the silent thought and watched her eyes widen a split second before she seemed to relax.

"It's from someone male," she added.

I unfolded the white vellum and read the black scrawl:

> *Sorry I haven't called. Things have been crazy. Call me . . . Ty.*

"I knew he liked you," Evie said, peering over my shoulder. "I *knew* it. Are you going to call him?"

"Maybe." I picked up the flowers and walked back into my office. *Maybe not.*

Indecision rolled through me as I set the vase on my desk, sank down into my chair, and reached for the card again.

Call me.

Where was the undying emotion? The feeling? The *love?* At the very least, he could have written *Love, Ty.*

But no . . .

Because he doesn't love you.

I drew a deep breath and the sweet, sultry scent of

roses spiraled through my nostrils and made my heart pump faster.

Then again, he did have good taste in flowers, and he had gone to the trouble of sending them and filling out the card himself rather than using a computer-generated message.

That had to mean something. Right? There was only one way to find out.

I gathered my courage and reached for the phone.

If you enjoyed JUST ONE BITE,
get ready to sink your fangs into this excerpt from
Kimberly Raye's next book

Sucker for Love

Available from Ballantine Books in May 2009

Chapter One

❤ ❤ ❤

*Are you tired of nursing down that bottle of O+ all
by your lonesome? Did you spend the last full moon
drinking Cosmos and lusting over the American Ken-
nel Club finals? Do you spend every evening scarfing
a Hungry-Man (or woman) and watching TiVo?*

*If you're first reaction was "uh-oh" or "How'd she
know that?" to any of the above, then you are cor-
dially invited to a meet-and-greet dinner party, hosted
by Dead End Dating, Manhattan's number one
matchmaking service for vampires, humans, and
Others. Join fantabulous host (and incredibly well-
dressed vampire) Lil Marchette for a night of dinner
and dancing and romance in the penthouse of the
Waldorf-Astoria.*

*Disclaimer—DED is an equal opportunity dating
service that does not discriminate based on race, sex,*

looks (or lack thereof) or appetite. Net worth, how-
ever, is an entirely different matter—i.e. don't forget
the checkbook, debit card, and/or Visa Gold.

I propped up the framed copy of the engraved vellum invitation I'd mailed out to every appropriate
single in Manhattan and tried to calm the butterflies
in my stomach.

I'm the Countess Lilliana Arrabella Guinevere du
Marchette (Lil for short), a five-hundred-year-old
(and holding) born-vampire. I've got super fab taste
in clothes, a to-die-for collection of MAC cosmetics,
and a hot, hunky, bounty-hunting boyfriend. I *so*
have it going on.

Ix-nay the nerves, right?

Wrong.

I'm also the owner of Dead End Dating, Manhattan's primo matchmaking service for vampires, weres,
Others, and even the occasional human. As of five
minutes ago, I had exactly one week to match up
more than a dozen paid-in-full clients, otherwise I
would fail to make good on my *Find your one and*
only in six months or your money back! guarantee.

Since I don't do refunds (not unless I want to return
half my wardrobe and say *bye-bye* to my new Black-
Berry), I had to pick up the pace. Pronto.

Hence, my latest super fantabulous brainstorm—
the meet-and-greet dinner party about to happen
right here. Right now.

I drew a deep breath (not because I had to, but hey,
when in Rome . . .), straightened my green Roberto
Cavalli dress (a floor-length, strappy chiffon number
a la Rihanna), and finished setting up the hostess
table. I added DED business cards, name tags, promotional pens, koozies and calendars, and even a few

pics and testimonials from previous clients. I sprinkled some rose petals and debated whether or not to hand out the Viagra samples in my bag or just spike the drinks when no one was looking.

The hornier the clients, the lower the standards, the sooner everyone paired up.

At the same time, I was desperate, not depraved.

Not yet.

I stored my bag, complete with samples, under the table. What? So I'm a romantic. I freely admit it (to anyone except my Ma, that is).

"Help!"

The frantic voice drew my attention and I turned just as a frustrated blonde rushed at me.

Evie Dalton could man the phones, key in profiles, and suck down a steaming latte, all without smudging her lip gloss. She was the best assistant a vampire could ask for. She was also human, and completely unaware of my fanged-and-fabulous status.

The 4-1-1 on tonight?

She thought it was just another movie theme party. Like the toga fever spawned by *Animal House* and the '50s sock hops a la *Grease*. Tonight's brain candy? Contemporary monster mania courtesy of the barrage of recent horror movies such as *30 Days of Night* and *The Mist*.

In honor of the occasion, she'd donned a silver jacket with eight sparkly "legs," a sequined mini smock dress, and three-inch glitter sandals. She looked like Spidie's wet dream. So good in fact that, with the exception of a fading bruise on her neck and some seriously rank breath, it was impossible to tell that just two short weeks ago she'd been possessed by a demon. *And* that she'd come this close to heading downtown (way, *way* downtown) to become Satan's own personal bee-yotch.

I'd been so busy hiding her from the long arms of the Prince brothers (a hot, hunky trio of demon hunters who just so happened to be demons themselves) that I'd sort of let the rest of my work pile up.

The demon was now back in hell, Evie was back in the office (and munching Tic Tacs), and I was making up for lost time.

"The fangs are melting on the ice sculpture," she informed me. "I need you to take these," she handed me a clipboard and a copy of the invitation, "and brief Nina while I find the catering manager and get them to relocate the flambé table asap."

"Why not just hike the air-conditioning up?"

"But won't the guests be cold?"

"They'll be more inclined to pair up and snuggle."

She grinned. "I knew there was a reason you were the boss." She handed me a small box with a corsage. "Make sure Nina puts this on, too—if you can find her." She glanced around. "One minute she was at the bar sucking down a Bloody Mary and the next—poof—gone. Vanished into thin air."

Or the nearest storage closet.

"I knew it," I declared when I threw open the door a few seconds later to find the MIA Nina.

Nina Lancaster aka Nina One—the blond half of The Ninas who'd been my best friends for the past four hundred and ninety-eight years—was the daughter of filthy rich hotelier Victor Lancaster, who owned the Waldorf along with several five-star establishments throughout New York and Connecticut. Nina was rich, beautiful (big surprise, right?), and living with my middle brother, Rob. They'd been seeing each other since I'd hooked them up a few months ago. Judging by the spaghetti straps that sagged near her elbows and my brother's untucked button-down shirt, they'd been about to see a lot more of each other in the next five minutes.

I glanced at Rob. His eyes were glazed and hooded. His fangs gleamed. A hungry growl vibrated the air.

Okay, make that the next five *seconds*.

Anxiety rushed through me. "Can you please boff my brother on your own time?"

"I'm not boffing him." She grinned and tugged her straps back into place. "Not yet." She touched a hand to her mussed hair. "Besides, this isn't your time. I donated the ballroom, so that makes it *my* time."

She had a point.

I traded in pissed-off client for desperately needy friend. "But I need you to screen guests at the entrance."

"Get Evie to do it."

"I'm sending her back to the office on a 'dating emergency' as soon as the party's in full swing." I'd scheduled a new client this evening and I was going to pretend I'd forgotten all about it and needed her to conduct the meeting while I dealt with the party. "She's the best assistant I've got. I can't have her wind up some vampire's sex slave, or the midnight snack for a hungry werewolf."

Or worse, realize that the fangs I was sporting were the real deal. I wasn't ready to break the born-vamp's number one commandment—Thou Shalt Keep a Low Profile—and come out of the closet to Evie. My mother would kill me. Even worse, I wasn't sure if Evie was ready to work for a vamp. So far, she'd been wonderful. But it was a lot to swallow and I just wasn't sure if she'd take me out for chocolate martinis to celebrate, or call in the rowdy villagers. I hadn't gone into mucho credit card debt decorating my office to have the whole thing wind up torched.

"Evie won't be here. You have to do it."

"Who says?"

"Your best friend in the entire universe." I gave her a knowing smile. "We're practically sisters. You know you'd do anything to help me."

"Which is why I loaned you the ballroom for free."

"But I still need this one teensy, tiny favor."

"Tonight's my night off." In addition to being Daddy's Little Vamp, Nina was also the hotel's chief hostess. "I just showed up to tell you to make sure that nobody gets blood on the white settees. Daddy will kill me."

"I'm willing to beg."

"I'm a born-vampire. We're not genetically wired for sympathy."

"Are we genetically wired for greed? Because I'm willing to pay."

She grinned. "What'd you have in mind?"

I did a mental check of my most recent purchases, singling out the key items that I knew would melt her hard-ass resolve. "Ferragamo sunglasses?"

"I've got three pairs."

"Michael Kors bangle bracelets?"

"Got 'em."

"Hermès lipstick compact."

She shook her head. "There's no such thing."

"If you think so." I shrugged a shoulder. "But I just happen to have one from the insanely small, limited edition collection purchased by a select few clients who have the right connections." In this case, a bisexual sales assistant at Barneys that I'd glammed ages ago. I'd been scamming primo purchases ever since. "But if you're not interested—"

"Okay, okay. I'm going." She shrugged at Rob. "Sorry, babe. What can I say? I'm shallow."

He grinned and dropped a kiss on her lips. "Just one of the many things I love about you."

Awwww . . .

My heart swelled for about an eighth of a second before I remembered who was actually in the closet with Nina.

My very own flesh and blood *brother*.

Middle born son of Countess Jacqueline and Count Pierre Gustavo Marchette.

Descendant of one of the first (and snottiest) born-vamp families in existence.

Propagator of the species and all-around playa playa.

And he'd just used the *L* word.

Shut. *Up*.

Before I could find my voice, Nina grabbed my hand and hauled me off toward the entrance to the ballroom. "What color?"

Rob. Nina. Love? "What color what?"

"The lipstick case." She nudged me, shattering my thoughts. "What color is it?"

I shook away my sudden excitement and focused on the here and now. "Hot pink with rhinestones and Swarovski crystals."

"No way!"

"And there's even a tiny diamond inlay on the inside mirror near the Hermès logo."

She squealed and snatched the corsage from my hands. A few seconds later, she had a single red rose pinned near the collar of her Carolina Herrera original and the clipboard in hand. "I'm ready. What do you want me to do?"

"Just greet everyone and take invitations. No one gets inside without one."

"What if he's cute?"

"It doesn't matter. No invitation, no party."

"Well dressed?"

"Hand him a business card, talk us up, and send him on his way."

"Rich?"

"Stick a nametag on him and send him in." What can I say? This vamp had her priorities.

After leaving a few more instructions (pass out an extra pack of DED promotional mints to all weres, ask blood type preference for all vamps), I left Nina at the entrance and headed inside to see the end result of eight days of wicked stress and frantic planning.

The room was huge, with ornate frieze work and a marbled floor. A large dance area had been set up in the very center, the circular area surrounded by clusters of round tables covered in crisp white linens. Polished silver candelabras dominated the center of each table. Candlelight flickered, making the china and crystal place settings sparkle. Moonlight filtered through the wall of glass windows behind the small (I'm on a budget, all right?), but tasteful orchestra I'd booked for tonight. The place oozed romantic ambiance and for the first time since I'd started planning the event, I actually believed that it might work. Up to that point I'd been running on sheer desperation and crazy hope.

My gaze shifted to the huge silver fountain flowing with champagne that dominated the far corner of the room. Next to that sat a Bloody Mary bar. No, Mary herself wasn't in attendance (not yet, anyway—my mother *had* sent her an invitation on my behalf), but there was plenty of AB-, vodka, and Tabasco sauce to keep the vamps happy. Next to that sat a meat lover's buffet sporting everything from roast beef to lamb chops. The food was barely cooked (we're talking *rare*) and plentiful for the weres. Add a dessert bar with everything from fudge overboard to raspberry cheesecake for the few humans who'd been invited, and there was a little something for everyone.

In fact, the entire room reminded me of one of those It's a Small World rides at Disneyland. I had the sudden urge to sing "Kumbaya."

Or, in this case, "The Monster Mash."

Everything looked absolutely perfect.

Which should have been my first clue of the coming disaster. I mean, really. A roomful of vamps and weres and humans? Talk about a massacre just waiting to happen.

The first to draw blood? A hot-looking demon. At least, I thought he was a demon since I couldn't smell him (nix vamp), nor could I read his thoughts (forget human), and he didn't look ready to howl at the moon (so *not* a were).

His name was Jordan Barrett Finley and he was über hot. I wasn't sure where he'd come from (he wasn't on my guest list), but I wasn't about to argue with the whopping cash retainer he presented to Nina or the fact that he was desperate to find a plus-sized made vampire. Not when I just so happened to have the perfect woman for him.

Esther Crutch was a nice, sweet, stylishly chic made vampire I'd met while getting a spray tan at my favorite salon. Unfortunately, the stylishly chic packaged a size-fourteen body and so Esther didn't get as much nooky as the rest of her kind.

Made male vamps were so shallow.

Ahem.

Okay, so were born male vamps, but enough with the details.

Esther and Jordan. Talk about a perfect match. I introduced them and stepped back to let Cupid do his thing.

One minute they were dancing and gazing into

each other's eyes and the next . . . I wasn't sure what happened next. I just knew judging by the blood-stained sofa that it wasn't good.

"I knew someone was going to spill a drink," Nina said as she came up behind me. "Daddy's going to take it out of my allowance for sure."

"Nobody spilled a drink," I said, picking at a torn piece of Esther's dress that had caught on the edge of a mirrored coffee table. The fabric was soaked with blood, the edges jagged where it had ripped on the table. Or where someone had ripped it.

An image flashed and I remembered Esther, a strange expression on her face as Jordan had led her out of the ballroom. I'd been five steps behind them because I'd wanted a pic to add to my wall of success back at the office. I'd stopped to calm down an overly excited were who'd been upset because we'd run out of au jus for the roast beef. By the time I'd reached the sitting area outside the ballroom, they were gone.

"Lil?" Nina asked. "If it's not a spilled drink, what is it?"

"It's Esther." Goosebumps crawled up and down my arms and a strange sense of doom settled in the pit of my stomach. "I think she's been kidnapped." The ripe smell of fresh blood teased my nostrils. "Or worse."